PRA...
The Shadow Year

"Doomed though i... Ford
thralling places I'v...

WITHDRAWN

"Think Ray Bradbu...
a Mockingbird, and
Stand by Me) and y...
work. Grade A."

—*Rocky Mountain News*

"Ford travels deep into the wild coun...
novel. . . . The observations and adv...
ward children provide more than eno...

"The setup is perfect. . . . Setting has always played a central role in Ford's work, and he clearly knows this yellowed glimpse of Long Island very well—the streets, the trees, the frozen lakes all bear the imprimatur of reality. That's what keeps you turning pages."

—*Los Angeles Times*

"Children are the original magic realists. The effects that novelists of a postmodern bent must strive for come naturally to the young, a truth given inventive realization in this wonderful quasi-mystery tale by Jeffrey Ford."

—*Boston Globe*

"Surreal, unsettling, and more than a little weird. Ford has a rare gift for evoking mood with just a few well-chosen words and for creating living, breathing characters with only a few lines of dialogue."

—*Booklist*

"If little Ralphie, the everykid hero of that classic film *A Christmas Story*, wandered into one of Ray Bradbury's darker tales, his adventures might resonate with the quirky, creepy, and quite poignant vibes of Jeffrey Ford's latest—and most accomplished—novel."
—Hartford Courant

"*The Shadow Year* accumulates so great a simultaneous charge of the commonplace and the bizarre that it constitutes an epic of unlikely immediacy. . . . [It] belongs to the distinctively American subgenre of nostalgia for small towns and suburbs, for innocence and youthful energy lost, à la Ray Bradbury and Stephen King. . . . *The Shadow Year* captures the totality of a lived period, its actualities and its dreams, its mundane essentials and its odd subjective imperatives; it is a work of episodic beauty and mercurial significance."
—Locus

"Spooky and hypnotic. . . . Recommended for all public libraries."
—Library Journal

"Properly creepy, but from time to time deliciously funny and heartbreakingly poignant too. For those of you—and you know who you are—who think the indispensable element for good genre fiction is good writing, this is not to be missed."
—Kirkus Reviews (starred review)

"Ford keeps the reader turning pages at a rapid pace, trying to separate event from illusion as three kids with an absent father and a mother whose heart is permanently out to lunch come to grips with the enemy. Better yet, he finishes off *The Shadow Year* with a surprise you won't likely see coming."
—Chicago Sun-Times

© Lynn Gallagher-Ford

About the Author

Jeffrey Ford is the author of seven previous novels, including the Edgar Award–winning *The Girl in the Glass*. He is a professor of writing and early American literature at a college in New Jersey. Visit his blog at http://14theditch.livejournal.com.

Also
by
Jeffrey Ford

NOVELS

The Girl in the Glass

The Cosmology of the Wider World

The Portrait of Mrs. Charbuque

The Beyond

Memoranda

The Physiognomy

Vanitas

STORY COLLECTIONS

The Dreamed Life

The Empire of Ice Cream

The Fantasy Writer's Assistant

The
Shadow
Year

Jeffrey Ford

HARPER ⬤ PERENNIAL

NEW YORK • LONDON • TORONTO • SYDNEY • NEW DELHI • AUCKLAND

HARPER ● PERENNIAL

A hardcover edition of this book was published in 2008 by William Morrow, an imprint of HarperCollins Publishers.

FIRST HARPER PERENNIAL EDITION PUBLISHED 2009.

Designed by Janet M. Evans

The Library of Congress has catalogued the hardcover edition as follows:
Ford, Jeffrey 1955–
   The shadow year : a novel / Jeffrey Ford. — 1st ed.
      p. cm.
   ISBN 978-0-06-123152-0
   1. Teenage boys—Fiction. 2. Cities and towns—Fiction. 3. Domestic fiction.
I. Title.
   PS3556.O6997S47 2008
   813'.54—dc22
                                                                    2007037319

ISBN 978-0-06-123153-7 (pbk.)

09 10 11 12 13 OV/RRD 10 9 8 7 6 5 4 3 2 1

For **Jim, Mary,** and **Dool,**

whose love was like a light

in the shadow years

The Shadow Year

The Eyes

■ It began in the last days of August, when the leaves of the elm in the front yard had curled into crisp brown tubes and fallen away to litter the lawn. I sat at the curb that afternoon, waiting for Mister Softee to round the bend at the top of Willow Avenue, listening carefully for that mournful knell, each measured *ding* both a promise of ice cream and a pinprick of remorse. Taking a cast-off leaf into each hand, I made double fists. When I opened my fingers, brown crumbs fell and scattered on the road at my feet. Had I been waiting for the arrival of that strange changeling year, I might have understood the sifting debris to be symbolic of the end of something. Instead I waited for the eyes.

That morning I'd left under a blue sky, walked through the woods and crossed the railroad tracks away from town, where the third rail hummed, lying in wait, like a snake, for an errant ankle. Then along the road by the factory, back behind the grocery, and up and down the streets, I searched for discarded glass bottles in every open garbage can, Dumpster, forgotten corner. I'd found three soda bottles and a half-gallon milk bottle. At the grocery store, I turned them in for the refund and walked away with a quarter.

All summer long, Mister Softee had this contest going. With each purchase of twenty-five cents or more, he gave you a card:

On the front was a small portrait of the waffle-faced cream being pictured on the side of the truck. On the back was a piece
of a puzzle that when joined with seven other cards made the
same exact image of the beckoning soft one, but eight times
bigger. I had the blue lapels and red bow tie, the sugar-cone-
flesh lips parted in a pure white smile, the exposed towering
brain of vanilla, cream-kissed at the top into a pointed swirl,
but I didn't have the eyes.

A complete puzzle won you the Special Softee, like Coney
Island in a plastic dish—four twirled Softee-loads of cream,
chocolate sauce, butterscotch, marshmallow goo, nuts, party-
colored sprinkles, raisins, M&M's, shredded coconut, bananas,
all topped with a cherry. You couldn't purchase the Special
Softee—you had to win it, or so said Mel, who through the
years had come to be known simply as Softee.

Occasionally Mel would try to be pleasant, but I think the
paper canoe of a hat he wore every day soured him. He also
wore a blue bow tie, a white shirt, and white pants. His face was
long and crooked, and at times, when the orders came too fast
and the kids didn't have the right change, the bottom half of his
face would slowly melt—a sundae abandoned at the curb. His
long ears sprouted tufts of hair as if his skull contained a hedge
of it, and the lenses of his glasses had internal flaws like dia-
monds. In a voice that came straight from his freezer, he called
my sister, Mary, and all the other girls "sweetheart."

Earlier in the season, one late afternoon, my brother, Jim,
said to me, "You want to see where Softee lives?" We took our
bikes. He led me way up Hammond Lane, past the shoe store
and the junior high school, up beyond Our Lady of Lourdes.
After a half hour of riding, he stopped in front of a small house.
As I pulled up, he pointed to the place and said, "Look at that
dump."

Softee's truck was parked on a barren plot at the side of the
place. I remember ivy and a one-story house, no bigger than a

good-size garage. Shingles showed their zebra stripes through fading white. The porch had obviously sustained a meteor shower. There were no lights on inside, and I thought this strange because twilight was mixing in behind the trees.

"Is he sitting in there in the dark?" I asked my brother.

Jim shrugged as he got back on his bike. He rode in big circles around me twice and then shot off down the street, screaming over his shoulder as loud as he could, "Softee sucks!" The ride home was through true night, and he knew that without him I would get lost, so he pedaled as hard as he could.

We had forsaken the jingle bells of Bungalow Bar and Good Humor all summer in an attempt to win Softee's contest. By the end of July, though, each of the kids on the block had at least two near-complete puzzles, but no one had the eyes. I had heard from Tim Sullivan, who lived in the development on the other side of the school field, that the kids over there got fed up one day and rushed the truck, jumped up and swung from the bar that held the rearview mirror, invaded the driver's compartment, all the while yelling, "Give us the eyes! The fuckin' eyes!" When Softee went up front to chase them, Tim's brother Bill leaped up on the sill of the window through which Softee served his customers, leaned into the inner sanctum, unlatched the freezer, and started tossing Italian ices out to the kids standing at the curb.

Softee lost his glasses in the fray, but the hat held on. He screamed, "You little bitches!" at them as they played him back and forth from the driver's area to the serving compartment. In the end, Mel got two big handfuls of cards and tossed them out onto the street. "Like flies on dog shit," said Tim. By the time they'd realized there wasn't a pair of eyes in the bunch, Softee had turned the bell off and was coasting silently around the corner.

I had a theory, though, that day at summer's end when I sat at the curb, waiting. It was my hope that Softee had been holding out on us until the close of the season, and then, in the final days before school started and he quit his route till spring, some kid was going to have bestowed upon him a pair of eyes. I had faith like I never had at church that something special was going to happen that day to me. It did, but it had nothing to do with ice cream. I sat there at the curb, waiting, until the sun started to go down and my mother called me in for dinner. Softee never came again, but as it turned out, we all got the eyes.

Will There Be Clowns?

■ My mother was a better painter than she was a cook. I loved her portrait of my father in a suit—the dark red background and the distant expression he wore—but I wasn't much for her spaghetti with tomato soup.

She stood at the kitchen stove over a big pot of it, glass of cream sherry in one hand, a burning cigarette with a three-quarter-inch ash in the other. When she turned and saw me, she said, "Go wash your hands." I headed down the hall toward the bathroom and, out of the corner of my eye, caught sight of that ash falling into the pot. Before I opened the bathroom door, I heard her mutter, "Could you possibly . . . ?" followed hard by the mud-sucking sounds of her stirring the orange glug.

When I came out of the bathroom, I got the job of mixing the powdered milk and serving each of us kids a glass. At the end of the meal, there would be three full glasses of it sitting on the table. Unfortunately, we still remembered real milk. The mix-up kind tasted like sauerkraut and looked like chalk water with froth on the top. It was there merely for show. As long as no one mentioned that it tasted horrible, my mother never forced us to drink it.

The dining-room walls were lined with grained paneling, the knots of which always showed me screaming faces. Jim sat across the table from me, and Mary sat by my side. My mother sat at the end of the table beneath the open window. Instead of a plate, she had the ashtray and her wine in front of her.

"It's rib-stickin' good," said Jim, adding a knifeful of margarine to his plate. Once the orange stuff started to cool, it needed constant lubrication.

"Shut up and eat," said my mother.

Mary said nothing. I could tell by the way she quietly nodded that she was being Mickey.

"Softee never came today," I said.

My brother looked up at me and shook his head in disappointment. "He'll be out there at the curb in a snowdrift," he said to my mother.

She laughed without a sound and swatted the air in his direction. "You've got to have faith," she said. "Life's one long son of a bitch."

She took a drag on her cigarette and a sip of wine, and Jim and I knew what was coming next.

"When things get better," she said, "I think we'll all take a nice vacation."

"How about Bermuda?" said Jim.

In her wine fog, my mother hesitated an instant, not sure if he was being sarcastic, but he knew how to keep a straight face. "That's what I was thinking," she said. We knew that, because once a week, when she hit just the right level of intoxication, that's what she was always thinking. It had gotten to the point that when Jim wanted me to do him a favor and I asked how he was going to pay me back, he'd say, "Don't worry, I'll take you to Bermuda."

She told us about the water, crystal blue, so clear you could look down a hundred yards and see schools of manta rays flapping their wings. She told us about the pure white beaches with palm trees swaying in the soft breeze filled with the scent of wildflowers. We'd sleep in hammocks on the beach. We'd eat pineapples we cut open with a machete. Swim in lagoons. Washed up on the shore, amid the chambered nautilus, the sand dollars, the shark teeth, would be pieces of eight from galleons wrecked long ago.

That night, as usual, she told it all, and she told it in minute detail, so that even Jim sat there listening with his eyes half closed and his mouth half open.

"Will there be clowns?" asked Mary in her Mickey voice.

"Sure," said my mother.

"How many?" asked Mary.

"Eight," said my mother.

Mary nodded in approval and returned to being Mickey.

When we got back from Bermuda, it was time to do the dishes. From the leftovers in the pot, my mother heaped a plate with spaghetti for my father to eat when he got home from work. She wrapped it in waxed paper and put it in the center of the stove where the pilot light would keep it warm. Whatever was left over went to George the dog. My mother washed the dishes, smoking and drinking the entire time. Jim dried, I put the plates and silverware away, and Mary counted everything a few dozen times.

Five years earlier the garage of our house had been converted into an apartment. My grandparents, Nan and Pop, lived in there. A door separated our house from their rooms. We knocked, and Nan called for us to come in.

Pop took out his mandolin and played us a few songs: "Apple Blossom Time," "Show Me the Way to Go Home," "Goodnight, Irene." All the while he played, Nan chopped cabbage on a flat wooden board with a one-handed guillotine. My mother rocked in the rocking chair and drank and sang. The trilling of the double-stringed instrument accompanied by my mother's voice was beautiful to me.

Over at the little table in the kitchenette area, Mary sat with the Laredo machine, making cigarettes. My parents didn't buy their smokes by the pack. Instead they had this machine that you loaded with a piece of paper and a wad of loose tobacco from a can. Once it was all set up, there was a little lever you pulled forward and back, and presto. It wasn't an easy operation. You had to use just the right amount to get the cigarettes firm enough so the tobacco didn't fall out the end.

When my parents had first gotten the Laredo, Mary watched them work it. She was immediately expert at measuring out the brown shag, sprinkling it over the crisp white paper, pulling the lever. Soon she took over as chief roller. She was a cigarette factory once she got going; Pop called her R. J. Reynolds. He didn't smoke them, though. He smoked Lucky Strikes, and he drank Old Grand-Dad, which seemed fitting.

Jim and I, we watched the television with the sound turned down. Dick Van Dyke mugged and rubber-legged and did pratfalls in black and white, perfectly synchronized to the strains of "Shanty Town" and "I'll Be Seeing You." Even if Pop and my mother weren't playing music, we wouldn't have been able to have the sound up, since Pop hated Dick Van Dyke more than any other man alive.

The Shadow Year

■ My room was dark, and though it had been warm all day, a cool end-of-summer breeze now filtered in through the screen of the open window. Moonlight also came in, making a patch on the bare, painted floor. From outside I could hear the chug of the Farleys' little pool filter next door and, beneath that, the sound of George's claws, tapping across the kitchen linoleum downstairs.

Jim was asleep in his room across the hall. Below us Mary was also asleep, no doubt whispering the times tables into her pillow. I could picture my mother, in the room next to Mary's, lying in bed, the reading light on, her mouth open, her eyes closed, and the thick red volume of Sherlock Holmes stories with the silhouette cameo of the detective on the spine open and resting on her chest. All I could picture of Nan and Pop was a darkened room and the tiny glowing bottle of Lourdes water in the shape of the Virgin that sat on the dresser.

I was thinking about the book I had been reading before turning out the light—another in the series of adventures of Perno Shell. This one was about a deluge, like Noah's flood, and how the old wooden apartment building Shell lived in had broken away from its foundation and he and all the other tenants were sailing the giant ocean of the world, having adventures.

There was a mystery about the Shell books, because they were all published under different authors' names, sometimes by different publishing companies, but you only had to read a few pages to tell that they were all written by the same person. The problem was finding them in the stacks, because the books were shelved alphabetically, according to the authors' last names. I would never have discovered them if it wasn't for Mary.

Occasionally I would read to her, snatches from whatever book I was working through. We'd sit in the corner of the backyard by the fence, in a bower made by forsythia bushes. One day, amid the yellow flowers, I read to her from the Shell book I had just taken out: *The Stars Above* by Mary Holden. There were illustrations in it, one per chapter. When I was done reading, I handed the book to her so she could look at the pictures. While paging through it, she held it up to her face, sniffed it, and said, "Pipe smoke." Back then my father smoked a pipe once in a while, so we knew the aroma. I took the book from her and smelled it up close, and she was right, but it wasn't the kind of tobacco my father smoked. It had a darker, older smell, like a cross between a horse and a mildewed wool blanket.

When I walked to the library downtown, Mary would walk with me. She rarely said a word during the entire trip, but a few weeks after I had returned *The Stars Above*, she came up to me while I was searching through the four big stacks that lay in the twilight zone between the adult and children's sections. She tugged at my shirt, and when I turned around, she handed me a book: *The Enormous Igloo* by Duncan Main.

"Pipe smoke," she said.

Opening the volume to the first page, I read, "'Perno Shell was afraid of heights and could not for the world remember why he had agreed to a journey in the Zeppelin that now hovered above his head.'" Another Perno Shell novel by someone completely different. I lifted the book, smelled the pages, and nodded.

Tonight I wanted Perno Shell to stay in my imagination until I dozed off, but my thoughts of him soon grew as thin as paper, and then the theme of my wakeful nights alone in the dark, namely death, came clawing through. Teddy Dunden, a boy who'd lived up the block, two years younger than me and two years older than Mary, had been struck by a car on Montauk Highway one night in late spring. The driver was drunk and swerved onto the sidewalk. According to his brother, Teddy was thrown thirty feet in the air. I always tried to picture that: twice again the height of the basketball hoop. We had to go to his wake. The priest said he was at peace, but he didn't look it. As he lay in the coffin, his skin was yellow, his face was bloated, and his mouth was turned down in a bitter frown.

All summer long he came back to me from where he lay under the ground. I imagined him suddenly waking up, clawing at the lid as in a story Jim had once told me. I dreaded meeting his ghost on the street at night when I walked George around the block alone. I'd stop under a streetlight and listen hard, fear would build in my chest until I shivered, and then I'd bolt for home. In the lonely backyard at sundown, in the darkened woods behind the school field, in the corner of my night room, Teddy Dunden was waiting, jealous and angry.

George came up the stairs, nudged open my bedroom door, and stood beside my bed. He looked at me with his bearded face and then jumped aboard. He was a small, schnauzer-type mutt, but fearless, and having him there made me less scared. Slowly I began to doze. I had a memory of riding waves at Fire Island, and it blurred at the edges, slipping into a dream. Next thing I knew, I was falling from a great height and woke to hear my father coming in from work. The front door quietly closed. I could hear him moving around in the kitchen. George got up and left.

I contemplated going down to say hello. The last I'd seen him was the previous weekend. The bills forced him to work three jobs: a part-time machining job in the early morning, then his regular job as a gear cutter, and then nights part-time as a janitor in a department store. He left the house before the sun came up every morning and didn't return until very near midnight. Through the week I would smell a hint of machine oil here and there, on the cushions of the couch, on a towel in the bathroom, as if he were a ghost leaving vague traces of his presence.

Eventually the sounds of the refrigerator opening and closing and the water running stopped, and I realized he must be sitting in the dining room, eating his pile of spaghetti, reading the newspaper by the light that shone in from the kitchen. I heard the big pages turn, the fork against the plate, a match being struck, and that's when it happened. There came from outside the house the shrill scream of a woman, so loud it tore the night open wide enough for the Shadow Year to slip out. I shivered, closed my eyes tight, and burrowed deep beneath the covers.

A Prowler

■ When I came downstairs the next morning, the door to Nan and Pop's was open. I stuck my head in and saw Mary sitting at the table in the kitchenette where the night before she had made cigarettes. She was eating a bowl of Cheerios. Pop sat in his usual seat next to her, the horse paper spread out in front of him. He was jotting down numbers with a pencil in the margins, murmuring a steady stream of bloodlines, jockeys' names, weights, speeds, track conditions, ciphering what he called "the McGinn System," named after himself. Mary nodded with each new factor added to the equation.

My mother came out of the bathroom down the hall in our house, and I turned around. She was dressed for work in her turquoise outfit with the big star-shaped pin that was like a stained-glass window. I went to her, and she put her arm around me, enveloped me in a cloud of perfume that smelled as thick as powder, and kissed my head. We went into the kitchen, and she made me a bowl of cereal with the mix-up milk, which wasn't as bad that way, because we were allowed to put sugar on it. I sat down in the dining room, and she joined me, carrying a cup of coffee. The sunlight poured in the window behind her. She lit a cigarette and dragged the ashtray close to her.

"Friday, last day of vacation," she said. "You better make it a good one. Monday is back to school."

I nodded.

"Watch out for strangers," she said. "I got a call from next door this morning. Mrs. Conrad said that there was a prowler at her window last night. She was changing into her nightgown, and she turned and saw a face at the glass."

"Did she scream?" I asked.

"She said it scared the crap out of her. Jake was downstairs watching TV. He jumped up and ran outside, but whoever it was had vanished."

Jim appeared in the living room. "Do you think they saw her naked?" he asked.

"A fitting punishment," she said. And as quickly added, "Don't repeat that."

"I heard her scream," I said.

"Whoever it was used that old ladder Pop keeps in the back-yard. Put it up against the side of the Conrads' house and climbed up to the second-floor window. So keep your eyes out for creeps wherever you go today."

"That means he was in our backyard," said Jim.

My mother took a drag of her cigarette and nodded. "I suppose."

Before she left for work, she gave us our list of jobs for the day—walk George, clean our rooms, mow the back lawn. Then she kissed Jim and me and went into Nan and Pop's to kiss Mary. I watched her car pull out of the driveway. Jim came to stand next to me at the front window.

"A prowler," he said, smiling. "We better investigate."

A half hour later, Jim and Mary and I, joined by Franky Conrad, sat back amid the forsythias.

"Did the prowler see your mother naked?" Jim asked Franky.

Franky had a hairdo like Curly from the Three Stooges, and he rubbed his head with his fat, blunt fingers. "I think so," he said, wincing.

"A fitting punishment," said Jim.

"What do you mean?" asked Franky.

"Think about your mother's ass," said Jim, laughing.

Franky sat quietly for a second and then said, "Yeah," and nodded.

Mary took out a Laredo cigarette and lit it. She always stole one or two when she made them. No one would have guessed. Mary was sneaky in a way, though. Jim would have told on me if I'd smoked one. All he did was say to her, "You'll stay short if you smoke that." She took a drag and said, "Could you possibly . . . ?" in a flat voice.

Jim, big boss that he was, laid it out for us. "I'll be the detective and you all will be my team." Pointing at me, he said, "You have to write everything down. Everything that happens must be recorded. I'll give you a notebook. Don't be lazy."

"Okay," I said.

"Mary," he said, "you count shit. And none of that Mickey stuff."

"I'm counting now," she said in her Mickey voice, nodding her head.

We cracked up, but she didn't laugh.

"Franky, you're my right-hand man. You do whatever the hell I tell you."

Franky agreed, and then Jim told us the first thing we needed to do was search for clues.

"Did your mother say what the prowler's face looked like?" I asked.

"She said it was no one she ever saw before. Like a ghost."

"Could be a vampire," I said.

"It wasn't a vampire," Jim said. "It was a pervert. If we're going to do this right, it's got to be like science. There's no such things as vampires."

Our first step was to investigate the scene of the crime. Beneath the Conrads' second-floor bedroom window, on the side of their house next to ours, we found a good footprint. It was big, much larger than any of ours, and it had a design on the bottom of lines and circles.

"You see what that is?" asked Jim, squatting down and pointing to the design.

"It's from a sneaker," I said.

"Yeah," he said.

"I think it's Keds," said Franky.

"What does that tell you?" asked Jim.

"What?" asked Franky.

"Well, it's too big to be a kid, but grown-ups usually don't wear sneakers. It might be a teenager. We better save this for if the cops ever come to investigate."

"Did your dad call the cops?" I asked.

"No. He said that if he ever caught who it was, he'd shoot the son of a bitch himself."

It took us about a half hour to dig up the footprint, carefully loosening the dirt all around it and scooping way down beneath it with the shovel. We went to Nan's side door and asked her if she had a box. She gave us a round pink hatbox with a lid that had a picture of a poodle and the Eiffel Tower.

Jim told Franky, "Carry it like it's nitro," and we took it into our yard and stored it in the toolshed back by the fence. When Franky slid it into place on the wooden shelf next to the bottles of bug killer, Mary said, "One."

As God Is My Judge

■ Nan made lunch for us when the fire whistle blew at noon. She served it in our house at the dining-room table. Her sandwiches always had butter, no matter what else she put on them. Sometimes, like that day, she just made butter-and-sugar sandwiches. We also had barley soup. Occasionally she would make us chocolate pudding—the kind with an inch of vinyl skin across the top—but usually dessert was a ladyfinger.

Nan had gray wire-hair like George's, big bifocals, and a brown mole on her temple that looked like a squashed raisin. Her small stature, dark and wrinkled complexion, and the silken black strands at the corners of her upper lip made her seem to me at times like some ancient monkey king. When she'd fart while standing, she'd kick her left leg up in the back and say, "Shoot him in the pants. The coat and vest are mine."

Every morning she'd say the rosary, and in the afternoon when the neighborhood ladies came over to drink wine from teacups, she'd read the future in a pack of playing cards.

Each day at lunch that summer, along with the butter sandwiches, she'd also serve up a story from her life. That first day of our investigation, she told us one from her childhood in Whitestone, where her father had been the editor of the local paper, where the fire engines were pulled by horses, where Moishe Pipik, the strongest man alive, ate twelve raw eggs every morning for breakfast, where Clementine Cherenete, whose hair was a waterfall of gold, fell in love with a blind man who could not see her beauty, and where John Hardy Farty, a wandering vagrant, strummed a harp and sang "Damn the rooster crow." All events, both great and small, happened within sight of a local landmark, Nanny Goat Hill.

"A night visitor," she said when we told her about the footprint we had found and preserved in her pink hatbox. "Once there was a man who lived in Whitestone, a neighbor of ours. His name was Mr. Weeks. He had a daughter, Louqueer, who was in my grade at school."

"Louqueer?" said Jim, and he and I laughed. Mary looked up from counting the grains of barley in her soup to see what was so funny.

Nan smiled and nodded. "She was a little odd. Spent all her time staring into a mirror. She wasn't vain but was looking for something. Her mother told my mother that at night the girl would wake up choking, blue in the face, from having dreamed she was swallowing a thimble."

"That wasn't really her name," said Jim.

"As God is my judge," said Nan. "Her father took the train every day to work in the city and didn't come home until very late at night. He always got the very last train that stopped in Whitestone, just before midnight, and would stumble home drunk through the streets from the station. It was said that when he was drunk at a bar, he was happy-go-lucky, not a care in the world, but when he got drunk at home, he hit his wife and cursed her.

"One night around Halloween, he got off the train at Whitestone. The wind was blowing, and it was cold. The station was empty but for him. He started walking toward the steps that led down to the street, when from behind him he heard a noise like a voice in the wind. *OOOOoooo* was what it sounded like. He turned around, and at the far end of the platform was a giant ghost, eight feet tall, rippling in the breeze.

"It scared the bejesus out of him. He ran home screaming. The next day, which was Saturday, he told my father that the train station was haunted. My father printed the story as kind of a joke. No one believed Mr. Weeks, because everyone knew he was a drunk. Still, he tried to convince people by swearing to it, saying he knew what he saw and it was real.

"On the way into the city on the following Friday, he told one of the neighbors, Mr. Laveglia, who took the same train in the morning, that the ghost had been there on both Monday and Wednesday nights and that both times it had called his name. Weeks was a nervous wreck, stuttering and shaking while he told of his latest encounters. Mr. Laveglia said Weeks was a man on the edge, but before getting off the train in the city, Weeks leaned in close to our neighbor and whispered to him that he had a plan to deal with the phantom. It was eight o'clock in the morning, and Mr. Laveglia said he already smelled liquor on Weeks's breath.

"That night Weeks returned from the city on the late train. When he got off onto the platform at Whitestone, it was deserted as usual. The moment he turned around, there was the ghost, moaning, calling his name, and coming straight at him. But that day, in the city, Weeks had bought a pistol. *That* was his plan. He took it out of his jacket, shot four times, and the ghost collapsed on the platform."

"How can you kill a ghost?" asked Jim.

"It was eight feet tall," said Mary.

"It wasn't a ghost," said Nan. "It was his wife in a bedsheet, standing on stilts. She wanted to scare her husband into coming home on time and not drinking. But he killed her."

"Did he get arrested for murder?" I asked.

"No," said Nan. "He wept bitterly when he found out it was

his wife. When the police investigation was over and he was shown to have acted in self-defense, he abandoned his home and Louqueer and went off to live as a hermit in a cave in a field of wild asparagus at the edge of town. I don't remember why, but eventually he became known as Bedelia, and kids would go out to the cave and scream, 'Bedelia, we'd love to steal ya!' and run away when he chased them. Louqueer got sent to an orphanage, and I never saw her again."

"What happened to the hermit?" asked Jim.

"During a bad winter, someone found him in the middle of the field by his cave, frozen solid. In the spring they buried him there among the wild asparagus."

Sewer Pipe Hill

■ After lunch we put George on the leash and took him out into the backyard. Mary didn't go with us because she decided to have a session with her make-believe friends, Sally O'Malley and Sandy Graham, who lived in the closet in her room. Once in a while, she'd let them out and she would become Mickey and they would go to school together down in the cellar.

Jim had the idea that we could use George to track the pervert. We'd let him smell the ladder, he'd pick up the scent, and we'd follow along. Franky Conrad joined us in our backyard where the ladder again lay propped against the side of the toolshed. For a while we just stood there waiting for the dog to smell the ladder. Then I told Jim, "You better rev him up." To rev George up, all you had to do was stick your foot near his mouth. If you left it there long enough, he'd start to growl. Jim stuck his foot out and made little circles with it in the air near George's mouth. *"Geoorgieee,"* he sang very softly. When the dog had had enough, he went for the foot, growling like crazy and fake-biting all over it—a hundred fake bites a second. He never really chomped down.

When he was revved, he moved to the ladder, smelled it a few times, and then pissed on it. We were ready to do some tracking. George started walking, and so did we. Out of the backyard, we went through the gate by Nan's side of the house and under the pink blossoms of the prehistoric mimosa tree into the front yard.

Around the corner was East Lake School, a one-story red-brick structure, a big rectangle of classrooms with an enclosed courtyard of grass at its center. On the right-hand side was an alcove that held the playground for the kindergarten—monkey bars, swings, a seesaw, a sandbox, and one of those round, turning platform things that if you got it spinning fast enough, all the kids would fly off. The gym was attached to the left-hand side of the building, a giant, windowless box of brick that towered over the squat main building.

The school had a circular drive in front with an elongated, high-curbed oval of grass at its center. Just west of the drive and the little parking lot there were two asphalt basketball courts, and beyond that spread a vast field with a baseball backstop and bases, where on windy days the powdered dirt of the baselines rose in cyclones. At the border of the field was a high barbed-wire-topped fence to prevent kids from climbing down into a craterlike sump. Someone long ago had used a chain cutter to make a slit in the fence that a small person could pass through. Down there in the early fall, among the goldenrod stalks and dying weeds, it was a kingdom of crickets.

Behind the school were more fields of sunburned summer grass cut by three asphalt bike paths. At the back the school fields were bounded by another development, but to the east lay the woods: a deep oak-and-pine forest that stretched well into the next town and south as far as the railroad tracks. Streams ran through it, as well as some rudimentary paths that we knew better than the lines on our own palms. A quarter mile in lay a small lake that we had been told was bottomless.

That day George led us to the boundary of the woods, near the pregnant swelling of ground known as Sewer Pipe Hill. We stood on the side of the hill where a round, dark circle of the pipe protruded and faced the tree line. Some days a trickle of water flowed from the pipe, but today it was bone dry. Jim walked over to the round opening, three feet in circumference, leaned over, and yelled, *"Hellooooo!"* His word echoed down the dark tunnel beneath the school fields. George pissed on the concrete facing that held up the end of the pipe.

"X marks the spot," said Jim. He turned to Franky. "You better crawl in there and see if the prowler is hiding underground."

Franky rubbed his head and stared at the black hole.

"Are you my right-hand man?" asked Jim.

"Yes," said Franky. "But what if he's in there?"

"Before he touches you, just say you're making a citizen's arrest."

Franky thought about this for a moment.

"Don't do it," I said.

Jim glared at me. Then he put his hand on Franky's shoulder and said, "He saw your mom's ass."

Franky nodded and went to the pipe opening. He bent down, got on his knees, and then crawled forward into the dark a little way before stopping. Jim went over and lightly tapped him in the rear end with the toe of his sneaker. "You'll be a hero if you find him. They'll put your picture in the newspaper." Franky started crawling forward again, and in seconds he was out of sight.

"What if he gets lost in there?" I said.

"We'll just have everyone in town flush at the same time, and he'll ride the wave out into the sump behind the baseball field," said Jim.

Every few minutes one of us would lean into the pipe and yell to Franky, and he would yell back. Pretty soon we couldn't make out what he was saying, and his voice got smaller and smaller. Then we called a few more times and there was no answer.

"What do you think happened to him?" I asked.

"Maybe the pervert got him," said Jim, and he looked worried. "He could be stuck in there."

"Should I run home and get Pop?" I asked.

"No," said Jim. "Go up to that manhole cover on the bike path by the playground and call down through the little hole. Then put your ear over the hole and see if you hear him. Tell him to come back."

I took off running up the side of Sewer Pipe Hill and across the field as fast as I could. Reaching the manhole cover, I got on all fours and leaned my mouth down to the neat round hole at its edge. "Hey!" I yelled. I turned my head and put my ear to the hole.

Franky's voice came up to me quite clearly but with a metallic ring to it, as if he were a robot.

"What?" he said. "I'm here." It sounded as if he were right beneath me.

"Come out," I called. "Jim says to come back."

"I like it in here," he said.

In that moment I pictured his house; his sister, Lily, with her crossed eyes; his mother's prominent jaw and horse teeth, her crazy red hair; the little figures his father fashioned out of the wax from his enormous ears. "You gotta come back," I said.

A half minute passed in silence, and I thought maybe he had moved on, continuing through the darkness.

Finally his voice sounded. "Okay," he said, and then, "Hey, I found something."

Jim was sitting on the lip of the sewer pipe reading a magazine, while George sat at his feet staring up at him. As I eased down the side of the hill, he said, "Look what George tracked down by that fallen tree." He pointed into the woods. "There were some crushed beer cans and cigarette butts over there."

I came up next to him and looked over his shoulder at the magazine. It was wrinkled from having been rained on, and there was mud splattered on the cover. He turned the page he was looking at toward me, and I saw a woman with red hair, black stockings, high-heeled shoes, a top hat, and an open jacket but nothing else.

"Look at the size of those tits," said Jim.

"She's naked," I whispered.

Jim picked the magazine up to his mouth, positioning it right in the middle of her spread-out legs, where the little hedge of red hair grew over her pussy, and yelled, *"Hellooooooo!"*

We laughed.

I forgot to tell Jim that I'd made contact with Franky. Instead we moved on to the centerfold. Three full pages of a giant blonde bending over a piano bench.

"Aye-aye, Captain," said Jim, and rapidly saluted her ass four times. Then we flipped the pages quickly to the next naked woman, only to stare and swoon.

As I reached down to pet the dog for his discovery, we heard Franky inside the pipe. Jim got up and turned around, and we both stared into the opening. Slowly the soles of his shoes appeared out of the dark, and then his rear end, as he backed out into daylight. When he stood up and turned to face us, he was smiling.

"What's your report?" asked Jim.

"It was nice and quiet in there," said Franky.

Jim shook his head. "Anything else?"

Franky held out his hand and showed Jim what he'd found. It was a green plastic soldier, carrying a machine gun in one hand and a grenade in the other. I moved closer to see the detail and noticed that the figure wore no helmet, which was unusual for an army man. He wore cartridge belts over each shoulder, and his lips were pulled back so that you could see his teeth gritted tight.

Jim took the soldier out of Franky's hand, looked at it for a second, said, "Sergeant Rock," and then put it into his pocket.

Franky's brow furrowed. "Give it back," he said. His hands balled into fists, and he took a step forward as a challenge.

Jim said, "Let me ask you a question. When the prowler saw your mother's ass . . ."

"Stop saying my mother's ass," said Franky, and took another step forward.

". . . did it look like this?" asked Jim, and he flipped the magazine so that the centerfold opened.

Franky saw it and went slack. He brought his hands up to his cheeks, his fingers partially covering his eyes. "Oh, no," he said, and stared.

"Oh, yes," said Jim. He ripped off the bottom third, the page containing the big ass, and handed it to Franky. "This is your reward for bravery in the sewer pipe."

Franky took the torn page in his trembling hands, his gaze fixed on the picture. Then he looked up and said, "Let me see the magazine."

"I can't," said Jim. "It's Exhibit A. Evidence. You'll get your fingerprints on it." He rolled it up and put it under his arm the way Mr. Mangini carried the newspaper as he walked down the street coming home from work every evening.

We spent another couple of hours looking for clues all around the school field and through the woods, but George lost the scent, and we eventually headed home. At every other driveway we passed, Franky would take his piece of centerfold out of his back pocket and stop to stare at it. We left him standing in front of Mrs. Grimm's house, petting the image as if it were flesh instead of slick paper.

Botch Town

■ When we got home, Jim made me go in first and see if the coast was clear. My mother wouldn't be home for about two hours, and Nan and Pop were in their place. I didn't see Mary around, but that didn't matter anyway.

Up in his room, Jim slid the loose floorboard back and stowed the magazine. Then he got up and went to his desk. "Here," he said, and turned around holding a black-and-white-bound composition book. "This is for the investigation." He walked over and handed it to me. "Write down everything that's happened so far."

I took the book from him and nodded.

"What are you gonna do with the soldier?" I asked.

Jim took the green warrior out of his pocket and held it up. "Guess," he said.

"Botch Town?" I asked.

"Precisely," he said.

I followed him out of the room, down the stairs, through the living room, to the hallway that led to the first-floor bedrooms. At the head of this hall was a door. He opened it, and we descended the creaking wooden steps into the dim mildew of the cellar.

The cellar was lit by one bare bulb with a pull string and whatever light managed to seep in from outside through the four window wells. The floor was unpainted concrete, as were the walls. The staircase bisected the layout, and there was an area behind the steps, where a curtain hung, that allowed access from one side to the other. Six four-inch-thick metal poles positioned in a row across the center of the house supported the ceiling.

It was warm in the winter and cool in the summer down there in the underground twilight, where the aroma of my mother's oil paints and turpentine mixed with the pine and glittering tinsel scent of Christmas decorations heaped in one corner. It was a treasure vault of the old, the broken, the forgotten. Stuff lay on shelves or stacked along the walls, covered with a thin layer of cellar dust, the dandruff of concrete, and veiled in cobwebs hung with spider eggs.

On Pop's heavy wooden workbench, complete with crushing vise, there sat coffee cans of rusted nuts and bolts and nails, planes, rasps, wrenches, levels with little yellow bubbles encased to live forever. Riding atop this troubled sea of strewn tools, seemingly abandoned in the middle of the greatest home-repair job ever attempted, was a long, curving Chinese junk carved from the horn of an ox, sporting sails the color of singed paper, created from thin sheets of animal bone, and manned by a little fellow, carved right out of the black horn, who wore a field worker's hat and kept one hand on the tiller. Pop told me he had bought it in Singapore, when he traveled the world with the merchant marine, from a woman who showed him my mother as a little girl dancing, years before she was born, in a piece of crystal shaped like an egg.

Leaning against the pipe that ran along the back wall and then out of the house to connect with the sewer line were my mother's paintings: a self-portrait standing in a darkened hallway, holding me when I was a baby; the flowering bushes of the Bayard Cutting Arboretum; a seascape and view of Captree Bridge. All the colors were subdued, and the images came into focus slowly, like wraiths approaching out of a fog.

Crammed into and falling out of one tall bookcase that backed against the stair railing on the right-hand side were my father's math books and used notebooks, every inch filled with numbers and weird signs, in his hand, in pencil, as if through many years he had been working the equation to end all equations. I remember a series of yellow journals, each displaying in a circle on the cover the bust of some famous, long-dead genius I would have liked to know more about, but when I pulled one journal off the shelf and opened it, that secret language inside told me nothing.

In the middle of the floor to the right of the stairs sat an old school desk, with wooden chair attached, and a place to put your books underneath. Around this prop Mary created the school that her alter ego, Mickey, attended. Sometimes, when I knew she was playing this game, I would open the door in the hallway and listen to the strangely different voices of the teacher, Mrs. Harkmar, of her classmates, Sally O'Malley and Sandy Graham, and naturally of Mickey, who knew all the answers.

Back in the shadows where the oil burner hummed stood a small platform holding the extreme-unction box, a religious artifact with hand-carved doors and a brass cross protruding from the top. We had no idea what unction was, but Jim told me it was "holy as hell" and that if you opened the door, the Holy Ghost would come out and strangle you, so that when they found your dead body it'd look like you just swallowed your tongue the wrong way.

To the left of the stairs, beneath the single bare bulb like a sun, lay Jim's creation, the sprawling burg of Botch Town. At one point my father was thinking of getting us an electric-train set. He went out and bought four sawhorses and the most enormous piece of plywood he could find. He set these up as a train table, but then the money troubles descended and it sat for quite a while, smooth and empty. One day Jim brought a bunch of cast-off items home with him, picked up along his early-morning paper route. It had been junk day, and he'd delivered his papers before the garbagemen had come. With coffee cans, old shoe boxes, pieces from broken appliances, Pez dispensers, buttons, Dixie cups, ice cream sticks, bottles, and assorted other discarded items, he began to build a facsimile of our neighborhood and the surrounding area. It became a project that he worked on a little here, a little there, continuously adding details.

He'd started by painting the road (battleship gray) that came down straight from Hammond Lane and then curved around to the school, made from a shoe box with windows cut in it, a flagpole outside, the circular drive, basketball courts, and fields. Neatly written on the building in black Magic Marker above the front doors was RETARD FACTORY. The rest of the board he painted green for grass, with the exception of the lake in the woods, whose deep blue oval was covered with glitter.

I left Jim there, contemplating his miniature world, and went back upstairs to record what we'd so far discovered.

Dead Man's Float

■ I sat at the desk in my room, the open notebook in front of me, a pencil in my hand, and stared out the window, trying to recall all the details surrounding the prowler. There was the old ladder and the footprint, sitting, like a dirt layer cake, in a pink hatbox in the shed. I could have started with Mrs. Conrad and her ass, or just her scream.

But, in fact, I didn't know where to start. Although from the time I was six, I had always loved writing and reading, I didn't feel much like recording evidence. Then, through the open window, I heard the Farleys' back screen door groan open and slam shut. I stood and looked out to see what was going on. It was Mr. Farley, carrying a highball in one hand and a towel in the other. He was dressed in his swimming trunks, his body soft and yellow-white. His head seemed too heavy for the muscles of his neck, and it drooped forward, making him look as if he were searching for something he'd dropped in the grass.

The Farleys' pool was a child's aboveground model, larger than the kind you blow up but no bigger than three feet deep and no wider than eight across. Mr. Farley set his drink down on the picnic table, draped his towel over the thickest branch of the cherry tree, shuffled out of his sandals, and stepped gingerly over the side into the glassy water.

He trolled the surface, inspecting every inch for beetles and bees that might have escaped the draw of the noisy little filter that ran constantly. He fetched up blackened cherry leaves from the bottom with his toes and tossed them into the yard. Only then did he sit, cautiously, the liquid rising to accommodate his paunch, his sagging chest and rounded shoulders, until his head bobbed on the surface. Gradually he dipped forward, bringing his legs underneath him. His arms stretched out at his sides, his legs straightened behind him, his back broke the surface, and his face slipped beneath the water, leaving one bright bubble behind in its place.

He floated there for a moment, his body stretched tautly across the center of the pool, and there came an instant when the rigid raft of his form gave way to death. His arms sank slowly, and his body curled like a piece of dough in a deep fryer. Mr. Farley really could do a mean dead man's float. I wondered if he left his eyes open, letting them burn with chlorine, or if he closed them in order to dream more deeply into himself.

I sat back down at my desk, and instead of writing about the investigation I wrote about Mr. Farley. After describing him getting into the pool and fake-drowning, I recorded two other incidents I remembered. The first had to do with his older son, Gregory, who had since moved away from home. When the boy was younger, Farley, an engineer who made tools for flights into outer space, tried to get his son interested in astronomy and science. Instead the kid wanted to be an artist. Mr. Farley didn't approve. Before Gregory left home for good, he made a giant egg out of plaster of paris and set it up in the middle of the garden in the backyard. It sat there through months of wind and rain and sun and eventually turned green. On the day after the astronauts walked on the moon, Mr. Farley sledgehammered the thing into oblivion.

The second incident happened one day when my father and I were raking leaves on the front lawn. Suddenly the Farleys' front door opened and there he stood, weaving slightly, highball in hand. My father and I both stopped raking. Mr. Farley started down the steps tentatively, and with each step his legs buckled a little more until he stumbled forward, his knees landing on the lawn. He remained kneeling for an instant and then tipped forward, falling face-first onto the ground. Throughout all this, and even when he lay flat, he held his drink up above his head like a man trying to keep a pistol dry while crossing a river. I noticed that not a drop was spilled, as did my father, who looked over at me and whispered, "Nice touch."

I put the pencil down and closed the notebook with a feeling of accomplishment. Jim had Botch Town, Mary had her imaginary world, my mother had her wine, my father his jobs, Nan the cards, and Pop his mandolin. Instead of writing about the footprint or Mrs. Conrad's scream, I planned to fill the notebook with the lives of my neighbors, creating a Botch Town of my own between two covers.

When I went down into the cellar to tell Jim about my decision, I found him holding the plastic soldier up to the lightbulb. Big white circles had been painted over his eyes, and his hands, which had once held the machine gun and grenade, had been chopped off and replaced with straight pins that jutted dangerously, points out, from the stubs of his arms.

"Watch this: glow-in-the-dark paint," said Jim, standing the figure upright on the board between our house and the Conrads'. He then leaned way out over Botch Town and pulled the lightbulb string. The cellar went dark.

"The eyes," he said, and I looked down to see the twin circles on the soldier's face glowing in the shadows of the handmade town. The sight of him there, like something from a nightmare, gave me a chill.

Jim stood quietly, admiring his creation, and I told him what I had decided to do with the notebook. I thought he would be mad at me for not following his orders.

"Good work," he said. "Everyone is a suspect."

He Walks the Earth

■ Saturday afternoon I sat with Mary back amid the forsythias and read to her the descriptions of the people I had written about in my notebook so far. That morning I'd gone out on my bike early, scouring the neighborhood for likely suspects to turn into words, and had caught sight of Mrs. Harrington, whom I had nicknamed "the Colossus" for her mesmerizing girth, and Mitchell Erikson, a kid who shared my birthday and who, for every school assembly and holiday party, played "Lady of Spain" on his accordion.

I doled them out to Mary, starting with Mr. Farley, reading in the same rapid whisper I used when relaying a chapter of a Perno Shell adventure. Mary was a good audience. She sat still, only nodding occasionally as she did when she sat with Pop while he figured the horses. Each nod told me that she had taken in and understood the information up to that point. She was not obviously saddened when Mrs. Harrington's diminutive potato-head husband died, nor did she laugh at my description of Mitchell's smile when bowing to scanty applause. Her nod told me she was tabulating the results of my effort, though, and that was all I needed.

When I was done and had closed the notebook, she sat for a moment in silence. Finally she looked at me and said, "I'll take Mrs. Harrington to place."

Our mother called us in then. Since it was the weekend, my father had just gotten home from work, and it was time for us to visit our aunt Laura. We piled into the white Biscayne, Jim and me in the back with Mary between us. My father drove with the window open, his elbow leaning out in the sun, a cigarette going between his fingers. I hadn't seen him all week, and he looked tired. Adjusting the rearview mirror, he peered back at us and smiled. "All aboard," he said.

St. Anselm's was somewhere on the North Shore of Long Island, nearly an hour's drive from our house. The ride was usually solemn, but my father sometimes played the radio for us, or if he was in a good mood, he'd tell us a story about when he was a boy. Our favorites were about the ancient, swaybacked plow horse, Pegasus, dirty white and ploddingly dangerous, that he and his brother kept as kids in Amityville.

This hospital was not a single modern building, smelling vaguely of Lysol and piss. St. Anselm's was like a small town of stone castles set amid the woods, a fairy-tale place of giant granite steps, oaken doors, stained glass, and dim, winding corridors that echoed in their emptiness. There was a spot set amid a thicket of poplars where a curved concrete bench lay before a fountain whose statuary was a pelican piercing its own chest with its beak. Water geysered forth from the wound. And the oddest thing of all was that everyone there, save the patients and old, bent Dr. Hasbith of the bushy white sideburns, was a nun.

I'd never seen so many nuns before, all of them dressed in their flowing black robes and tight headgear. If one of them came toward you from out of the cool shadows and your eyes weren't yet adjusted to the dark interior, it was like a disembodied face floating in midair. They moved about in utter silence, and only rarely would one smile in passing. The place was haunted by God. I couldn't help thinking that our aunt was being held prisoner there, enchanted like Sleeping Beauty, and that on some lucky Saturday we would rescue her.

As usual, we were not allowed to accompany our parents to the place where Aunt Laura was kept. Jim was left in charge, and we were each given a quarter to buy a soda. We knew that if we went down a set of winding steps that led into what I thought of as a dungeon, we would find a small room with a soda machine and two tables with chairs. Our typical routine was to descend, have a drink, and then go and sit on the bench by the fountain to watch the pelican bleed water for two hours. But that day, after we'd finished our sodas, Jim pointed into the shadow at the back wall of the small canteen to a door I'd never noticed before.

"What do you think is in there?" he asked as he walked over to it.

"Hell," said Mary.

Jim turned the knob, flung the door open, and jumped back. Mary and I left our seats and stood behind him. We could see a set of stone steps leading downward, walls close on either side like a brick gullet. There was no light in the stairway itself, but a vague glow shone up from the bottom of the steps. Jim turned to look at us briefly. "I order you to follow me."

At the bottom of the long flight of steps, we found a room with a low ceiling, a concrete floor, and a row of pews that disappeared into darkness toward the back. Up front, near the entrance to the stairway, was a small altar and above it a huge painting in a golden frame. The dim light we had seen from above was a single bulb positioned to illuminate the picture, which showed a scene of Jesus and Mary sitting next to a pool in the middle of a forest. The aquamarine of Mary's gown was radiant, and both her and Christ's eyes literally shone. The figures were smiling, and their hair, along with the leaves in the background, appeared to be moving.

"Let's go back," I said.

Mary inched away toward the stairs, and I started to follow her.

"One second," said Jim. "Look at this, the holy fishing trip."

We heard a rustle of material and something clunk against the heavy wood of one of the pews behind us. I jumped, and even Jim spun around with a look of fright on his face.

"It's a lovely scene, isn't it?" said a soft female voice. From out of the dark came a nun, whose face, pushing through the black mantle of her vestments, was so young and beautiful it confused me. She, too, was smiling, and her hands were pale and delicate. She lifted one as she passed by us and climbed onto the altar. "But you mustn't miss the message of the painting," she said, pointing.

"Do you see here?" she asked, and turned to look at us.

We nodded and followed her direction to gaze into the woods behind Mary and Jesus.

"What do you see?"

Jim stepped closer and a few seconds later said, "Eyes and a smile."

"Someone is there in the woods," I said as the figure became evident to me.

"A dark figure, spying from the woods," said the nun. "Who is it?"

"The devil," said Mary.

"You're a smart girl," said the nun. "Satan. Do you see how much this looks like a scene from the Garden of Eden? Well, the painter is showing us that just as Adam and Eve were subject to temptation, to death, so were the Savior and His mother. So are we all."

"Why is he hiding?" asked Jim.

"He's waiting and watching for the right moment to strike. He's clever."

"But the devil isn't real," said Jim. "My father told me."

She smiled sweetly at us. "Oh, the devil is real, child. I've seen him. If you don't pay attention, he'll take you."

"Good-bye now," whispered Mary, who took my hand and pulled me toward the steps.

"What does he look like?" asked Jim.

I didn't want to be there, but I couldn't move. I thought the nun would get angry, but instead her smile intensified, and her face went from pleasant to scary.

Mary pulled my arm, and we took off up the stairs. Not bothering to stop in the canteen, we kept going up the next set of steps to the outside and only rested when we made it to the bench by the fountain. We waited there for some time, hypnotized by the cascading water, before Jim finally showed up.

"You chickens should be hung for mutiny," he said as he approached.

"Mary was afraid," I said. "I had to get her out of there."

"Check your own shorts," he said, shaking his head. "But she told me a secret."

"What?" I asked.

"How to spot the devil when he walks the earth. That's what Sister Joe said, 'when he walks the earth,'" said Jim, and he started laughing.

"She was the devil," said Mary, staring into the water.

That night, back at home, the wine flowed, and my parents danced in the living room to the Ink Spots on the Victrola. Something dire was up, I could tell, because they didn't talk and there was a joyless gravity to their spins and dips.

Before we turned in, Nan came over from next door and told us that while we were out she had heard from Mavis across the street that the prowler had struck again. When Mavis's husband, Dan, had taken out the trash, he heard something moving in their grape arbor. He called out, "Who's there?" Of course there was no answer, but he saw a shadow and a pair of eyes. Dan was an airline pilot who flew all over the world, and one of his hobbies was collecting old weapons. He ran inside and fetched a long knife from Turkey that had a wriggled blade

like a flat, frozen snake. Mavis had told Nan that he charged
out the back door toward the arbor, but halfway there tripped
on a divot in the lawn, fell, and stabbed his own thigh. By the
time he was able to hobble back beneath the hanging grapes,
the prowler had vanished.

While my mother sat in her rocker, eyes closed, rocking to
the music, Jim and I arm-wrestled my father a few times, and
then Mary danced with him, her bare feet on his shoes. "Bed,"
my mother finally said, her eyes still closed.

At the top of the stairs before Jim and I went into our separate rooms, he said to me, "He walks the earth." I laughed, but
he didn't. George followed me to bed and lay by my feet, falling
asleep instantly. He kicked his back leg three times and growled
in his dreams. I stayed awake for a while, listening to my parents' hushed conversation down in the living room, but I
couldn't make anything out.

I wasn't the least bit tired, so I got up and went over to my
desk. Nan's talking about Mavis and Dan gave me the idea to
capture them in my notebook before I forgot. All I found interesting about Dan were the things that he owned: the leopard-
skin rug, the shrunken head, the axes and knives and ancient
pistols. Otherwise he was a pretty blank person, save for his
toupee, which sat on his head like a doily. Mavis, on the other
hand, had been born in Ireland, in the town of Cork, and had
the most beautiful way of talking. She had grown up with the
actor Richard Harris, who sang the song about the cake in the
rain.

By the time I was done, it was quiet downstairs, and I knew
that my parents had finally gone to bed. Still, I wasn't tired, and
on top of that I was a little spooked by the day's events. Any
thought of death was capable of conjuring the angry spirit of
Teddy Dunden. To dispel his gathering presence, I got out of
bed and tiptoed quietly down the stairs. In the kitchen I stole a
cookie, and that's when I decided to visit Botch Town.

Every old wooden step on the way to the cellar groaned miserably, but my father's snoring, rolling forth from the bedroom at the back of the house, covered my own prowling. Once below, I inched blindly forward, and when my hip touched the edge of the plywood world, I leaned way over and grabbed the pull string. The sun came out in the middle of the night in Botch Town. I half expected the figures to scurry, but no, they must have heard me coming and froze on cue. Peering down on the minute lives made me think for an instant about my own smallness.

Scanning the board, I found the prowler, with his straight-pin hands, on the prowl, hiding in the toothpick grape arbor netted with vines of green thread behind Mavis and Dan's house across the street from ours, his clever, glowing eyes like beacons searching the dark.

The Retard Factory

■ School started on a day so hot it seemed stolen from the heart of summer. The tradition was that if you got new clothes for school, you wore them the first day. My mother had made Mary a couple of dresses on the sewing machine. Because he'd outgrown what he had, Jim got shirts and pants from Gertz department store. I got his hand-me-downs, but I did also get a new pair of dungarees. They were as stiff as concrete and, after months of my wearing nothing but cutoffs, seemed to weigh fifty pounds. I sweated like the Easter pig, shuffling through school zombie style, to the library, the lunchroom, on the playground, and all day long that burlap scent of new denim smelled like the spirit of work.

Jim was starting seventh grade and was going to Hammond Road Junior High. He had to take a bus to get there. Mary and I were still stuck at the Retard Factory around the corner. None of us was a good student. I spent most of my time in the classroom either completely confused or daydreaming. Mary should have been in fourth grade but instead was in a special class in Room X, basically because they couldn't figure out if she was really smart or really simple. The kids they couldn't figure out, they put in Room X. Although all the other classrooms had numbers, this one had just the letter that signaled something cut-rate, like on the TV commercials: Brand X. When I'd pass by that room, I'd look in and see these wacky kids hobbling around or mumbling or crying, and there would be Mary, sitting straight up, focused, nodding every once in a while. Her teacher, Mrs. Rockhill, whom we called "Rockhead," was no Mrs. Harkmar and didn't have the secret to draw the Mickey of all right answers out of her. I knew Mary was really smart, though, because Jim had told me she was a genius.

Once they called Jim into the psychologist's office and made my mother go over to the school and witness the tests they gave him. They showed him pages of paint blobs and asked him what he saw in them. "I see a spider biting a woman's lip," he said, and, "That's a sick three-legged dog, eating grass." Then they asked him to put pegs of various shapes into appropriate holes in a block of wood. He shoved all the wrong pegs into all the wrong holes. Finally my mother smacked him in the back of the head, and then he and she started laughing. Throughout sixth grade he incorporated something about Joe Manygoats, a Navajo boy written about in the fifth-grade social-studies book, into all his test answers, no matter the subject, and signed all yearbooks with that name. Still, he never failed a grade, and this gave me hope that I, too, would someday leave East Lake.

My teacher for sixth grade was the fearsome Mr. Krapp. To borrow a phrase from Nan, "as God is my judge," that was his name. He was a short guy with a sharp nose and a crew cut so flat you could land a helicopter on it. Jim had had him for sixth grade, too, and told me he screamed a lot. My mother had diagnosed Krapp with a Napoleonic complex. "You know," she said, "he's a little general." He assured us on the first day that he "wouldn't stand for any of it." The third time he repeated the phrase, Tim Sullivan, who sat beside me, whispered, "He'd rather get down on his knees."

Krapp also had big ears, and he heard Tim, who he made get up in front of the classroom and repeat for everyone what he'd said. That day we all learned an important lesson in how not to laugh no matter how funny something is.

School brought a great heaviness to the hours of my days as if they, too, had put on new dungarees. By that year, though, it was business as usual, so I weathered it with a grim resignation. The only thing drastic that happened in that first week occurred on the way home one afternoon: Will Hinkley, a kid with a bulging Adam's apple and curly hair, challenged me to a fight. I tried to walk away, but before I knew what was going on, a bunch of kids had surrounded us and Hinkley started pushing me. The whirl of voices and faces, the evident danger, made me light-headed, and what little strength I had quickly evaporated. Mary was with me, and she started crying. I was not popular and had no friends there to help me; instead everyone was cheering for me to get beat up.

After a lot of shoving and name-calling and me trying to back out of the circle and getting thrown into the middle again, he hit me once in the side of the head, and I was dazed. Clenching my fists, I held my hands up in front of my face, assuming a position I had seen in fights on TV, and Hinkley circled me. I tried to follow his movements, but he darted in quickly, and his bony knuckle split my lip. There was little pain, just an over-whelming sense of embarrassment, because I felt tears welling in the corners of my eyes.

As Hinkley came toward me again, I saw Jim pushing through the crowd. He came up behind Hinkley, reached around, and grabbed him by the throat with one hand. In a second, Jim wrestled him to the ground, where he punched him again and again in the face. When Jim got up, blood was running from Hinkley's nose and he was quietly whimpering. All the other kids had taken off. Jim lifted my book bag and handed it to me.

"You're such a pussy," he said.

"How?" was all I could manage, I was shaking so badly.

"Mary ran home and told me," he said.

"Did you kill him?"

He shrugged.

Hinkley lived, and his mother called our house that night complaining that Jim was dangerous, but Mary and I had already told our mother what had happened. I remember her telling Mrs. Hinkley over the phone, "Well, you know, you play with fire, you're liable to get burned." When she hung up the phone, she flipped it the middle finger and then told us she didn't want us fighting anymore. She made Jim promise he would apologize to Hinkley. "Sure," he said, but later, when I asked him if he was really going to apologize, he said, "Yeah, I'm going to take him to Bermuda."

His Air Was Cold

■ In reality, the start of school was anticlimactic, because the prowler had surfaced twice more. The Hayeses' teenage daughter, Marci, spotted him spotting her sitting on the toilet late one night. The Mason kid, Henry, who regularly proclaimed in school that he would someday be president, found the shadow man in their darkened garage, crouching in the corner behind the car when he took out the empty milk bottles after dinner. As he told Jim and me later when we went to talk to him about it, "He ran by me so fast I didn't see him, but his air was cold."

"What do you mean, 'his air was cold'?" asked Jim.

"It smelled cold."

"Unlike yours?" said Jim.

Henry nodded.

That evening, down in the cellar, Jim made tiny red flags out of sewing needles and construction paper and stuck them into the turf of Botch Town in all the spots we knew that the prowler had been. When he was done, we stepped back and he said, "I saw this on *Dragnet* once. Just the facts. It's supposed to reveal the criminal's plan."

"Do you see any plan?" I asked.

"They're all on our block," he said, "but otherwise it's just a mess."

Apparently we weren't the only ones concerned about the prowler, because somebody called the cops. Thursday afternoon a police officer walked down the block, knocking on people's doors, asking if they'd seen anything suspicious at night or if they'd heard someone in their backyard. When he got to our house, he spoke to Nan. As usual, Nan knew everything that happened on the street, and she gave the cop an earful. We hid in the kitchen and listened, and in the process we learned something we hadn't known. It so happened that the Farleys had found a human shit at the bottom of their swimming pool, as if someone had sat on the rim and dropped it.

When the cop was getting ready to leave, Jim stepped out of hiding and told him we had a footprint we thought belonged to the prowler. He smiled at us and winked at Nan but asked to see it. We led him back to the shed, and Jim went in and brought out the hatbox. He motioned for me to take the lid off, and I did. The cop bent over and peered inside.

"Nice job, fellas," he said, and took the box with him, but later on, when I walked George around the block that night, I saw the pink cardboard box with its poodle and the Eiffel Tower jutting out of the Manginis' open garbage can at the curb. I went over to it and peeked under the lid. The footprint was ruined, and I decided not to tell Jim.

As George and I continued on our rounds, autumn came. We were standing at the entrance to East Lake beneath a full moon, and suddenly a great burst of wind rushed by. The leaves of the trees at the boundary of the woods beyond Sewer Pipe Hill rattled, some flying free of their branches in a dark swarm. Just like that, the temperature dropped. I realized that the crickets had gone silent, and I smelled a trace of Halloween.

Down the block a wind chime that had been silent all summer sounded its cowbell call. I looked up at the stars and felt my mind start to wander, so I sat down at the curb. George sat next to me.

That day in school, they had herded us into the cafeteria and showed us a movie, *The Long Way Home from School*. It was about kids playing on the train tracks and getting flattened by speeding trains or electrocuted on the third rail. The guy who narrated the stories looked like the father from *Leave It to Beaver*. He told one about kids thinking it was fun to climb on train cars and run across the tops. Little did they know that the train was about to pull out. When the movie showed the train starting to move, he said, "Oops, Johnny fell in between the cars and was crushed to death by tons of steel. It's not so much fun when you're flat as a pancake." After that came a scene of a kid shooting a slingshot at a moving train crosscut with another scene of a little girl in a passenger compartment pressing her hand to her eye as blood dripped down her face while the landscape rolled by. "Nice shooting, cowboy," Mr. Cleaver said.

After the movie they made us line up out in the hallway on our knees with our heads down and pressed into the angle where the floor met the wall. "Cover the back of your head by locking your fingers behind it. This will protect you from flying debris," said Mr. Cleary, the principal, one hand lightly stroking his throat. We were led to believe that this crouching maneuver would save us if the Russians dropped an atomic bomb on our town.

My mother had told us that if the air-raid siren ever really went off, I was to get home. She and my father had devised a plan. The minute the siren sounded, someone was supposed to shovel dirt into the window wells of the cellar and then get all the mattresses from the house and lay them out on the first floor to block the radiation from seeping down into the basement. At one time they had stocked a bunch of cans of food in the cellar and gallon bottles of water, each with a drop of bleach in it to keep them fresh. But as time went on, the supplies dwindled to a single can of Spam and a bottle of water that had gone green.

As George and I got up and headed back home, I day-dreamed a *Twilight Zone* scenario of us projecting ourselves into the world of Botch Town to escape the horrible devastation of atomic bombs.

When George and I got home, the wine bottle sat on the kitchen counter, empty, and my mother was passed out on the couch. There was a cigarette between her fingers with an ash almost as long as the cigarette. Jim went and got an ashtray that was half a giant clamshell we had found on the beach the previous summer, and Mary and I watched as he positioned it under the ash. He gave my mother's wrist the slightest tap, and the gray tube dropped perfectly whole into the shell.

I wedged a pillow under her head as Jim took her by the shoulders and settled her more comfortably on the couch. Mary fetched the *Sherlock Holmes.* Jim opened it to *The Hound of the Baskervilles,* the story that obsessed her, and gently placed the volume binding up, its wings open like those of a giant moth, on her chest.

We went next door to say good night to Nan and Pop.

"Where's your mother?" asked Pop.

"She's out cold," said Jim.

Nan's lips did that kissing-fish thing that they did whenever she was trying to trick you into ignoring the truth. I had first noticed it that past summer on the day the ladies came over and she read the cards for them. The widow, old Mrs. Restuccio, who lived by herself next to the Curdmeyers across the street, had drawn the ace of spades. Nan's lips started going, and she quickly pulled the card from the table and exclaimed, "Misdeal." There was a moment where the room went stone quiet, and then, as if someone flipped a switch, the ladies started chattering again.

Never Eat a Peach Leaf

■ The first Saturday morning after school started, I followed Pop around the yard holding a colander as he harvested the yield of the trees. Before he picked each piece of fruit, he'd take it lightly in his hand as if it were a live egg with a fragile shell.

As we moved from tree to tree, he told me things about them. "Never put a peach leaf near your mouth," he said. "They're poisonous." When we came to the yellow apple tree: "This tree grew from seeds that no one sells anymore. It's called Miter's Sun, and I bought the sapling from an old coot who told me there were only a half dozen of them left in the world. It's important to take care of it, because if it and the few others that remain die off, this species will be gone from the face of the earth forever." He picked a small, misshapen yellow apple from a branch, rubbed it on his shirt, and handed it to me. "Take a bite of that," he said. From that ugly marble came a wonderful sweetness.

We continued on to the plum tree, and he said to me, "I heard you were in a fight this week."

I nodded.

"Do you want me to teach you how to box?" he asked.

I thought about it for a while. "No," I said, "I don't like to fight."

He laughed so loud that the crow sitting on the TV antenna atop the house was frightened into flight. I felt embarrassed, but he reached down and put his hand on my head. "Okay," he said, and laughed more quietly.

After retiring from the Big A, Aqueduct Racetrack, where he had worked in the boiler room for years, Pop had taken up an interest in trees, especially ones that gave fruit. On our quarter-acre property, he planted quite a few—a peach, a plum, three apples, a cherry, an ornamental crabapple, and something called a smoke bush that kept the mosquitoes away—and spent the summer months tending to them: spraying them for bugs, digging around their bases, pulling up saplings, getting rid of dead branches. I'd never seen him read a book on the subject or study it in any way; he just started one day within the first week after leaving his job.

Nan had shown us old, yellowing newspaper clippings from when Pop was a boxer in Jamaica Arena and photographs of him standing on the deck of a ship with an underwater suit and a metal diving helmet that had a little window in it. Once when my parents thought I was asleep on the couch but I just had my eyes closed, I learned that he had spent time in a mental institution, where they'd given him electroshock therapy. Supposedly, when he was fifteen, his mother had sent him out around the corner for a loaf of bread. He went and joined the merchant marine, lying about his age, and returned home after three years, carrying the loaf of bread. Later, when he was asked how his mother had reacted, his answer was "She beat the shit out of me."

He was powerfully built, with a huge chest and wide shoulders. Even when he was in his old age, I couldn't circle one of his biceps with both my hands. Every once in a while, we'd ask to see his tattoos, vein-blue drawings he could make dance by flexing his muscles: a naked woman on his left forearm, an eagle on his chest, and a weird fire-breathing dragon-dog, all curlicue fur and huge lantern eyes, on his back, which he had gotten in Java from a man who used whalebone needles. He told Jim and me that the dragon-dog was named Chimto and that it watched behind him for his enemies.

The trees may have been Pop's hobby, but his true love was the horses. He studied the *Daily Telegraph,* the horse paper, as if it were a sacred text. When he was done with it, the margins were filled with the scribble of horses' names, jockeys' names, times, claiming purses, stacks of simple arithmetic, and strange symbols that looked like Chinese writing. Whatever it all stood for, it allowed him to pick a fairly high percentage of winners. There was one time when he went to the track and came home in a brand-new car, and another when he won so much he took us all on vacation to Niagara Falls. Pop's best friend was his bookie, Bill Pharo, and Pop drove over to Babylon to see him almost every day.

Mr. Blah-Blah

■ That Saturday afternoon, when my father got home from work, he called us kids into the living room and made us sit on the love seat. My mother and he sat on the couch across the marble coffee table from us. Before they spoke, my mind raced back through the recent weeks to try to remember if we could be in trouble for something.

All I could think of, besides the incident with Hinkley, which seemed to have blown over by then, was a night a week or so before school started when Jim and I had made a dummy out of old clothes—shirt and pants—stuffed with newspapers and held together with safety pins. The head was from a big, mildewed doll, an elephant stuffed with sawdust someone had won at the Good Samaritan Hospital fair that had been lying around in the cellar for as long as I could remember. We cut the head off, removed some of the sawdust, tied the neck in a knot, and pinned it to the collar of the shirt. The figure was crude, but we knew that it would serve our purposes, especially in the dark. We got it out of the cellar unseen by pushing it through one of the windows into the backyard.

We'd named our floppy elephant guy Mr. Blah-Blah and tied a long length of fishing line around his chest under the arms of the shirt. We laid him at the curb on one side of the street and then payed out the fishing line to the other side of the street and through the bottom of the hedges in front of the empty house that had, until a little more than a year earlier, belonged to the Halloways. We knew that it wouldn't pay to do what we were planning in front of our own house, and the one we chose had the benefit of having a southern extension of the woods right behind its backyard. We could move along the trails in the pitch black, and anyone who tried to chase us would be hopelessly lost and have to turn back.

Hiding behind the hedges, we waited until we saw the lights of a car coming down the street. When the car neared the hedges, we pulled on the line, reeling in the bum, and in the dark it looked like he was crawling across the road in fits and starts, like maybe he'd already been hit by a car.

The car's brakes screeched, and it swerved, almost driving up onto the curb and nearly hitting the telephone pole. The instant I heard the brakes, I realized that the whole thing was a big mistake. Jim and I ran like hell, bent in half to gain cover from the hedges. We stopped at the corner of the old Halloway house, in the shadows.

"If they come after us, run back and jump the stream, and I'll meet you at the fork in the main path," Jim whispered.

I nodded.

From where we stood, we had a good view of the car. I was relieved to see it wasn't one I recognized as belonging to any of the neighbors. It was an old model, from before I was born, shiny white, with a kind of bubble roof and fins that stuck up in the back like a pair of goalposts. The door creaked open, and a man dressed in a long white trench coat and hat got out. It was too dark and we were too far away to see his features, but he came around the side of the car and discovered Mr. Blah-Blah in the road. He must have seen the fishing line, because he looked up and stared directly at us. Jim pulled me back deeper into the shadows. The man didn't move for the longest time, but his face was turned straight toward us. My heart was pounding, and only Jim's hand on the back of my shirt kept me from running. Finally the man got back into the car and drove away. When we were sure the car was gone, we retrieved Mr. Blah-Blah and threw him back in the woods. But that had happened more than a week earlier.

My father cleared his throat, and I looked at Jim, who sat on the other side of Mary. He looked back at me, and I knew that his memory was stuffed with that mildewed elephant head.

"We just wanted to tell you that we don't think Aunt Laura is going to be with us much longer," said my father. His elbows were on his knees, and he was looking more at our feet than at us. He rubbed his hands together as if he were washing them.

"You mean she's going to die?" said Jim.

"She's very sick and weak. In a way it will be a blessing," said my mother. I could see the tears forming in the corners of her eyes.

We nodded, but I was unsure if that was the right thing to do. I wondered how dying could be a good thing. Then my father told us, "Okay, go and play." Mary went over to where my mother was sitting and climbed into her lap. I left before the waterworks really got started.

Later that afternoon I took George and my notebook, and we traveled far. When I set out, I felt the weight of a heavy thought in my head. I could feel it roosting, but when I tried to realize it, reach for it with my mind, it proved utterly elusive, like trying to catch a killifish in the shallows with your bare hands. On my way up to Hammond Lane, I saw Mr. and Mrs. Bishop being screamed at by their ten-year-old tyrant son, Reggie; passed by Boris, the janitor from East Lake, who was fixing his car out in his driveway; saw the lumbering, moon-eyed Horton kid, Peter, big and slow as a mountain, riding a bike whose seat seemed to have disappeared up his ass.

We crossed Hammond Lane and went down the street lined on both sides with giant sycamores, leaves gone yellow and brown. To the left of me was the farm, cows grazing in the field; to the right was a plowed expanse of bare dirt where builders had begun to frame a line of new houses. Beyond that another mile, down a hill, amid a thicket of trees, next to the highway, we came to a stream.

I sat with my back to an old telephone pole someone had dumped there and wrote up the neighbors I'd seen on my journey—told about how Mrs. Bishop had Reggie when she was forty-one; told about how the kids at school would try to fool Boris, who was Yugoslavian and didn't speak English very well, and his invariable response: "Boys, you are talking dogshit"; told about the weird redneck Hortons, whom I had overheard described by Mrs. Conrad once as "incest from the hills."

When I was finished writing, I put my pencil in the notebook and pulled George close. I petted his head and told him, "It's gonna be okay." The thought I'd been carrying finally broke through, and I saw a figure, like a human shadow, leaning over Aunt Laura's bed in the otherwise empty room at St. Anselm's and lifting her up. He held her to him, enveloping her in his darkness and then, like a bubble of ink bursting, vanished.

Maybe He'll Show Up for Lunch

■ That night, well into her bottle of wine, my mother erupted, spewing anger and fear. During these episodes she was another person, a stranger, and when they were done. I could never remember what the particulars of her rage were, just that the experience seemed to suck the air out of the room and leave me unable to breathe. In my mind I saw the evil queen gazing into her talking mirror, and I tried to rebuff the image by conjuring the memory of a snowy day when I was little and she pulled Jim and me to school on the sled, running as fast as she could. We laughed, she laughed, and the world was covered in white.

We kids abandoned our father, leaving him to take the brunt of the attack. Jim fled down the cellar to lose himself in Botch Town. Mary went instantly Mickey, encircled herself with a whispered string of numbers for protection, and snuck next door to Nan and Pop's house. As I headed up the stairs to the refuge of my room, I heard the sound of a smack and something skittering across the kitchen floor. I knew it was either my father's glasses or his teeth, but I wasn't going downstairs to find out. I knew he was sitting there stoically, waiting for the storm to pass. I shoved off with Perno Shell down the Amazon in search of El Dorado.

Some time later, just after Shell had taken a curare dart in the neck and paralysis was setting in, there was a knock on my door. Mary came in. She curled up at the bottom of my bed and lay there staring at me.

"Hey," I said, "want me to read you some people from my notebook?"

She sat up and nodded.

So I read her all the ones I had recently added, up to the Horton kid on his bike. I spoke my writing at a slow pace in order to kill time and allow her a long stint of the relief she found in the mental tabulation of my findings. When we finished, the house was silent.

"Any winners in that bunch?" I asked.

"Boris the janitor," she said.

"Go to bed now," I told her.

The next morning my mother was too hungover to take us to church, so she told us to each say a good act of contrition and a Hail Mary. We raced through them. When we were finally gathered at the breakfast table, my father recounted some of his stories from the army. I wondered if my mother's assault the night before had put him in mind of other battles. The phone rang, and my mother, now light and smiling, as if suffering amnesia of last night, answered it.

When she hung up, she told us the news—yesterday Charlie Edison, who was in my class at East Lake, had gone out to play and never returned. At dinnertime, when he didn't appear, his mother had started to worry. When night fell and he still hadn't gotten home, his father called the police. My mother said, "Either something happened to him or he's been abducted." Nan's lips moved in and out, and she said, "Maybe he'll show up for lunch."

Charlie Edison was even more weak and meek than me. We'd had the same teachers since kindergarten. In class photographs he was clearly the runt of the litter. His arms were as thin as pipe cleaners, and he was short and skinny, with a pencil neck and a face that looked like Tommy the Turtle from the old cartoons. His glasses were so big it was as if he had stolen them from his old man, and every time I thought of him, I pictured him pushing those huge specs up on the bridge of his nose with one extended twiglike finger. Charlie's daily project was trying to achieve invisibility, because the meaner kids liked to pick on him. I felt sympathy for him and also relief that he existed, since without him those same kids would probably have been picking on me.

For gym we had Coach Crenshaw, who for some reason always had at least one hand in his sweatpants, and I'm not talking about the pocket. When it rained or the weather was too cold to go outside, we'd stay in the gym and play dodgeball. We divided into two teams, one on either side of the gym. You couldn't cross the dividing line, and you had to bean someone on the other side with one of those hard red gym balls in order to get him out. If he managed to catch the ball, then you were out and had to sit on the side.

One day, right before Christmas, Crenshaw got that glint in his eye, blew his whistle, and called for dodgeball. The usual game ensued, and Charlie managed to hide out and practice his powers of invisibility long enough so he was the last one left on his side of the line. On the other side of the line, the last one left was Bobby Harweed. No one knew how many times he'd been left back, but it was certain he'd already been arrested once before he'd made it to fifth grade. His arm muscles were like smooth rocks, and he had a tattoo he had given himself with a straight pin and india ink: the word "Shit" scrawled across the calf of his left leg. When Crenshaw saw the final match-up, he blew his whistle and instituted a new rule—the two remaining players could go anywhere they wanted; the dividing line no longer mattered.

Charlie had the ball, but Bobby stalked toward him, unworried. Charlie threw it with all his might, but it just kind of floated on the air, and Bobby grabbed it like he was picking an apple off a tree. That should have ended the game, but Crenshaw didn't blow the whistle. Everyone in the gym started chanting Bobby's name. Bobby wound up, and as he did, Charlie backed away until he was almost to the wall. He brought his hands up to cover his face. When it came, the ball hit him with such force in the chest that it knocked the air out of him and slammed him backward so his head hit the concrete wall. His glasses flew off and cracked in half on the hardwood floor, and he slumped unconscious. An ambulance was called, and for that Christmas, Charlie got a broken rib.

My father and Pop went out in the car to join the search for Charlie, and Jim and I hooked up George and headed for the woods to see if we could track him there. On the way we passed a lot of parents and kids from the neighborhood either in cars or on bikes out looking for him, too.

Jim told me, "He must have just gotten lost somewhere and couldn't remember how to get home. You know Charlie."

I didn't say anything, as my imagination was spinning with images of myself, lost, unable to find my way home, or worse, being tied up and taken away to a place where I would never see my family or home again. I was frightened, and the only thing that prevented me from running back to the house, besides the daylight, was that we had George with us. I said, "Maybe the prowler took him."

We were, by then, at the entrance to the school, and Jim stopped walking. He turned and looked at me. "You know what?" he said. "You might be right."

"Do you think they thought of it?"

"Of course," he said, but I remembered the hatbox in the garbage can and had my doubts.

Our tour of the woods was brief. It was a beautifully clear and cool day, the trees all turning red, but the idea that the prowler was now doing more than just peeping kept us on edge.

We ventured only as far as the bend in the stream before giving up. Once out from under the trees, we peered into the sewer pipe, inspected the basketball courts, gazed briefly down into the sump, and followed the perimeter of the fence around the school yard back to the entrance.

"I have thirty cents," said Jim. "You want to go to the deli and get a soda?"

Is That You?

■ There were cops all over the neighborhood for the next week or so, interviewing people about the disappearance of Charlie Edison and trying to piece together what might have happened to him. The story was on the nightly news, and they included a shot of East Lake in the report. It looked different in black and white, almost like some other school a kid would want to go to. Then they flashed a photo of Charlie, smiling, from behind his big glasses, and I had to look away, aware of what he'd been through since I'd known him.

There had been honest grief over his absence and the anguish it caused his family, but at the end of the second week the town started to slip into its old ways, as if some strong current were pulling us back to normalcy. It distressed me, though I couldn't so easily put my finger on the feeling then, how ready everyone was to leave Charlie behind and continue with the business of living. I can't say I was any different. My mind turned to worrying about Krapp's math homework and the troubles of my own family. I suppose the investigation into Charlie's disappearance continued, but it no longer entranced the neighborhood.

Even though the hubbub surrounding the tragedy was quickly receding, I'd still get a chill at school whenever I'd look over to Charlie's desk and see his empty chair, or when out on my bike I'd pass his mother, who had certainly lost her mind when she lost her son. Every day she'd wander the neighborhood, traipsing through people's backyards, inspecting the Dumpsters behind the stores downtown, staggering along the railroad tracks. She was one of the youngest mothers on the block, but the loss had drained her, and overnight she became haggard, her blond hair frizzed, her expression blank.

In the evenings she'd walk around the school yard and stand by the playground calling Charlie's name. One night, as darkness fell and we were eating dinner, my mother, quite a few glasses of sherry on her way to Bermuda, looked up and saw, through the front window, Mrs. Edison heading home from East Lake. She stopped talking and got up, walked through the living room and out the front door. Jim and Mary and I went to the window to watch. She met Mrs. Edison in the street and said something to her. Then she stepped in close, put her arms around the smaller woman, and held her. They stood like that for a very long time, swaying slightly, until night came, and every now and then my mother would lightly pat her back.

Since it involved going out before sunrise each morning, Jim had to quit his paper route, and certain precautions were taken, even including locking the front and back doors at night. We weren't allowed to go anywhere off the block without another kid with us, and if I went to the woods, I'd have to get Jim to go with me. Still, I continued to walk George by myself at night and now felt another specter lurking behind the bushes with Teddy Dunden.

On the first really cold night, near the end of September, the wind blowing dead leaves down the block, I went out with George and started around the bend toward the school. As we passed Mrs. Grimm's darkened house, I heard a whisper: "Is that you?" The sudden sound of a voice made me jump, and George gave a low growl. I looked over at the yard, and there, standing amid the barren rosebushes, was Mrs. Edison.

"Charlie, is that you?" she said, and put her hand out toward me.

The sudden sight of her scared the hell out of me. I turned, unable to answer, and ran as fast as I could back to my house. When I got home, my mother was asleep on the couch, so just to be near someone else I went down to the cellar to find Jim. He was there, sitting beneath the sun of Botch Town, fixing the roof on Mrs. Restuccio's house. On the other side of the stairs, Mickey and Sandy Graham and Sally O'Malley were working hard in Mrs. Harkmar's class.

"What do you want?" asked Jim.

My heart was still beating fast, and I realized it wasn't so much the sight of Mrs. Edison that had scared me, since we were by now used to her popping up anywhere at just about any time, but it was the fact that she thought I was Charlie. I didn't want to tell Jim what was wrong, as if to give voice to it would make the connection between me and the missing boy a real one.

"I guess the prowler is gone now," I said to him. There had been no reported sightings of him since Charlie's disappearance. I scanned the board to find the shadow man's figure, those painted eyes and straight-pin hands, and found him standing behind the Hortons' place up near Hammond Lane.

"He's still around, I bet," said Jim. "He's lying low because of all the police on the block in the last couple of weeks."

My eyes kept moving over the board as he spoke. Botch Town always drew me in. There was no glancing quickly at it. I followed Willow Avenue down from Hammond and around the corner. When I got to Mrs. Grimm's house on the right side of the street, I was brought up short. Standing in her front yard was the clay figure of Mrs. Edison.

"Hey," I said, and leaned out over the board to point. "Did you put her there?"

"Why don't you go do something?" he said.

"Just tell me, did you put her *there*?"

I knew he could tell from the tone of my voice that I wasn't kidding.

"No," he said, "Why?"

"'Cause I was just out with George, and that's exactly where I saw her a few minutes ago."

"Maybe she walked over there after I turned the lights out last night," said Jim.

"Come on," I said. "Did you move her?"

"I swear I didn't touch her," he said. "I haven't moved any of them in a week."

We looked at each other, and out of the silence that followed, we heard, from the other side of the cellar, the voice of Mrs. Harkmar say, "Mickey, you have scored one hundred on your English test."

A few seconds passed, and then I called out, "Hey, Mary, come here."

The voice of Sally O'Malley said, "I'll have to do better next time."

Jim got up and took a step toward the stairs. "Mickey, we need you over here," he said.

A moment later Mary came through the curtain behind the stairs and over to where we were standing.

"I'm not going to be mad at you if you did, but did you touch any of the stuff in Botch Town?" he asked, smiling.

"Could you possibly . . . ?" she said in her Mickey voice.

"Did you move Mrs. Edison here?" I asked, and pointed to where the clay figure stood.

She stepped up to the board and looked down at the town.

"Well?" asked Jim, resting his hand lightly on her shoulder.

She stared intently and then nodded.

The McGinn System

■ The next day on the playground at school, I over-heard Peter Horton telling Chris Hackett that there had been someone at his mother's window the night before.

"Who was it?" asked Chris. "Batman?"

Peter thought for some time and then laughed so his whole giant body jiggled. "No, course not," he said. "She thought she was lookin' at a full moon, but then it was a face."

"What a dip," said Chris.

Peter thought just as long again and then said, "Hey," reaching out one of his man-size hands for Chris's throat. Hackett took off, though, running across the field, yelling, "Your mom's got a fart for a brain!" Horton ran four steps and then either forgot why he was running or became winded.

The minute I heard what Peter had said, I thought back to the board the previous night and remembered the shadow man's pins scratching the back wall of the Hortons' house. When I got home that afternoon, I told Jim, and we went to find Mary. At first she was nowhere to be found, but then we saw little clouds of smoke rising from the forsythias in the corner of the backyard. We crossed the leaf-covered grass and crawled in to sit on either side of her.

"How do you know where to put the people in Botch Town?" asked Jim.

Mary flicked the ash off her cigarette exactly the way my mother did and said, "Ciphering the McGinn System."

"You're handicapping them?" I asked.

"From your morning line," she said.

"What do you mean?" I asked.

"You read them to me," she said.

"My notebook?"

She nodded.

"A town full of horses," said Jim.

"It's not a race," I said.

"Yes it is, in the numbers," she said, staring straight ahead.

"Do you figure it in your head or on paper?" I asked.

"Sometimes," she said.

Mary stamped out her cigarette. We sat there quiet for a time, the wind blowing the branches of the bushes around us. Above, the dying leaves of the oak tree scraped together. I tried to understand what she was doing with the information I was giving her but couldn't stretch my imagination around it.

"Where's Charlie Edison?" asked Jim.

"Gone," said Mary.

"But where does he belong on the board?" he persisted.

"I don't know. You never read him to me," she said, turning to me.

"I never read you his mother either," I said.

"I saw her," said Mary. "Saw her on the street and saw her with Mommy."

For the next fifteen minutes we told her everything we knew about Charlie Edison: all of his trials and tribulations in school, what color bike he rode, what team insignia was on his baseball hat (the Cleveland Indians), and so on. She nodded as we fed her the information. When we were done, she said, "Good-bye now," and got up and left the forsythias.

Jim started laughing. "It's all luck," he said. "There's only so much space in Botch Town, and the figures have to go somewhere. There's a good chance you'll get it right sometimes."

"I don't know," I said.

"You think she's Dr. Strange," he said, and laughed so hard at me I was convinced I'd been a fool. For my trouble he gave me a Fonseca Pulverizer in the side muscle of my right arm that deadened it for a good five minutes. As he left me behind in the bushes, he called back, "You'll believe anything."

In silent revenge I thought back to the night a few years earlier when my parents had told Jim and me that there was no Santa Claus. Just that afternoon Jim and I had been lying on our stomachs in the snow, trying to peer into the cellar, which had been off limits since Thanksgiving. "I see a bike," said Jim. "Christ, I think I see Robot Commando." But when my mother dropped the bomb that there was no Santa Claus, I was the one who simply nodded. Jim went to pieces. He sat down in the rocking chair by the front window, the snow falling in huge flakes outside in the dark, and he rocked and sobbed with his hands covering his face for the longest time.

I left the bushes and went inside to dig around in the couch cushions for change. I found a nickel and decided to ride to the store and get a couple pieces of Bazooka. There was still an hour left before my mother got home from work and made dinner. The sun was already setting when I left the house. Night was coming sooner and sooner each day, and I rode along wondering what I should be for Halloween. I took the back way to the store, down Feems Road, and wasn't paying much attention to what was going on around me when I suddenly woke up to the scent of a vaguely familiar aroma.

A few feet in front of me, parked next to the curb, was a white car. I knew I had seen it before but couldn't recall where. Only when I was next to it and looked in the open passenger-side window to see a man sitting in the driver's seat, did I remember. The fins, the bubble top, the old curved windshield—it was the car that had stopped the night we dragged Mr. Blah-

Blah across the street. As I passed, I saw the man inside, wearing a white trench coat and white hat. He was smoking a pipe. His face was thin, with a sharp nose, and his eyes squinted as if he were studying me.

I panicked and took off down the sidewalk, pedaling as fast as I could. Behind me I heard the car start up, and that pushed me to pump even faster. I made it around the turn that led to the stores but didn't stop. Instead of heading left to the deli, I made a right on Hammond and rode all the way down to Willow and back home. I was almost home and thoroughly winded when I finally stopped to see if he was still behind me. The street was empty, and night was only a few minutes away.

I didn't want to tell Jim what had happened, because I knew he would laugh, but I couldn't shake the memory of the way that guy had stared at me. It took a lot of effort to put him out of my mind. Mom came home, we had dinner and did our homework and went next door to listen to Pop play the mandolin, and after a few hours I was able to forget him. When I went to bed, though, and opened the novel about Perno Shell in the Amazon, that face came floating back into my mind's eye. Pipe smoke! The same exact scent that had made me look up during the bike ride now emanated from the pages of my book.

It Must Have Been the Black Olives

■ The next day Pop had to drive over to the school and pick Mary up. She was running a high fever and feeling sick to her stomach. Something was definitely making the rounds at East Lake. When my class was in the library that afternoon, Larry March, the boy who smelled like ass, puked without warning all over the giant dictionary that old Mr. Rogers, the librarian, kept on a pedestal by the window. Larry was escorted to the nurse's office, and Boris the janitor was called in, pushing his barrel of red stuff and carrying a broom. I don't know what that red stuff was, but in my imagination it was composed of grated pencil erasers and its special properties absorbed the sins of children. He used about two snow shovels full in the library that day. As Boris disposed of the ruined dictionary, much to Mr. Rogers's obvious sadness, he said, "It must have been the black olives."

Back in Krapp's classroom, though, after library, Patricia Trepedino puked, and then after watching her, Felicia Barnes upchucked. Boris and his barrel of red stuff were in hot demand, because reports of more puking came in from all over the school. Krapp was visibly shaken, his nostrils flaring, his eyes darting. After everything was cleaned up, a lingering vomit funk pervaded the room. He opened all the windows and put on a filmstrip for us about the uses of fossil fuels, featuring a talking charcoal briquette. He sat in the last row in the dark, dabbing his forehead with a handkerchief.

When I got home, Dr. Gerber was there. He had pulled the rocker over by the living-room couch, where Mary was sleeping wrapped in a blanket with a bed pillow under her head. A big steel pot we knew as "the puke bucket" was on the floor next to her. He opened his eyes and waved to me as I came through the door. He was smoking a cigar, which he took out of his mouth momentarily to put his finger to his lips, and cautioned me to be quiet.

Gerber was the town doctor. He was a heavyset man with a thick wave of black hair, a wide face, and glasses. I never saw him without his black suit on and his black leather bag sitting next to him or in his hand. He gave us kids all our shots, choked us on flat sticks, rubber-hammered our knees, listened to our hearts, and came to our houses when we were too sick to make it to the office. When my mother first brought Mary, small and weak, home from the hospital, he stopped by every day for a month to help my mother administer a special medicine and to assure us that Mary would live. It was not unusual to find him, morning or night, dozing for a few minutes in our rocking chair, pocket watch in hand.

Once, during a snowstorm, when it was impossible to drive and my mother thought Jim was having an appendicitis attack, Gerber came the half mile from his office on foot, trudging through the snow. When he pronounced that Jim was merely suffering from a bad case of gas, he shook his head and laughed. Then he went next door to see Pop, with whom he shared an interest in horses, had a glass of Old Grand-Dad and a cigar, and was off. I watched him through the front window as he left, the darkness falling hard with the snow.

He didn't stay long the day Mary was sick but told Nan that he had another dozen kids to see, all of whom had the same thing. When he left, I sat at the end of the couch and watched cartoons on TV with the sound off. Just when I was about to get up and go outside, Mary opened her eyes. She was shivering slightly. Her mouth started to move, and she mumbled something. I got up and went to the hall closet where the towels were kept. Taking a washrag, I wet it with cold water and placed it on her forehead. She grabbed my hand.

"The boy," she said. "He's to show. I found him." She pointed one finger down at the floor.

"Okay," I said. "Okay."

She fell back to sleep and seemed to be more comfortable. I went out into the yard, bored, and looked for something to do. Jim, I knew, would not be home soon, as he had joined the wrestling team and now took the late bus. In the middle of smacking the cherry tree's trunk with an old yellow Wiffle ball bat, it suddenly came to me what Mary had meant.

I ran back inside and went into the cellar. Leaning out over Botch Town, I pulled the string for the sun. I started at Hammond Lane and scanned up and down the block, searching for the clay figure of Charlie Edison. Mrs. Harrington was standing, round as a marble, in her front yard. Mr. Conrad was out of place, standing next to Mrs. Hayes in the Hayeses' backyard. Mr. Mason had fallen over in his driveway, Boris the janitor worked on his car. I did find Mrs. Edison making her way down Willow Avenue toward the school but didn't see Charlie anywhere. Most of the characters usually just milled around by their houses, but Charlie was no longer there.

I was about to turn out the light and give up my search when I finally saw him. All the way on the other side of the board, beyond the school field and the woods, his figure lay on its side, directly in the center of the glittering blue waters of the lake.

Back upstairs, I put the leash on George, and we were out the door in a flash. Down the block and around the corner we went, moving quickly toward the school. It was getting late in the afternoon, and the temperature had dropped. The woods were somewhat forbidding to me since Charlie had gone missing, and I wasn't supposed to enter them alone, but I hesitated for only a moment before plunging in beneath the trees.

We took the main trail and after ten minutes of fast walking stood at the edge of the lake. All the neighborhood kids' parents told them it was bottomless, but the older I got, the more I suspected that was just a story to keep us from swimming in it or trying to set sail on a raft.

Its surface was littered with fallen leaves, and in those places where the water peeked through, the reflection of the surrounding trees was rippled by the wind moving over its surface. It was so peaceful. I didn't know what I expected to find—maybe a body floating out in the middle—but it looked just like it always did in autumn. I stood there for quite a while, listening to acorns and twigs falling in the woods around me, thinking about Charlie. I imagined him resting lightly on his back at the bottom, his eyes wide, his mouth open as if crying out. His hands reached up for the last rays of sunlight that came in over the treetops, cutting the water and revealing the way through his murky nightmare back up to the world. The gathering dusk chased George and me down the path and back out of the woods.

That night I woke from sleep shivering. The wind was blowing, and the antenna on the roof above my room vibrated with a high-pitched wail, as if the very house were moaning. I made it to the bathroom, got sick, and staggered back to bed, where I fell into feverish dreams—a tumbling whirl of images punctuated with scenes of the sewer pipe, the lake, the descending brick stairway at St. Anselm's. Teddy Dunden paid me a visit. Charlie, his mother, the man in the white car, a pale face at the window, and Perno Shell himself chased me, befriended me, betrayed me, until it all suddenly stopped. I heard the birds singing and opened my eyes to see a hint of red through the window. There was a wet cloth on my forehead, and then I noticed the shadowy form of my father, sitting at the end of my bed, hunched forward, eyes closed, one hand lying atop the covers next to my ankle. He must have felt me stir. He whispered, "I'm here. Go back to sleep."

Although the fever had broken and I was feeling much better by nine o'clock in the morning, the virus bought me a day off from school. Mary didn't go either, and my mother stayed home from work to take care of us. It was like the old days, before the drinking and the money trouble. Nan came in, and we all sat for an hour after breakfast at the dining-room table, playing cards: old maid and casino. I had a great adventure with my plastic soldiers, which I hadn't bothered with for months, on the windowsill in the living room while the brilliant, cold day shone in around me. We watched a mystery movie on TV with Peter Lorre as the sauerkraut-eating detective Mr. Moto, and my mother made spaghetti with butter.

Around three o'clock I lay back down on the couch and closed my eyes. Mary sat on the floor in the kitchen putting together a puzzle, while my mother sat in the rocker beside me and dozed. All was quiet save for the murmur of the wind outside.

I thought back to when I was in fourth grade and had stayed out of school off and on for forty-five days. My mother wasn't working then, and if I didn't feel like going to school, she let me stay home. I had genuinely discovered reading that year, and I lay in bed much of the time, devouring one book after another: *Jason and the Argonauts, Treasure Island, The Martian Chronicles, Charlotte's Web.* It didn't matter what type of story it was; the characters were more alive to me than all the students and teachers at East Lake.

At lunchtime I would come out into the living room, and my mother would make the spaghetti, and we would watch an old movie. I was the only fourth grader who could identify Paul Muni or Leslie Howard on sight. I loved the mystery movies, their plots and the sense of suspense. My favorites were the ones with the Thin Man, and my mother, of course, was partial to Basil Rathbone as Holmes. Mr. Cleary threatened to keep me from passing fourth grade, but my mother went over to the school and told him I was passing, and I did.

Remembering that year, I realized how different my mother was from other parents. That difference was like a light that always shone in the back of my mind no matter how dim things got when she'd drink. She scared me, and I hated what she became, but that light was like the promise of an eventual return to the way things once were. Those memories protected me as I fell a thousand stories down into sleep.

I woke from that peaceful nap of no dreams only because Jim pried open my left eye with his thumb. "This one's dead, Doctor," he said. I came to and noticed twilight at the window, heard the sound of the wine bottle pinging the rim of a glass in the kitchen. The first thought I had was of Charlie at the bottom of the lake. Who could I tell who would believe what I thought I knew?

After dinner my mother put the Kingston Trio on the Victrola and sat at the dining-room table drinking and reading the newspaper. Mary was on her roller skates, going round and round, following the outer curve of the braided rug in the living room. Inside her orbit, Jim showed me some of his wrestling moves.

"Could you possibly . . . ?" I heard my mother say, and then she called us over to her.

Jim and I each went to one side of the chair. She pointed at a small photograph in the newspaper. "Look who that is," she said.

I didn't recognize him at first because he wasn't wearing his paper hat, but Jim finally said, "Hey, it's Softee."

Then the long, haggard face came into focus, and I could just about hear him say, "What'll it be, sweetheart?"

My mother told us that he'd been arrested because he was wanted for child molestation in another state. For a while he'd been a suspect in the Charlie Edison case but had been cleared of that suspicion.

"What's child molestation?" I asked

"It means he's a creep," said my mother, and she turned the page.

"He gave some kid a Special Softee," said Jim.

My mother lifted the paper and swung it at him, but he was too fast.

"What's the world coming to?" she said, and took another sip of wine.

That night I couldn't get to sleep, partly because I had slept during the day and partly because my thoughts were full of all the dark things that had burrowed into my world. I pictured a specimen of Miter's Sun fresh from the branch but riddled with wormholes. The antenna moaned in the wind, and it didn't matter how close Perno Shell was to the golden streets of El Dorado—the aroma of pipe smoke made it impossible to concentrate on the book.

I got up and went to my desk, opened the drawer, and took out my stack of Softee cards. The vanilla-cone head now struck me as sinister; leering with that frozen smile. I took them over to the garbage pail and dropped them in. Back in bed, though, all I could think of was the one card—the eyes—that I had never owned. I was unable to throw that card out, bury it, burn it with the rest of the deck, those eyes were always gaining power, and they watched me from inside my own head. I hunkered down under the covers and waited to hear my father come in from work.

Instead I heard a scream—Mary downstairs—and the sound of George barking. I jumped out of bed and took the steps. Jim was right behind me. When we got to her darkened room, she was sitting upright in bed with a terrified look on her face.

"What?" said Jim.

"Someone's outside," she said. "There was a face at the window."

George snorted and growled.

I felt someone at my back and turned quickly. It was Nan, standing there in her quilted bathrobe and hairnet, holding a carving knife in her hand.

Jim took George by the collar and led him to the kitchen. "Get 'em, George," he said, and opened the back door. The dog ran out, growling. Mary, Nan, Jim, and I waited to hear if he caught anyone. After some time passed, Nan told us to stay put and went out, holding the knife at the ready. A few seconds later, she came back, George at her heels.

"Whoever it was is gone," she said. She sent Jim and me back to bed and told us she'd sit with Mary until our father got home. My mother had never even opened an eye, and as I passed her bedroom, next to Mary's, I saw her lying there, mouth open, the weight of *Holmes* holding her down.

You'd Be Surprised

■ By the time I was in the kitchen the next morning, fixing a bowl of cereal, Jim had already been out in the backyard studying the scene of the crime.

"The ladder was up against the house," he said.

"Any footprints?" I asked.

He shook his head.

"Your father is contacting the police about it from work today," called my mother from the dining room.

Jim leaned in close to me and whispered, "We gotta catch this guy."

I nodded.

I went to school, my head full of worry, only to learn something that almost made me laugh with joy. At recess Tim Sullivan told me that his father had said that the police were going to dredge the lake for Charlie Edison. I couldn't believe how lucky I was. It was as if someone had read my mind, and not just that, they were doing something about it. I suppose it only made sense, given the circumstances of Charlie's disappearance, but for me it was a relief.

That afternoon Krapp announced that the police were going to be "searching" the lake for Charlie on Saturday and they had asked all the teachers to announce that no kids were allowed near the school field or in the woods on the weekend. Part of our homework assignment was to tell our parents.

"We'll go into the woods behind the Halloways' house," Jim said later that day after I'd told him. We were in his room, and he was supposed to be doing his homework. "The cops will have guys at the school field and maybe over on Minerva, but they probably won't be that far into the woods. We'll take the binoculars."

I nodded.

"Can you imagine if they pull him out of the lake?" he said, staring at the floor as if he were seeing it before his eyes. "We'll have to get up and go early."

I wasn't so sure I wanted to see them dredge Charlie up, but I knew I had to go. "If they find him, does that mean he fell in or someone threw him in there?" I asked.

"Who do I look like, Sherlock Holmes?" he said.

After that he gave me instructions to rig the ladder the next day after school. "Get two old soda cans and fill them with pebbles," he said. "Tie one to one end of the ladder with fishing line and one to the other end the same way. If he comes at night and tries to take it, we'll hear him and let George out."

The week dragged in anticipation of the Saturday dredging. Mary sat with me the following afternoon as I worked at setting up the ladder. It lay along the fence on the right-hand side of the yard, near the clothesline. She had counted the number of pebbles I put into the first can and would not let me tie the second one on until it contained the exact same number.

"Two more," she said when I figured I was done. I looked over at her, and she lifted her hand. First the index finger came up and then, slowly, the thumb. I laughed and put another two in.

"So Charlie's in the lake," I said as I tied the second can

in place. I had not yet spoken to her about her Botch Town revelation.

"He'll be in the lake," she said.

"Are you sure?" I asked.

"He'll be in the lake."

I went out on my bike looking for someone to write about and passed Mr. Barzita's house. He was such a quiet old man that I'd almost forgotten he lived on our block. There he was, though, raking leaves in his front yard. He had lived alone since his wife died, back when I was only seven. His property was surrounded by a chain-link fence, and instead of opting for the usual open lawn, he had long ago planted rows of fig trees, so that his house was obscured by a small orchard. Even though he lived in solitude, rarely emerging from his front gate, he always smiled and waved to us kids when we rode by on our bikes, and he would come to the fence to talk to grown-ups.

Mr. Barzita was one of those old people who seemed to be shrinking and would simply fade away rather than die of old age. During the winter I never saw him, but every spring he reappeared, more wizened than the year before. On the hottest summer days, he'd sit in his chaise lounge among the fig trees, sipping wine, holding a loaded pellet pistol in his lap. When squirrels invaded his yard to get at the figs, he'd shoot them. If you yelled to him, "How many?" he'd hold whatever his kill was up by the tails.

One Sunday when my father and I were driving by the old man's house, I asked what he thought of Barzita killing the squirrels. My father shrugged. He told me, "That guy was in the medical corps in the army during the Second World War. He was stationed at a remote mountain base in Europe, and there was an outbreak of meningitis—a brain disease, very contagious, very deadly. They asked for volunteers to take care of the sick. He volunteered. They put him and another guy in a locked room with fifteen infected soldiers. When it was over, he was the only one who came out alive."

I tried to imagine what it must have been like in that room, the air stale with the last exhalations of dying men.

"A lot of these old farts you see scrabbling around town . . ." he said. "You'd be surprised."

Hand Me the Camera

■ Jim looked both ways up and down Willow to check for cars or anyone who might be watching, and then he and I ducked into the Halloways' driveway and behind the hedges. We ran around the side of the house, through the backyard, and down a slope that led to the stream. Jumping the stream, we moved in under the trees. It was a little before eight o'clock on Saturday morning. The sky was overcast, and there was a cold breeze that occasionally gusted, lifting the dead leaves off the floor of the woods and loosing more from the branches above.

We followed a winding path toward East Lake. Jim suggested we not take the most direct route that passed closest to the school yard but that we arc out on a lesser-used trail through moss patches and low scrub. He had Pop's old binoculars slung around his neck, and I carried the Brownie camera. As we neared the lake, Jim warned me to keep quiet and said that if we were spotted, we should split up; he'd head toward the railroad tracks, and I'd go back the way we came. I nodded, and from that point on, we only whispered.

After jumping the snaking stream twice more, from mossy hillock to root bole, from sandbank to solid dirt, we came in view of the lake. Jim crouched and motioned for me to get down too.

"The cops are there already," he said. "We'll have to crawl."

We made our way to within thirty yards of the southern bank of the lake and hunkered down behind a fallen oak. My heart was pounding, and my hands were shaking. Jim peeked up over the trunk and put the binoculars to his eyes.

"It looks like they just got started," he said. "There's five guys. Two on the bank and three in a flat-bottom boat with a little electric motor."

I looked and saw what he had described. Coming off the back of the boat were two ropes attached to winches with hand cranks. The boat was moving along slowly, trolling the western side of the lake. Then I noticed some of the neighbors standing on the opposite bank. Mr. Edison was there, a big man with a bald head and a mustache. He wore his gas-station uniform and stood, eyes downcast, arms folded across his chest. It was the first I'd seen of him since Charlie had gone missing. Beside him was his next-door neighbor, Mr. Felina. There were a few other people I didn't recognize, but when one of them moved to the side, I caught sight of Krapp. There he stood, dressed in his usual short-sleeved white shirt and tie, his hairdo flatter than his personality.

"Krapp's here," I whispered.

Jim turned the binoculars to focus on the group I'd been looking at. "Jeez, you're right," he said.

"Wonder what he's doing here?" I said.

"I think he's crying," said Jim. "Yeah, he's drying his eyes. Man, I always knew he was a big pussy."

"Yeah," I said, but the thought of Krapp both showing up and crying struck me.

Jim swung the binoculars back to see what the cops were doing. He reported to me that at the ends of those ropes they had these big steel hooks with four claws each. Every once in a while, they'd stop moving and reel them in by turning the hand cranks. He gave me an inventory of what they brought up—pieces of trees, the rusted handlebars of a bike, the partial skeleton of either a dog or fox . . . and on and on. They slowly covered the entire lake and then started again.

"He's not down there," said Jim. "So much for Mary's predictions."

I peered back over the fallen trunk and watched for a while, braver now that I probably wasn't going to see Charlie. We sat there in the cold for two straight hours, and I started to shiver. "Let's go home," I whispered.

"Okay," said Jim. "They're almost done." Still he sat watching, and our hiding and spying reminded me of the prowler.

From out on the lake, one of the cops yelled, "Hold up, there's something here!" I stuck my head up to watch. The cop started turning the crank, reeling the rope. "Looks like clothing," he called to the other cops on the bank. "Wait a second. . . ." he said. He reeled more quickly then.

Something broke the surface of the water near the back of the boat. It looked like a soggy body at first, but it was hard to tell. There were definitely pants and a shirt. Then the head came into view, big and gray, with a trunk.

"Shit," said Jim.

"Mr. Blah-Blah," I whispered.

"Hand me the camera," said Jim. "I gotta get a picture of this."

He snapped it, returned the camera to me, and then motioned for me to follow him. We got down on all fours and crawled slowly away from the fallen tree. Once our escape was covered by enough trees and bushes, we got to our feet and ran like hell.

We stood behind the Halloways' place, still in the cover of the woods, and worked to catch our breath.

"Blah-Blah," said Jim, and laughed.

"Did you put him in there?" I asked.

"Blah," he said, and shook his head. "Nah, Softee molested him and threw him in there."

"Get out," I said.

"Probably Mason and his horrible dumpling sisters found him and took him to the lake. They're always back here in the woods," he said. "We should have had Mary predict where Mr. Blah-Blah would be."

"But then where's Charlie?" I asked.

He brushed past me and jumped the stream.

I followed him and stayed close as we ran through the Halloways' backyard and around the house to the street.

When we got home, I was relieved to find that my mother wasn't sitting at the dining-room table. The door to Nan and Pop's was open. I could hear Pop in there figuring his system out loud, and, without looking, I knew that Mary was beside him. Jim took the camera and binoculars upstairs, and I walked down the hallway toward my parents' room to see if my mother was up yet. She wasn't in her bed, but when I passed by the bathroom door, I heard her in there retching.

I knocked once. "Are you all right?" I called.

"I'll be out in a second," she said.

You'll Need This

■ It had been obvious since the start of the school year that Mr. Rogers, the librarian, had been losing his mind. During his lunch break, when we were usually laboring over math in Krapp's class, the old man would be out on the baseball diamond walking the bases in his rumpled suit, hunched over, talking to himself as if he were reliving some game from the distant past. That loose dirt that collected around the bases, the soft brown powder that Pinky Steinmacher ate with a spoon, would lift up in a strong wind, circling Rogers, and he'd clap as if the natural commotion were really the roar of the crowd. Krapp would look over his shoulder from where he stood at the blackboard and see us all staring out the window, shake his head, and then go and lower the blinds.

The loss of his giant dictionary seemed to be the last straw for Rogers, as if it had been an anchor that kept him from floating away. With that gone, as my father would say, "he dipped out." Each week we would be delivered to the library by Krapp and spend a half hour there with Rogers. Of late the old man had been smiling a lot, like a dog on a hot day, and his eyes were always busy, shifting back and forth. Sometimes he'd stand for minutes on end, staring into a beam of light shining in through the window, and sometimes he'd be frantic, moving here and there, pulling books off the shelves and shoving them into kids' hands.

Bobby Harweed was brutal to him, making gestures behind the librarian's back, coaxing everyone to laugh (and you had to laugh if Bobby wanted you to). Bobby would knock books off the shelf onto the floor and just leave them there. For Rogers to see a book on the floor was a heartache, and one day Harweed had him nearly in tears. I secretly liked Rogers, because he loved books, but he was beginning to put off even me with his weirdness.

On the Monday morning following the dredging, we had library. Rogers sat in his little office nearly the entire time we were there, bent over his desk with his face in his hands. Harweed started the rumor that he kept *Playboy* magazines in there. When the half hour was almost up, Rogers came out to stamp the books kids had chosen to borrow. Before he sat down at the table with his stamp, he walked up behind me, put one hand on my shoulder, and reached up over my head to the top shelf, from which he pulled a thin volume.

"You'll need this," he said, and handed it to me. He walked away to the table then and began stamping books.

I glanced down at the book. On the cover, behind the library plastic, was a drawing of a mean-looking black dog; above the creature, in serif type, *The Hound of the Baskervilles.* I wanted to ask him what he meant, but I never got the chance. News spread quickly through the school the next day that he had been fired because he went nuts.

Having the *Baskervilles* in my possession was, at first, an unsettling experience. It felt like I had taken some personal belonging of my mother's, just as if I had stolen my father's watch or Nan's hairnet. The book itself had an aura of power that prevented me from simply opening the cover and beginning. I hid it in my room, between the mattress and box spring of the bed. For the next few days, I'd take it out every now and then and hold it, look at the cover, gingerly flip the pages. Although by this time my mother used the big red volume of *The Complete Sherlock Holmes* only as an anvil in her sleep, there had been a time when she'd read it avidly over and over. She'd read a wide range of other books as well but always returned to detective stories. She loved them in every form and, before we went broke, spent Sunday mornings consuming five cups of coffee and a dozen cigarettes, solving the mystery of the *New York Times* crossword puzzle.

Painting, playing the guitar, making bizarre collages—those were mere hobbies compared to my mother's desire to be a mystery writer. Before work became a necessity for her, she'd sit at the dining-room table all afternoon, the old typewriter in front of her, composing her own mystery novel. I remembered her reading some of it to me. The title was *Something by the Sea,* and it involved her detective Milo, a farting dog, a blind heiress, and a stringed instrument to be played with different-colored glass tubes that fit over one's fingers. Something by the Sea was the name of the resort where the story took place. All the while she wrote it, she kept *Holmes* by her side, opened to *The Hound of the Baskervilles.*

Thinking about my mother one night, I wondered if maybe there was something in *The Hound of the Baskervilles* that could tell me something secret about her. I passed up Perno Shell and pulled the book out from under the mattress. That night I stayed up late and read the first few chapters. In them I met Holmes and Watson. The book wasn't hard to read. I was interested in the story and liked the character of Watson very much, but Holmes was something else.

The great detective came across to me like a snob, the type my father once described as "believing that the sun rose and set from his asshole." I imagined him to be a cross between Perno

Shell and Phileas Fogg, but his personality was pure Krapp. When told about the demon hound, Holmes replied that it was an interesting story for those who believed in fairy tales. He was obviously "not standing for it." Still, I was intrigued by his voluminous smoking and the fact that he played the violin.

Delicious

■ The days sank deeper into autumn, rotten to their cores with twilight. The bright warmth of the sun only lasted about as long as we were in school, and then once we were home, an hour later, the world was briefly submerged in a rich honey glow, gilding everything from the barren branches of willows to the old wreck of a Pontiac parked alongside the Hortons' garage. In minutes the tide turned, the sun suddenly a distant star, and in rolled a dim gray wave of neither here nor there that seemed to last a week each day.

The wind of this in-between time always made me want to curl up inside a memory and sleep with eyes open. Dead leaves rolled across lawns, scraped along the street, quietly tapped the windows. Jack-o'-lanterns with luminous triangle eyes and jagged smiles turned up on front steps and in windows. Rattle-dry cornstalks bore half-eaten ears of brown and blue kernels like teeth gone bad, as if they had eaten themselves. Scarecrows hung from lawn lampposts or stoop railings, listing forward, disjointed and drunk, dressed in the rumpled plaid shirts of long-gone grandfathers and jeans belted with a length of rope. In the true dark, as I walked George after dinner, these shadow figures often startled me when their stitched and painted faces took on the features of Charlie Edison or Teddy Dunden.

Halloween was close, our favorite holiday because it carried none of the pain-in-the-ass holiness of Christmas and still there was free candy. The excitement of it crowded all problems to the side. The prowler, Charlie, schoolwork—everything was overwhelmed by hours of decision as to what we would be for that one night, something or someone who wasn't us, but who we wished to be, which I supposed ended up being us in some way. I could already taste the candy corn and feel my teeth aching. My father had given me a dollar, and with it I'd bought a molded plastic skeleton mask that smelled like fresh BO and made my cheeks sweat.

At the time the only thought I had about that leering bone face was that it was cool as hell, but maybe, in the back of my mind, I was thinking of all those eyes out there trying to look into me, and it was a good disguise because it let them think they were seeing deep under my skin even though it was only an illusion. I showed the mask to Jim, and he told me, "This is the last year you can wear a costume. You're getting too old. Next year you'll have to go as a bum." All the older kids went around trick-or-treating as bums—a little charcoal on the face and some ripped-up old clothes.

Mary decided she would be the jockey Willie Shoemaker. She modeled her outfit for Jim and me one night. It consisted of baggy pants tucked into a pair of white go-go boots, a baseball cap, a patchwork shirt, and a piece of thin curtain rod for a jockey's whip. She walked past us once and then looked over her shoulder. In the high nasal voice of a TV horse-racing announcer, she said, "And they're off. . . ." We clapped for her, but the second she turned away again, Jim raised his eyebrows and whispered, "And it's Cabbage by a head."

Only two days before the blessed event, Krapp threw a wet blanket on my daydreams of roaming the neighborhood by moonlight, gathering, door-to-door, a Santa sack of candy. He turned the joyous sparks of my imagination to smoke by assigning a major report that was to be handed in the day after

Halloween. Each of us in the class was given a different country, and we had to write a five-page report about it. Krapp pre-
sented me with Greece, as if he were dropping a steaming turd
into my open Halloween sack.

I should have gotten started that afternoon once school let
out, but instead I just sat in my room staring out the window.
When Jim got home from wrestling, he came into my room and
found me still sitting there like a zombie. I told him about the
report.

"You're going to be doing it on Halloween if you don't get
started," he said. "Here's what you do: Tomorrow, right after
school, ride down to the library. Get the G volume of the encyclopedia, open it to Greece, and just copy what they have there.
Write big, but not too big or he'll be onto you. If it doesn't look
like there's enough to fill five pages, add words to the sentences.
If the sentence says, 'The population of Greece is one million,'
instead write something like, 'There are approximately one million Greeks in Greece. As you can see, there are many, many
Grecians.' You get it? Use long words like 'approximately' and
say stuff more than once in different ways."

"Krapp warned us about plagiarism, though," I said.

Jim made a face. "What's he gonna do, go read the encyclopedia for every paper?"

The next afternoon I was in the public library copying from
the G volume. With the exception of the fact that I learned that
Greeks ate goat cheese, none of the information in the book
got into my head, as I had become merely a writing machine,
scribbling down one word after the next. The further I got into
the report, the harder it was to concentrate. My mind wandered
for long stretches at a time, and I stared at the design of the
weave in my balled-up sweater that lay on the table in front of
me. Then I'd look over at the window and see that the twilight
was giving way to night. I was determined to finish even if I got
yelled at for being late for dinner. When I hit the fourth page, I

could tell that the information in the encyclopedia was running out, and so I started adding filler the way Jim described. The last page and a half of my report was based on about five sentences from the encyclopedia. I didn't know how late it was when I finished, but I was so relieved I began to sweat. I rolled up my five handwritten pages and shoved them in my back pocket. Closing the big green tome, I went to reshelve it. As I was coming out of the stacks, I suddenly remembered my sweater and looked over at the table where I'd been working. Sitting there in my chair was the man in the white trench coat. He had my sweater in his hands, and he appeared to be sniffing it. My heart instantly began pounding. I was stunned for a second, but as soon as I came to, I ducked out of the aisle and behind the row of shelves to my right.

I ran down to the center aisle and made for the back of the stacks. I was pretty sure that when he came looking for me, he would head up the center aisle so that he could look down each row. Once I reached the back wall, I moved along it to the side of the building that held the front door. Checking my pocket, I touched the rolled-up report. I didn't care about leaving the sweater behind. I waited, while in my mind I pictured him walking slowly toward me, peering down each row. My breathing was shallow, and I didn't know if I would have the power to scream if he somehow cornered me. Then I saw the sleeve of his trench coat, the sneaker of his left foot, before he came fully into view, and I bolted.

I was down the side aisle and out the front door in a flash. I knew that whereas a kid might run in a library, an adult probably wouldn't, which might give me a few extra seconds. Outside, I sprinted around to the side of the building where my bike was chained up. Whatever time I had saved was spent fumbling with the lock. Just when I had the bike free and got my ass on the seat, I saw him coming around the side of the building. My only route to Hammond was now cut off. Instead of trying to ride past him, I turned and headed back behind the library, into the woods that led to the railroad tracks.

I carried my bike over the tracks in the dark, listening to the deadly hum of electricity coursing through the third rail and watching both ways for the light of a train in the distance. Although the wind was cold, I was sweating, trying not to lose my balance on the dew-covered wooden ties. All the time I cautiously navigated, grim scenes from *The Long Way Home from School* played in my memory. At any second I expected to feel a bony hand on my shoulder.

On the other side of the tracks, there was another narrow strip of woods, and I searched along it, walking my bike, until I found a path. I wasn't actually sure what street it would lead me to, since I had never gone this way before. Jim and I had occasionally crossed back and forth over the tracks, but always in daylight and always over on the other side of town behind the woods that started at the school yard. This was uncharted territory for me.

I walked clear of the trees onto a road that didn't seem to have any houses. My mind was a jumble, and I was on the verge of tears, but I controlled myself by trying to think through where I was in relation to the library and home. I figured I was west of Hammond and if I just followed the street I was on, it would finally meet up with the main road. Getting on my bike, I started off.

No sooner had I pedaled twenty feet than I saw, way up ahead, the lights of a car that had just turned onto the street, moving slowly. A moment later I noticed another car parked on the right-hand side of the road only a few feet ahead of me. I would have taken to the woods, but I couldn't see a path, and it was too dark to try to find one. I got off my bike, gave it a good shove, and watched it wheel into the tall grass and bushes, where it fell over, pretty well concealed from sight. I crouched low and scrambled to hide against the side of the parked car, an old station wagon with wood paneling.

The headlights of the approaching car came slowly closer. By the time it passed the parked car I was hiding behind, I was really hunkered down, my hands covering my head air-raid style, my right leg off the curb and under the car. The passing vehicle then picked up speed, almost disappearing around the bend at the opposite end of the road before I could get a look at it. Peeking out, I caught a glimpse of the fins of the old white car. I wasn't sure whether to sit tight in case the stranger reached a dead end and came back or to get on my bike and make a run for it.

I felt the car I was next to begin to gently rock. From inside there came a muffled moan. I lifted my head up carefully and peered in the window. Only then did I notice that all the windows were fogging over. The car's interior was dark, but the dashboard was glowing. Through one unfogged patch of glass, I could just make out something on the front seat. Lying there was Mrs. Hayes, her eyes closed, her blouse open, one big, pale breast visible in the shadows and one bare leg wrapped around the back of a small man. After seeing his grease-slicked hair and flapping ears, I didn't have to get a look at his face to know that it was Mr. Conrad.

I ran over to where my bike had fallen in the weeds and lifted it. In an instant I was on it and pedaling like a maniac up the street.

As it turned out, I found Hammond and made it back to the house safely, never seeing the white car along my way. When I pulled up in the front yard, I knew I was late and would get yelled at, perhaps sent to my room. Luckily, through all the turmoil, my report on Greece was still in my back pocket, and my hope was that this document could be used as proof that I hadn't just been goofing off.

I opened the door and stepped into the warmth of the living room. The house was unusually quiet, and I was inside no more than a few seconds when I could feel that something wasn't normal. The light in the dining room, where my mother usually sat drinking in the evenings, was off. The kitchen was also dark. I walked over and knocked on Nan's door. She opened it, and the aroma of fried pork chops wafted out around us. Her hairnet was in place, and she wore her yellow quilted bathrobe.

"Your mother's gone to bed already," she said.

I knew what she meant by this and pictured the empty bottle in the kitchen garbage.

"She told me to give you a kiss, though," she said. She came close and gave me one of those air-escaping-from-the-wet-mouthpiece-of-a-balloon kisses. "Jim told me you were at the library doing your homework. I left food for you in the oven. Mary's in with us."

And that was it. She went back into her apartment and closed the door. Like my father, I was left to get my own dinner, alone. It was all too quiet, too stark. I sat in the dining room by myself and ate. Nan wasn't a much better cook than my mother. Every dinner she made had some form of cabbage in it. Only George happened by while I sat there. I cut him a piece of meat, and he looked up at me as if wondering why I hadn't taken him out yet.

When I'd finished eating and put my plate into the kitchen sink, Jim came down from upstairs.

"Did you get your paper finished?" he asked.

"Yeah," I said.

"Let me see it," he said, and held out his hand.

I pulled it out of my back pocket and handed the rolled-up pages to him.

"You shouldn't have bent it all up. What was your country again?" he said, sitting down at the dining-room table in my mother's chair.

"Greece."

He read through it really quickly, obviously skipping half the words. When he got to the end, he said, "This last page is one hundred percent double-talk. Nice work."

"The Greece part in the encyclopedia ran out," I said.

"You stretched it like Mrs. Harrington's underwear," he said. "There's only one thing left to do. You gotta spice it up a little for the big grade."

"What do you mean?" I asked.

"Let's see," he said, and scanned the pages again. "It says the chief exports are cheese, tobacco, olives, and cotton. I saw a kid do this thing once for a paper, and the teacher loved it. He taped samples of the exports onto a sheet of paper. We've got all this stuff. Get me a blank sheet of paper and the tape."

Jim went to the refrigerator and took out a slice of cheese and the bottle of olives. I fetched the paper and tape for him, and then he told me to get a copy of a magazine and start looking for a picture of Greece to use as the cover of the report. Fifteen minutes later, as I sat paging through an old issue of *Life,* he showed me the sheet of paper he had been working on.

"Feast your eyes," he said. The page had the word "EXPORTS" written across the top in block letters. Below that a square of American cheese, half an olive (with pimiento), a crumpled old cigarette butt from the dining-room ashtray, and a Q-tip head, each affixed with three pieces of tape. The name of each item was printed beneath it.

"Wow," I said.

"No applause, just throw money," said Jim. "Did you find a picture for the cover?"

"There's nothing Greek in here," I said, "but this old woman's face looks kind of Greek." I showed him a picture of a woman who was probably about a hundred years old. She was in profile, wore a black shawl, and her face was a prune with eyes. "She's from Mexico, though," I said.

"I heard she was half Greek," said Jim. "Cut her out."

I did, pretty well, too, except that I hacked off the tip of her nose. He then told me to tape her face to a piece of paper and write the title of the report in a bubble coming out of her mouth, as if she were saying it. There was a subheading in the encyclopedia entry—"The Glory That Was Greece"—that he told me to use as the title of my paper. "Do it in block letters," he said. "Then take the whole thing and put six books on top of it to flatten it out, and you're all set. Krapp's gonna be caught between a shit and a sweat when he sees this one."

Mary cried at bedtime because my mother wasn't awake to tuck her in. Instead Nan sat with her until she dozed off. Jim and I were sent upstairs. Once the house was quiet, I got out of bed and snuck over to Jim's room and knocked on the open door.

"Yeah?" he said and opened one eye.

"I think I know who the prowler is," I whispered.

He told me to come in. I sat at the bottom of his bed and told him about the man in the white car and recounted what had happened at the library. When I told him about the old man sniffing my sweater, he breathed deeply through his nostrils, rolled his eyes upward, and said, "Delicious."

"I'm telling you, it's him," I said. "He travels around during the daytime in that old white car, and then at night he sneaks through the backyards looking for kids to steal. I bet he took Charlie. Not only that, but I think he might be some kind of evil spirit," I said.

"If he's an evil spirit," said Jim, "I doubt he'd be driving a car."

"Yeah, but remember, the nun said that the evil one walks the earth. Maybe he gets tired of walking and needs to drive."

"Hey," said Jim, "you said he always smells like smoke? That the books from the library he probably touched smell like smoke? That's what Sister Joe told me was the secret to knowing him when he came. She said he'd smell like the fires of hell. Fire doesn't smell, though, except for the smoke."

This revelation made me shiver, and I felt unsafe, even inside the house with Jim there. The old man could be anywhere—listening at the glass, sneaking in the cellar window, anywhere.

"So who is this guy?" asked Jim. "Where's he live?"

"I don't know his name," I said. "Do you remember the night we dragged Mr. Blah-Blah across the street? The guy who stopped and got out of his car? That's the guy."

"He was kind of creepy-looking," said Jim, "and I never saw him around here before." He yawned and lay back on his pillow. "We'll have to find out who he is."

"How?" I asked. I sat there for a long time, waiting for his answer.

"Somehow," he said, and turned over. I knew he was almost asleep.

The antenna cried mercilessly all night, and I tossed and turned, thinking of the man in the white car, my fear in the library, and spying Mrs. Hayes's tit. I could sense the evil as it crept forward day by day, dismantling my world, like a very slow explosion. I woke and slept and woke and slept, and it was still dark. The third time I awoke to the same night, I thought I heard the sound of pebbles jangling in soda cans. The plan had been to send George out after whoever it was who was taking the ladder, but I didn't move, save to curl up into a ball.

Every Shadowy Form

■ The next day, Halloween, was clear and cool and blue. My mother had to leave for work early, so Nan made us breakfast. Jim told Mary and me to request oatmeal instead of eggs, so the latter would be there to steal later on and use for ammo on the night streets. I could tell that Mary was excited because she wasn't being Mickey and wasn't counting or doing any of her strange antics but instead was pumping Jim for a rundown on what the coming night would be like. This was the first year she was allowed to go out with us, without our mother. The ugly oatmeal came, lumps of steaming khaki—with raisins in it, no less—and we all forced it down.

"The idea," he told Mary, "is to get as much candy as possible. You want candy, wrapped candy. If you get a candy bar, that's the best—a Hershey bar or a Milky Way. Mary Janes are okay if you don't mind losing a few fillings, little boxes of Good & Plenty, Dots, Chocolate Babies, packs of gum, all good. Then you've got your cheapskate single-wrapped candy—root-beer barrels, butterscotches, licorice drops—not bad, usually given out by people who are broke, but what can they do? They're trying.

"You don't eat anything that's not wrapped, except for Mr. Barzita's figs. Some people drop an apple in your bag. You can't eat it, but you can throw it at someone, so that's okay. Once in a while, someone will bake stuff to give out. Don't eat it—you don't know what they put in it. It could be the best-looking cupcake you ever saw, with chocolate icing and a candy corn on top, but who knows, they might have crapped in the batter. I've seen where people will throw a penny in your sack. Hey, a penny's a penny.

"You always stay where we can see you. If someone invites you into their house, don't go. When we tell you to run, run, 'cause kids could be coming to throw eggs at us. If you hear someone shout 'Nair bomb,' run like hell."

"What's a Nair bomb?" asked Mary.

"Nair is that chemical stuff women use to take the hair off their legs. Kids pour it into balloons and throw them. If you get hit on the head with it, all your hair will fall out. If it gets in your eyes, it could blind you for a while."

Mary nodded.

"I'm going to give you two eggs tonight. Save them until you see someone you really want to get. Aim for the head, 'cause if it hits their coat, it will probably bounce off and smash on the ground. Or you can throw it at the house of someone you hate. Who do you hate?" Jim asked.

"Will Hinkley," Mary said.

"Yeah," I said.

"We'll egg his house tonight for sure," said Jim. "Maybe I'll put one through his front window. One more thing: Kids will try to steal your sack of candy. Don't let them. Scream and kick them if they try to. I'll come and help you."

"Okay," said Mary.

We went in and said good-bye to Nan before leaving for school. She was at her table in the little dining area. Heaped on the table were three enormous piles of candy: rolls of Swee-Tarts, Mary Janes, and miniature Butterfingers. She took one from each pile, stuffed them in a little orange bag sporting a picture of a witch on a broomstick, and twisted the top. Pop was sitting in his underwear watching her, chewing a Mary Jane.

School was endless that day. We usually had a holiday party in the classroom on Halloween, but not that year. It was canceled because Krapp had to give us a series of standardized intelligence tests. It was a day of filling in little bubbles with a number-two pencil. The questions started off easy but soon became impossibly strange. There were passages to be read about sardine fishing off the coast of Chile and math problems where they showed you a picture of a weird shape and asked you to turn it around in your mind 180 degrees before answering questions about it.

I realized right when I was about to turn in one of the exams that I'd meant to skip an answer I didn't know but instead had filled in that bubble by mistake, so that all my answers from that point on would really be for the following question. I felt a fleeting moment of remorse as I put the test in Krapp's hand.

On the playground at lunch break, Tim Sullivan told me his theory about taking standardized tests. "I don't even bother reading the questions," he said. "I just guess. I've got to get at least some of them right."

Later, back in the classroom, Patricia Trepedino, the smartest girl in the class, referred Krapp to question number four. "It says," she said, "concrete is to peanut butter as . . ."

"Yes," said Krapp, checking his sheet.

"Chunky or plain?" she asked.

He stared at her with the same blank look that Marvin Gompers had worn after telling us in third grade that he was made of metal and then running headfirst into the brick wall behind the gym. Finally Krapp snapped out of it and said, "No talking, or I will have to invalidate your test."

The lingering twilight finally breathed its last, and that first moment of night was like a gunshot at the start of a race. Instantly, frantic kids in costumes streamed from lit houses, beginning their rounds, not to return until they had reached the farthest place they could and still remember how to get home. My mother and Nan stood at the front door and waved to us as Jim led the way, dressed in a baggy flannel shirt, ripped dungarees, a black skullcap, and a charcoal beard. Mary followed him in her jockey outfit, and I brought up the rear, stumbling on the curbs and across lawns because the eye slits in my skull mask drastically limited my view. Even though it was cold and windy, my face was sweating before we had climbed two front stoops and opened our bags. I could hear every breath I took, and each was laced with the hair-raising stench of molded plastic. Finally, after I walked into a parked car, I decided to push the mask back on my head and only pull it down over my face when we got to a house's front steps.

We traveled door-to-door around the block, joining with other groups of kids, splitting away and later being joined by others. Franky Conrad, dressed like a swami, with a bath towel wrapped in a turban around his head, eyeliner darkening his eyes, and a long purple robe, walked with us for a dozen houses. The Farley girls were angels or princesses, I couldn't tell which, but their costumes, made from flowing white material, glowed in the dark. President Henry Mason was dressed in his Communion suit, a button on the lapel that said VOTE FOR HENRY, and his sisters were ghosts with sheets over their heads. Reggie Bishop was a robot, wrapped in silver foil, wearing a hat with a lightbulb sticking out the top that went on and off without a switch, and Chris Hackett wore his father's army helmet and told us how his dad had gotten hand-grenade shrapnel in his ass and lost three fingers in Korea.

We worked the trick-or-treat with dedication that rivaled our father's for his three jobs, systematically moving up one side of the street and then down the other. Our pillowcases filled with candy. Old Lady Restuccio gave out Chinese handcuffs, a kind of tube woven from colored paper strips. You stuck a finger in each side and then couldn't pull them out. That's how we lost Franky Conrad. He was left behind, standing on Mrs. Restuccio's lawn, unable to figure out that you just had to twist your fingers to free them. The slow, the hobbled, the weak—all were left in our wake as we blitzkrieged Willow Avenue and moved on to Cuthbert.

When we finished with the last house on the last street in that part of the development, we took the secret trail through the dirt hills, through the waist-high weeds, to the path that led around the high fence of the sump, and came out on the western field of East Lake, just beyond the basketball courts. In the moonlight, a strong wind whipping across the open expanse and driving tatters of dark clouds above, we met up with Tim Sullivan and some of his friends. We rested for a while there and stuffed chocolate and licorice into our mouths as sustenance for the next leg of the journey.

Just as we were getting ready to head east toward Minerva Avenue on the other side of the school field over by the woods, we were attacked by Pinky Steinmacher, Justin Walsh, and about twenty other dirt eaters. The eggs flew back and forth. President Mason took one in the face and went down on his knees in tears. Someone yelled that Walsh had Nair bombs, and we fled. Jim had Mary by the hand, and I was right behind them. As we ran around the back of the school, I looked over my shoulder to see the enemy swarming toward Henry. His sisters, the horrible dumplings, had also abandoned him and were gaining on me. We would learn the next day that they beat him with flour socks until he went albino, split his lip, and stole his sack of treasure. Then Pinky peed on him.

We begged our way up Minerva and the street beyond that, and as we roamed farther from our own neighborhood, kids would break off and head back toward more familiar ground. Once when we left Mary standing on the sidewalk by herself for a minute, a kid tried to steal her sack, but she was able to keep him off by swinging her curtain rod/jockey whip until Jim got to her and pummeled the kid. We ended up taking his sack and splitting its contents three ways. Still, the run-in made Mary nervous, and she had to sit down on the curb for a while, mumble some numbers, and have a cigarette. The rest of the group went on without us. While we were waiting for Mary to relax, a bunch of Jim's junior-high friends came by, and just like that he left me in charge of Mary and went off with them.

By then it was late, and the street we were on, which I didn't know the name of, was deserted. Many of the houses had turned off their lights as a sign they either had gone to bed or were out of candy. That was the way Halloween always went: When you weren't watching, it lay back and went to sleep. It was quiet, eerie. I told Mary to get up, and she did. I vaguely remembered the direction home, and we started off, walking quickly, sticking to the shadows so as not to be noticed. We passed darkened houses whose trees were hung with wind-whipped strands of white toilet paper, smashed jack-o'-lanterns in the road, broken shells and the iridescent film of egg splatter reflected under streetlights where a battle had taken place. Every shadowy form startled me and brought to mind the prowler and Charlie and worse.

Mary hadn't worn a coat or a sweatshirt, having felt that without people seeing her baggy shirt, no one would be able to make out that she was Willie Shoemaker. It hadn't mattered, because kids kept asking me all night, "Hey, what's your sister supposed to be?" The guesses ranged from baseball player to clown to janitor, but no one hit on a jockey, even when Mary said, "They're coming around the back turn. . . ." It was getting colder by the minute, so I gave her my hooded sweatshirt.

Crossing the school field was harrowing, and we kept to the dark of the perimeter fence, in order to remain inconspicuous. Instead of striking out across the field and the lit basketball courts and front drive, I opted for the path that went around the sump. It took a little longer, but that vision of Henry Mason being attacked and the fact that Mary was with me made me cautious. The overgrown weed lot was lonesome enough to make me shiver, and the dirt hills were a strange, barren moonscape, but once I saw the street on the other side, I felt we were going to be okay. It was right then, as we stepped down onto the pavement, that lurching into the glow of the streetlight came a hulking form with a red and blistered face, its hair sloughing off, leaving huge bald spots. The creature whimpered as it tottered forward, its hands stretched out in front. Mary put her arms around me, pressing her face to my side, and I stood, unable to move, my mouth open. Then I realized it was poor Peter Horton, half blind and suffering the effects of a Nair attack, trying to grope his way home. We let him pass and then continued on.

As we came down a side street that opened onto Willow Avenue, I finally relaxed. Mary wasn't holding my hand anymore, as she could sense my ease and was calmer herself. All we had to do was get to Pine, turn left, and walk down seven houses. I wondered where Jim had gone and what adventures he had met, and then I gave myself over to thinking about the moment when I would empty my sack onto the dining-room table.

Mary interrupted me by pulling on my shirt. "Pipe smoke," she said.

I stopped walking and looked up. There, no more than twenty yards away, in the halo of a streetlight, was that old white car parked on Pine. At that moment it pulled away from the curb and rolled in the direction of our house. Grabbing Mary by the arm, I led her through a hole in the hedges we had been passing and whispered to her, "Don't make a sound." We stood motionless and waited. Only when I heard the car turn around and recede into the distance toward Hammond did I pull Mary back out to the street.

"Run," I told her, grabbing her hand. We sprinted around the corner onto Willow and all the way home. She'd been right:

Pervading the air at the spot where the two roads intersected was that smoldering scent of the man with the white coat. It followed us to the doorstep.

I sat at the dining-room table, chewing away like a cow with its cud, on both a Mary Jane and the contents of a miniature box of Good & Plenty, feeling slightly nauseated. My mind was vacant, and I was so weary I could hardly keep my eyes open. I had an animal fear that if I closed them, my pile of booty, which formed a small, colorful mountain, might disappear. Mary had already fallen asleep on the living-room floor, a melting Reese's Peanut Butter Cup smearing her outstretched hand. My mother sat across from me smoking a cigarette and picking through both my pile and Mary's for caramels, which, it was understood, were hers.

Jim finally came home, and my mother took Mary off to bed, telling Jim and me it was time to go upstairs. We gathered all the candy together and put it in the community pot, a huge serving bowl that otherwise got used only on Thanksgiving. As we headed up the stairs, Jim whispered behind me, "We egged the hell out of Hinkley's house and almost got away without anyone seeing us. But I saw Will's weasel face at the upstairs window. I doubt he'll tell his parents, since we'd kick his ass, but watch out for him. I'm sure he saw me."

That was the news I was left with at my bedroom door, and suddenly I was no longer tired. The threat of Hinkley's revenge and his sharp knuckles was enough to revive me, but since he wasn't there at that moment, it eventually receded, and I lay in bed, reviewing the night, the costumes, the thrill of running away across the field at East Lake, Peter Horton. Then, of course, I came to the incident with the pipe smoke, and the memory of the white car pulling away from the curb made me realize that something was missing. I got out of bed and quietly made my way downstairs to the dining room. There, I dug through the giant bowl of treats we had collected.

What was missing were the plump, ripe figs that each year Mr. Barzita wrapped in orange or black tissue paper and tied at the top with ribbon. I saw in my mind a fleeting image of his knotted old fingers, shaking slightly, making a bow. The figs were a Willow Avenue tradition, but this year there were none. I concentrated, searching my memory and realized that Mr. Barzita's house had been dark and he hadn't been at his front gate to meet us and drop one of his "beauties," as he called them, into our sacks. In the rush and fever of greed, we hadn't noticed his absence but had simply moved on to the Blairs' house. Then I worked away at a dark spot in my memory, trying to remember if the white car had been parked in front of his house when we had first passed it early on in our travels. It was Old Man Barzita's place the car had pulled away from when Mary and I noticed it. Perhaps I'd had my mask on, or my thoughts were on the handful of silver-wrapped Chunkies that Mrs. Harrington had dropped into my sack. No matter how I tried, I couldn't remember those minutes.

Instead I pictured Barzita as a young man, stepping out of that disease-laden room during the war. I wondered if the prowler, the man in the white coat, who had become, for me, Death himself, had appeared on Halloween to finally claim a man who by all accounts should have perished years before in another country.

For solace I walked down the hallway to my parents' bedroom. My mother had returned to the living room and passed out on the couch. My heart sank as I viewed the empty bedroom. The light was on, as it always seemed to be, but the bed was unmade, and my father's work clothes from earlier in the week lay in a pile on the floor.

As I stood in the doorway, the weariness that had enveloped me earlier returned, and I yawned. I tottered forward into the room and crawled into my parents' bed on my mother's side. The mattress was soft, and I sank into it. Immediately I noticed the aromas of machine oil and my mother's deep powder, and these scents combined, their chemistry making me feel safe. I lifted the red, bug-crushing weight of *The Complete Sherlock Holmes* from the night table and turned to *The Hound of the Baskervilles.*

The print was very small and set in double columns, the pages tissue thin. I found the place where I had left off in my own copy and started reading. Not even a minute went by, and the tiny letters began moving like ants. Then gravity took over, and my arms couldn't hold the volume up.

I dreamed Halloween and an egg battle on the western field beneath the moon at East Lake. Pinky Steinmacher's little brother, Gunther, hit me in the head with an egg and knocked me over. When I opened my eyes, all the kids from both sides were gone, and the man in the white coat was leaning over me to lift me up. I pretended to still be asleep as he carried me, the wind blowing fiercely, toward his car parked by the basketball court. He said in an angry voice, "Come on, open your eyes," and then I did, and it was morning, and I realized that his voice had been Jim's: "You'll be late for school." I was in my own bed, upstairs in my room.

It was a rush to get ready, and all three of us kids were groggy. I remembered at the last second to take my report for Krapp from beneath the pile of books. Mary and I made it to school just before the bell rang, and we hurried to our classrooms. I was in my seat no more than five minutes before Krapp stood up from his desk and said, with a grim smile on his face, "Hand me your reports." As soon as he said it, I looked around and could identify by the flush of red that spread across their faces all of those who'd let Halloween enchant them into inaction. "Who doesn't have it?" said Krapp. Five trembling hands went up. He lifted his grade book and recorded the zeros with excruciating precision, saying with each one, "A zero for you and two detentions." Someone behind me started crying, but I didn't dare turn around to look.

Krapp swept down the aisle, taking reports, and I held mine out to him. Just before his fingers closed on it, I noticed that on the front cover I'd misspelled "Greece," writing "The Glory That Was Grease." He took it all in in a second—the cutout picture of the old Mexican woman in the shawl, the misspelling—and shook his head in disgust. He added the paper to the stack in his other hand, and what he didn't notice, I did. The back of the bottom page, which held the samples of exports, was completely mottled with dark, greasy stains.

That paper came back to me the next day, bearing an F grade and the words "plagiarism" and "a stinking mess" written across the woman's wrinkled cheek. The stench of moldy cheese, rotten olive, and cigarette combined to make it smell like shit. I brought it home and showed it to Jim. He shrugged and said, "That's the breaks." He told me not to tell our parents about it. "They won't even notice, they're so busy with work and . . ." He tilted his head back and brought his arm up as if drinking from a big bottle. "Take it outside and bury it," he said. "It smells like a dead man's feet." So I did, knowing that no good would come of it. Mary watched me dig a hole with the shovel. When I was done laying the foul muddle to rest and had tamped down the dirt, she put a rock on top to mark the grave.

Sleeping Powder

■ I stood above Botch Town, surveying its length and breadth, and noticed that since Jim had started wrestling, taken up with a new group of friends, and stayed away from the house as much as possible, a thin film of dust had settled on his creation. I imagined it to be a sleeping powder, like a sprinkling of magic dust from an evil magician in a fairy tale. The town appeared quiet, as if in a deep sleep, and there was a certain loneliness that pervaded the entire expanse. Nothing much had moved since I'd last looked at it, before Halloween. Charlie still lay in the lake, Boris was still at work on his car, Mrs. Harrington had rolled forward onto her stomach to sleep.

The only change I noticed was that the prowler was now placed behind our house. I figured that Mary must have moved him after seeing his face at her window. Of course, in reality he was long gone and had probably spied on a dozen other families since he'd looked in on her. The repair to Mrs. Restuccio's roof still had not been completed, and although the Halloways had moved out of the neighborhood more than a year ago, the figure of Raymond, the oldest boy, still lay sleeping behind the house. I wondered if this was to be the end of Botch Town, if Jim, getting older now, would forsake it and it would continue to sleep and slowly decompose until the clay figures cracked and turned to dust and the cardboard houses wilted and fell.

I walked over to a corner of the cellar to a box of old toys we no longer played with. Rummaging through it, I found a Matchbox car, a reproduction of a hearse—long and black. The back doors opened, and there had once been a little coffin that you could slide in and out. Using Jim's supplies, I painted this car white and, while it was still wet, set it down on Willow Avenue, parked in front of Mr. Barzita's place. After taking one more look at the entire board, I reached out over it and turned off the sun.

We Didn't Go to Church Today

■ My father miraculously appeared in his bed Sunday morning. I happened to go down the hall to the bathroom, and on my way I noticed him lying there asleep next to my mother. The sight of him startled me, and I went upstairs to tell Jim, who was still sleeping. He got up and followed me downstairs. I went in and told Mary. Nudging her awake, I said, "Hey, Dad's home." She joined Jim and me, and we took up positions around the bed, staring and waiting. After quite a while, my father suddenly sat up and opened his eyes as if a nightmare had awakened him. He shook his head and breathed out, like a sigh of relief, and smiled at us.

We learned that not only was he there, but he would be home for the entire day. After he got up and had his coffee, he asked us if we wanted to go for a drive.

"Where?" asked Jim.

"I don't know. We'll find out when we get there," he said.

We all went and piled into his car, Jim on the passenger side of the front seat and Mary and me in the back. It was cold out, but they opened the windows up front, and we drove along with the radio blaring and the wind blowing wildly around us. No one said anything. My father pulled over at a roadside hot-dog stand. We ordered cream sodas and those hot dogs that snapped when you bit them, covered in cooked onions and mustard. Sitting on overturned milk crates a few feet from the hot-dog stand, we ate in silence. Then we got back into the car and drove fast, and I had a feeling of freedom, of skipping school and running away.

When we had gone many miles and there was no hope of going back, Mary leaned over the front seat and said, "We didn't go to church today."

My father turned and looked at her for a second, smiling, "I know," he said, and laughed out loud.

We wound up at a huge park on the North Shore. The lots were almost empty even though the day was beautifully clear. We left the car in the middle of the concrete expanse, surrounded by woods on three sides.

"Which way will we walk?" my father asked me.

I pointed to the west, because it seemed like it would take us the farthest from the road and away from the parking lots.

"Okay," he said, "and they're off. . . ."

We got out of the car, zipped up our coats, and started walking. Jim moved right up next to our father and tried to match him step for step. I had wanted to be there, next to him, but I didn't make a fuss about it. Mary and I brought up the rear. We left the concrete behind and stepped into the shadows beneath the tall pines. There was a half foot of fallen oak leaves and brown pine needles on the ground, and Mary and I shuffled our feet, occasionally kicking them into the air. She found a giant yellow leaf as wide as her face, poked two eyeholes into it, and held it up by the stem like a mask.

We walked along a path for quite a while, saw crows in the treetops, and came to a clearing where my father raised his hand and put his finger to his lips. We three kids stopped walking, and he crouched down and pointed into the trees on the other side of the clearing. Standing there staring at us was a huge deer with antlers. A whole minute went by, and then Mary said, "Hello," and waved to it. The deer sprang to the side and disappeared back into the woods.

My father looked down at the sandy ground. "Tracks," he said. "A lot of them came through here in the last few hours." He then found a fox track and showed that to us as well. After the clearing we changed direction, unanimously deciding, without saying so, that we'd follow the deer. We never saw it again for the rest of the day, but the trail we took led us to a huge hill. My father held Mary's hand to help her, and we all scrabbled up the hill, slipping on the fallen leaves and resting from time to time against the trunks of trees.

As it turned out, the deer had led us in the right direction, for as we crested the rise, the trees disappeared and we could see out across the Long Island Sound all the way to the Connecticut shore. The water was iron gray and choppy, dotted with whitecaps. A strong wind blew in our faces. The hill was covered in grass down the other side and devoid of trees. At its base was a little inlet that, farther west, skirted the set of sand dunes between us and the sound. It was as wide as two football fields and as long as four, its surface rippling in the wind. An army of white birds stood along its shore, pecking at the wet sand.

My father sat down at the top of the hill and took out his cigarettes. As he lit a match and cupped it in his hands, catching its spark at the end of his smoke, he said, from the side of his mouth, "You better go down there and investigate." We didn't need to be told twice but charged down the hill, whooping, and the birds took off, lifting into the sky in waves. It felt for a second as if I could lift into the air, just like the birds. Jim tripped and rolled a quarter of the way down, and, seeing him, Mary followed his lead, fell, and rolled the rest of the way.

We stayed there by the water for a long time, skipping stones, dueling with driftwood swords, watching the killifish swarm in the shallows. An hour or two passed, and when Jim and Mary decided to try to catch one of the fish with an old Dixie cup they found in the sand, I looked up at my father just sitting there. I sidled away from them and went back up the hill. During the climb I lost sight of him, as the steep incline prevented me from seeing more than a few feet ahead of me, but when I got to the top and he came into view, I noticed that he had his glasses in his hand. I think he'd been crying, because as soon as he saw me coming, he wiped his eyes and put the glasses back on.

"Come here," he said to me. "I need some help."

I walked over and stood next to him. He reached up and, placing a hand lightly upon my shoulder, stood, making believe he was using me as a crutch. "Thanks," he said, and for a brief moment he put his arm around me and hugged me to him. My face went into the side of his coarse plaid jacket, and I smelled the machine oil. Then he let go and called for Jim and Mary to come back.

We stopped on the way home and had dinner at a chrome-sided diner. My father ordered meat loaf, and the three of us ordered meat loaf, too. No one spoke through dinner, and when the ice cream came, he said to us, "How are you all doing in school?"

I felt Jim lightly kick my shin under the table as he said, "I'm doing great."

"Good," said Mary.

I said nothing at first, but Jim kicked me again, and I said, "Doing fine."

Mary, in her Mickey voice, said, "Could you possibly . . . ?" But my father didn't notice or chose not to notice and called for the check.

By the time we got back home, it was dark out. We got ready for bed and then sat in the living room. My mother was up and around and feeling good. She played the guitar and sang us a few songs. My father, like in the old days, read some poems to us from his collection of little red books—"The Charge of the Light Brigade," "The Ballad of Reading Gaol," and "Crossing the Bar." That night I slept well, no dreams, and the antenna whispered instead of moaned.

There He Is

■ I looked up Mr. Barzita's phone number in the directory and began calling his house every day after school, but there was never an answer. I asked Nan and Pop if they had seen him, but they both told me no. Pop asked me why I wanted to know, and I just shrugged and said, "Because I haven't seen him around."

"Do you ever see him in the cold weather?" asked Nan.

It was true, he rarely showed himself after Halloween, and the weather had really gotten frigid. Mid-November, and the temperature had dropped into the teens for a week straight. We prayed for a snowstorm, but it seemed like even the sky was frozen solid. Jim and I rode over to Babylon on our bikes one Saturday afternoon and went skating on Argyle Lake, but otherwise I just stayed inside, reading and catching up on my journal, filling in those members of our neighborhood I'd yet to capture in words.

There was one old lady who lived over by East Lake, and I couldn't remember her name. It was written on her mailbox, but I kept forgetting to check it on the way home from school. I had a good story about her occasionally going door-to-door, like she was trick-or-treating, asking everyone on the block for a glass of gin. Her dog, Tatel, a vicious German shepherd, was worth a few lines, especially concerning the time it chased the mailman up the Grimms' elm tree. I had a fine description of this old woman's white hag's hair, her skeletal body, and how her sallow skin fit her skull like a rubber glove, but no name. The cold snap had broken, and the temperature had risen slightly, so, just to get out of the house and get some fresh air, I put George on the leash and we took a quick walk around the block.

I wrote her name in my mind, in script, three times—*Mrs. Homretz*—while George peed on the post of her mailbox. The sky was overcast, and even though the wind blew, it was mild enough to keep my jacket open. When I was sure I had it memorized, I turned to start home. Lucky for me I looked behind me when I did, because just then, rounding the turn on Willow and heading straight for me, were three kids on their bikes— Will Hinkley, Pinky Steinmacher, and Justin Walsh.

"There he is!" cried Hinkley, and I saw all three of them lift their asses off their seats and press down hard on their pedals for a burst of speed. Even before my heart started pounding and I felt the fear explode inside me, I ran. They had blocked off my direct escape route and were gaining on me too fast for me to take the corner at Cuthbert in order to make my way around the block back to Willow. They'd have been on me before I reached the middle of that street. Instead I made a beeline for East Lake and the woods, thinking they might stop chasing me once they hit the tree line.

George easily kept pace with me as we made our way across the field and then down the slope of Sewer Pipe Hill. I chose the main path, thinking that if they did come after me, I'd get as far into the woods as possible before cutting into the trees and underbrush. At the last second, I would head south toward the spit of woods that extended into the backyards of the Masons and Halloways. If I could make it that far, I could get back onto Willow close to my house and be home before they caught me. I stopped for a second to listen for them. The pounding in

my cars was too loud at first, but then I heard Pinky give a
battle cry. The sound of bikes breaking twigs, rolling over fallen
leaves, followed.

We were off again, down the trail, branches whipping my
face, ruts making me stumble. I tried not to think about what
would happen if they caught us. George would hold his own
against them, but just picturing Hinkley's fists made me go
weak inside.

"He's right in front of us!" Walsh yelled, and I knew they
could see me. I left the path and cut into the trees. They continued behind me, but the underbrush and fallen logs slowed them
down, and it sounded as if they had left their bikes behind. If
you were a coward like I was, it was a good thing to be a fast
runner, which I also was. I ran for another five minutes at top
speed, and then I had to stop, not because I was winded but
because the lake spread out before me. I'd trapped myself.

I knew that if I had to turn either right or left, they would
catch me easily. The lake was still frozen from the cold snap,
but a thin layer of water slicked the top as it had begun to thaw.
I put a foot out onto the slippery surface and gradually eased
my weight down. It held me. George was uncertain of the ice,
and I had to drag him along behind me. I took slow, careful
steps forward. By the time my pursuers had broken through
the trees at the edge of the lake, I was about fifteen feet from
shore. I didn't look back, although they were calling my name
and saying I was a "fairy" and a "scumbag" and a "piece of
shit." George didn't like the situation at all and began to
growl.

"Egg my house?" I heard Hinkley scream, and then I saw a
rock whiz past my head, hit the ice, and slide three-quarters of
the way to the opposite shore.

"Let's go get him!" yelled Steinmacher, and they must have
stepped onto the ice together, because I felt the entire surface of
the lake undulate and make a growling sound like George did

just before chewing a sneaker. Following that, there was a cracking noise, like a giant egg hatching, and a splash. I looked over my shoulder and saw Walsh standing three feet from shore, up to his waist in brown water. I kept going forward as they helped him out of his hole and retreated.

Their extra weight on the ice must have made it unstable, because now with each step I took I could hear tiny splintering noises and see fissures spread like veins in the clear, frozen green beneath each foot. The wind was blowing fiercely in the middle of the open expanse, and my feeling of victory at their retreat suddenly vanished, replaced by the prospect that the lake might, at any moment, open up and swallow me. That's when the rock hit me in the back of the head, and I went down hard on my chest and face. I heard a great fracturing sound, and my mind went blank as much from fear as from the concussion.

When I finally opened my eyes, I remained splayed out, listening. I heard the wind, dead leaves blowing through the woods, George quietly whimpering, and a very distant sound of laughter, moving away. Every now and then, the ice made a cracking noise. I was soaked from having fallen into the film of water atop the frozen surface, and it came to me slowly that I was trembling. With the slowest and most cautious of movements, I got to my knees. Once I achieved that position, I rested for a moment. My head hurt and I was dizzy, so I closed my eyes. My next goal was to stand, and I told myself I would count to thirty, stand up, and get to shore.

When I reached twenty-five, I happened to look down, and staring up at me through the green ice was a pair of eyes. At first I thought it was my reflection. I leaned down closer to the surface to get a better look, and there, beneath the ice, was the pale, partially rotted face of Charlie Edison. His hair was fixed solid in a wild tangle. Much of the whites of his eyes had gone brown, and they were big and round like fish eyes. His mouth was open in a silent scream. Next to his face was the palm of one hand, and I could barely see past his wrist, as the forearm disappeared into the murk below. His glasses were missing, and so was the flesh of his right cheek.

When I screamed, I felt as though he was screaming through me. Dropping George's leash, I scrabbled to my feet, and, slipping and sliding, ice cracking everywhere around me, I ran straight toward the shore, twenty yards away. In the midst of one step, I felt the ice crack and give way beneath my heel, but I was already gone. The dog and I reached the shore at the same moment, and we both jumped the last few feet over the thin ice at the edge.

Chattering like mad and half frozen, I came out of the woods through the Halloways' backyard. My pant legs were stiff, as was the front of my shirt. When I walked through the front door of our house, the warmth thawed my fear, and I began to cry. My mother was cooking dinner in the kitchen, but she just said, "Hello," and didn't come in. I went upstairs to my room, pulled off my wet clothes, and got into bed. Until I was called to dinner, I lay under the covers, shivering.

Secrets

■ It was a Wednesday, but we were off from school because the next day was Thanksgiving. The weather was bad, and I couldn't sit still inside, so I decided to go with Nan to pick up Aunt Gertie at the Babylon train station. Nan drove at a crawl and made only right-hand turns. Pop called her style of driving, "Going there to get there." Sometimes when I was down at the candy store in town, I'd see the big blue Impala creeping by with Nan at the wheel, looking all around and smiling like Mr. Magoo. Once, when I was with her, an angry guy drove past us and yelled, "Get a horse and buggy!" Today the torture was compounded by sleet and hail.

An hour later we were somewhere in Brightwaters, over by the bay, searching for the correct series of right-hand turns that would send us back toward Babylon. Thankfully, the hail had stopped, but night was coming on.

"What do you think about secrets?" I said to her.

Her lips were going, and she was staring straight ahead. She jammed on the brakes at a stop sign, and then we made a turn. Right, of course. "Honesty's the best policy," she said.

A few minutes later, I said, "Aren't you talking about lies?"

"Maybe," she said, and laughed. She drove on for a while, eyes peeled for another right turn. "Did I ever tell you I was married before Pop?"

"I heard about it," I said.

"My first husband's name was Eddy. What a head of hair. He was a motorcycle cop in New York. A terrible drunk. Once he drove his motorcycle through a plate-glass window and was in the hospital for six months."

I waited for her to go on, but she didn't. "What happened to him?" I asked.

"Eventually he died of pneumonia," she said.

"Did you ever ride on his motorcycle?"

"Sure," she said. "He could be a lot of fun. But he was crazy. When he'd get drunk, he'd shoot his gun off in the street."

She laughed again, and so did I.

"I have his gun and badge and billy clubs in my closet. Remind me to show you."

"Cool."

"One of the clubs has dice inlaid into it. Beautiful. And there's a blackjack. Do you know what that is?"

"No."

"It's leather with a piece of lead rolled into it and stitched up. You can break somebody's skull with it."

"Wait till Jim sees that," I said.

"If you beat somebody with it, there's no black-and-blue marks. You can't play with it, though. It's deadly. I think it's illegal now," she said, and put her finger to her lips.

"When did you marry Pop?" I asked.

"A couple of months after Eddy died."

They'll Bring the Fetid Cheese Ball

■ Aunt Gertie was stout and pale, all bottom lip and jowls, like Winston Churchill with a hairnet, and Mary could face her only as Mickey. "Snap out of it, sweetie," Aunt Gertie told her. "You're acting simple." She handed me a five and said my hair was ridiculous. When she paid Jim, she just shook her head and winced. Then she ordered Nan, calling her Maisie, to hand out the black-and-white cookies in the bakery box on the table. She never came without them—platters of icing in half-moons. She asked us how we were doing in school and scowled at our reports. Aunt Gertie worked for the bishop in Rockville Centre, so when she asked if we said our prayers, we nodded.

"Yeah," said Jim. "We pray we do better in school."

Her body jiggled, and we knew she was laughing.

"We want to ask you about the hermit from where you and Nan grew up," I said.

"What hermit?" she said.

"Bedelia," said Nan.

Aunt Gertie made a sour face.

"The one who lived in a cave in the field of asparagus," said Jim.

Aunt Gertie laughed. "Heaven help us," she said, and folded her stubby arms across her chest.

"Remember, we'd go out there and call"—here Nan brought her hand up to the side of her mouth and wiggled her fingers—"Bedelia, we'd love to steal ya?'"

"Nothing of the sort," said her sister. "That never happened."

"God as my judge," said Nan.

"Malarkey," said Aunt Gertie.

As we retreated through the door to our house, Pop looked up over his paper and said, "Thanks."

The antenna gave me no sleep that night, and I knew there was something in the corner behind the open closet door. George must have felt it, too, because he growled in his sleep at the end of the bed. After what seemed a week passed in one night, each of my forced daydreams of Perno Shell lost in an arctic blizzard melted by fear, I finally heard my mother get up. Before going downstairs, I swung the closet door closed and then touched the bare wood of the floor with my foot. It was damp.

I squinted in the fluorescent light of the kitchen. My mother was at the sink, cleaning out the turkey. She wore her bathrobe, the sleeves rolled up, and her hair was crazy. There was a cigarette going in the ashtray on the counter, and next to it sat a cup of black coffee. The linoleum was cold. Out the window behind her, I saw a gray dawn with steam rising from the ground. I walked closer and looked at the massive pink and yellow bird, its cavern, its sharp wingtips, its nose and hairs. My father's work gave it to him for free, and he'd brought it home wrapped up in a towel like a baby.

"Twenty-six pounds," she said. She dropped the bird into the sink, pulled off a rubber glove, and took up her cigarette. "It's a real SOB."

She poured me a bowl of nameless flakes, drowned them in fake milk, added half a sliced banana, and covered it all with sugar. We sat in the dining room. She smoked and drank her coffee while I ate.

"What are you reading?" she asked me.

"Hound of the Baskervilles," I said.

As haggard as she looked, her face lit up.

"A. Conan Doyle," I said.

"What's your favorite part?" she asked.

In my imagination I saw the figure of Dr. Watson, his black bag in hand. He waved to me from across a snowy cobblestone street. "Watson," I said.

My mother smiled and took a drag on her cigarette. "I think the stories are really about Watson," she said. "He was wounded in the Afghan War, at the Battle of Maiwand. I think the stories are about Watson home from the war, using the writing of the stories to cure himself. He's a doctor, as was Conan Doyle."

"What about Sherlock Holmes?" I asked.

"He's a drug addict and he plays the violin," said my mother.

I nodded like I knew what she meant and quickly asked who was coming for dinner. She went through the list of guests, punctuating it with short comments: "They'll bring the fetid cheese ball again this year. . . ."

Amid a haze of cooking turkey, Jim and Mary and I watched every minute of the Macy's parade on the tube. Jim declared that the whole thing would rot if they didn't have the giant balloons.

"And Santa," Mary added.

"I hate the singers," I said.

"All they're doing is playing a record on a loudspeaker, and the singer just waves to people," said Jim.

"Stinks," said Mary.

George came in and got up on the couch between Jim and Mary. As soon as the dog lay down, Jim took to very, very lightly brushing just three of George's back hairs. Eventually George snarled. Jim laid off for a few seconds before doing it again. Three times later we all laughed, and suddenly George snapped. He hated to be made fun of.

Mary put an end to it by saying, "Stop. Santa's coming." But it wasn't for another hour. When he finally sailed past with his waving elves and bag of presents, it was as if attached to the back of his sleigh's runners was the movie *March of the Wooden Soldiers* with Laurel and Hardy. As Santa returned to the North Pole, he pulled that gray nightmare over us like a blanket, and Mary went Mickey. I could never decide which was creepier, the army of rouge-cheeked wooden soldiers or the hairy monsters that swarmed out of the caves beneath the story-land village. There was singing in it, and the singing didn't stink. Laurel and Hardy acted like idiots, and we enjoyed that.

To kill time before the company showed up, Jim and I took George for a walk to the school field. We messed around by the basketball court, peered down into the now-silent kingdom of crickets in the sump, and walked the perimeter. Eventually Jim said, "We're gonna be late," and started for home. I wanted to tell him about Charlie being in the lake, but when we reached the edge of the school yard, he started to tell me about this girl in his class in junior high. "She has tits like torpedoes," he said. "Up periscope."

And then we were home. The house was jangling with heat and voices. The smell of turkey roasting was as thick in the air as my mother's perfume on work mornings. Cars lined the curbs going both ways. My father let us in the front door and told us to hurry up and get dressed.

From the stairs I looked down on the scene through a cloud of smoke—people on the couches and chairs, standing in the dining room, leaning against the walls; ice cubes clinking, plates of cheese cubes impaled on toothpicks, celery with cream cheese and walnuts; a turquoise dress, a pile of hair, a strange deep laughter rising out of the noise of voices. I saw Nan's door open and knew there was a whole group of men in there watching football on television.

In minutes, with stiff white shirt and polished shoes, hair bear-waxed up, I dove into the party. Uncle Jack did magic tricks for Mary at the dining-room table, draping a handkerchief over his hands and making cards disappear. His mother, Grandma, my father's mother, sat straight as a statue, scanning the crowd. She had a big, smooth melted piece of skin under her chin that was supposedly transplanted there from her ass. Once she told me that when she was a girl in Oklahoma, she saw a woman with a disease that caused a cobweb to grow from her mouth and down across her chest. "Fine as frog's hair," she'd said to me, waving her hand in the air to show how the stuff caught the breeze.

Pop's sister, Aunt Irene, told about her trip to the psychic and blinked every other second. I also had an aunt who burped every other second, but she wasn't at the party. My father drank a whiskey sour with ice and a cherry in it and chatted with Aunt Gertie and her son, Bob, the priest. I went and stood near the back door, opening it a sliver to feel the cool air. In the kitchen my mother, surrounded by boiling pots and dirty dishes, a cigarette between her lips and a glass of cream sherry in her hand, knelt at the open oven, basting the sizzling bird.

My cousins Cillie and Ivy and Suzie, all in high school, sat with us at the kids' table set up in the living room. They liked to joke around with Jim, but their long blond hair and lemon perfume made me shy. There was this other kid there, the son of my father's friend. I forget his name, but no matter what you said to him, he'd say in return, "Naturally," like a big know-it-all. Jim threw a black olive at him and hit him in the eye. When the kid started crying, Jim told him to shut up. Then we ate.

After dinner everyone jammed around the living room, and my cousins played "The Twist," a record by Chubby Checker, on the Victrola, and taught everyone how to do the dance named after it. "Like you're putting out a cigarette with the toe of your shoe," they said. My mother even came out of the kitchen, drink in hand, and did the twist. Aunt Gertie laughed, Grandma stared, Edwin (I never really knew who he was related to or how) came in from the football room for another drink and fake-bit Nan on the head. Mary, talking to herself, snuck down the hallway to her room.

George circled the dancers, snarling. At one point Mrs. Farley dropped her glasses on the floor, and when she bent over to get them, George lunged for her ass. At that very second, my father, who was sitting on the couch and talking to someone, took it all in from the corner of his eye and stuck his foot out so that he caught the dog in midair, George's mouth closing on his loafer. I don't think anyone else saw it but me. My father, turning momentarily away from his conversation, looked over and raised his eyebrows.

Mary asked if it was okay, and we were allowed to go downstairs and check the Christmas lights. We did it every year on Thanksgiving night. My father led us into the basement, to the corner, back by the oil burner, on Mary's side of the stairs. The party above us sounded like a stampede. I heard Pop playing the mandolin in the background. My father showed Jim the boxes and instructed him in how to plug the strings of lights into the outlet. He gave us two rows of replacement bulbs— all orange. Then he left, and we just stood there in the mildew-dust scent, listening.

"Bubble lights," said Mary, and Jim moved into action.

"You know bubble lights are last," he said.

"Could you possibly . . . ?" said Mary.

Jim put one of the tattered red Nova boxes on the concrete floor. As soon as he flipped open its cover, I smelled the tinsel-pine scent of Christmases past. There they were, deep-colored glass heads asleep all in a row. He unstrung the cord and plugged them in. Mary sighed when they came on. "Wait a second," said Jim, and turned off the overhead light. We sat in the dark, in a circle around the box, just staring at the glow. As the lights heated, they baked that Christmas scent, and we breathed it in like a cure. We started replacing dead bulbs: I pulled out a burned one, Mary handed Jim a replacement, and he screwed it in.

I whispered, "Charlie Edison's in the lake, just like Mary said."

"How do you know?" asked Jim.

I told him about Hinkley chasing me out onto the ice.

"I hate Hinkley," said Mary.

"You probably saw your reflection," said Jim.

"I swear he's there," I said. "Mary knew it."

"What did he look like?"

I told him.

Jim stared at me through Christmas light. "I'll take care of Hinkley," he said.

"But what about the other?" I asked.

"Why didn't you tell Dad?"

"I don't want Charlie's mother to know," I said. "She still has hope."

"Don't tell," said Mary.

Jim shook his head.

"The guy in the car. I think he killed Mr. Barzita, too."

"Fig Man?" said Jim, and laughed.

I told him about what happened Halloween night.

My father came to the door then and called down to see if we were all right.

"Yeah," called Jim, and he got up and turned on the overhead light. Then he unplugged and put away the box of lights. "We'll do the bubble lights next," he told Mary.

"Naturally," she said.

He took a white and green box out of the stack and laid it on the floor. We gathered round as he opened it. They were rare, and there were no replacements for them—long glass fingers of colored liquid that boiled when they were lit. Jim plugged in the string, and it was so old and frayed we could hear the electricity running through it. Pop had bought them forty years back, and their glow was a message from the past. We watched carefully for the first bubble.

By the time we'd finished checking the lights and emerged from the basement, the guests were all gone. My mother was sitting in the recliner in her bathrobe sipping her wine, and my father, in his dress pants and black socks, sat on the couch smoking. They were talking about who looked good and who didn't. I lay down on the braided rug next to George and listened till I fell asleep.

They'll Go for That

■ In the days that followed Thanksgiving, Jim dusted off Botch Town and set to work on it again, fixing things that had fallen down, putting in a stop sign where Willow Avenue met Hammond Lane. He made figures for Mrs. Homretz and her dog, Tatel, and a new Mrs. Harrington. The old Mrs. Harrington had cracked from her own weight. I was his assistant. He saw the car I'd painted white and told me it was "almost good." We worked every night on the board after doing our homework. His plan was to let Mary have her way and show us where the prowler was. "Then we catch him," he said.

I asked around school if any of the kids had sighted the man in the white coat or seen a face at their window. I had to be careful the way I put it, so no one would get wise to what was going on. Not a trace, though. No one had seen anything. Hardly anybody remembered the prowler, and it had only been a couple of weeks since Mrs. Mangini had been "viewed in the altogether," as her husband, Joe, explained to Pop out on the front lawn. I'd been standing there when Joe went by wearing his Long Island Rail Road conductor's hat, his newspaper rolled up under his arm. After Joe had moved on, Pop said, "Christ."

One night Jim called Mary over to our side of the cellar. We heard her stop talking to herself, and then the curtain that separated the two halves opened. She took one step out on our side but didn't come any closer to the board.

"Do you get the plan?" Jim asked her.

"Yeah," said Mary.

I laughed.

Jim hit me in the arm and told me to shut up. "We want you to tell us where the prowler is," he said. He held up the figure he'd made from the army man—pin arms and bright eyes. "Show us," he said, holding the figure out to her.

She shook her head. "Not yet."

"Come on," he said.

"No comment till the time limit is up," she said.

We laughed because she'd stolen the line from an old *Superman* episode.

"What do you mean?" asked Jim.

She turned like a robot, walked past us, and went up the stairs.

The day I discovered the cheese ball in the kitchen garbage, we got our report cards. It was about a week before Christmas, and Krapp had done me wrong. When he handed it to me, he shook his head. I failed math and social studies, and the rest of the grades weren't too good either. After a long walk home and on the verge of tears, I entered the house. Jim was waiting for me. He immediately asked to see my card. One look and he smiled. "Nice work," he said. "They could use you at Harvard."

"What did you get?" I asked.

"I only failed one," he said. "And straight C's."

"Wait till they get home," I said.

"Don't worry, just tell them Krapp hates you. They'll go for that."

But they didn't. Even Mary, who spent all that extra time in her make-believe school, did lousy. There was a lot of yelling. My father, red in the face, poked me in the chest with his index finger and told me I'd have to learn math from him now. Jim sat quietly, no matter what happened, and nodded. When it was over, we were all sent to bed. Mary went down the hall, and I dried my tears as I followed Jim upstairs. He went toward his room and I toward mine. Just before I closed the door behind me, he whispered, "Hey." I turned around. He dropped into a squat, grunting and making faces. His hand was behind his back. Suddenly the report card fell to the floor between his legs. He stood, gave a sigh, and shut the door.

Snow Globe

■ Two days after Christmas, there was a blizzard. The heat went off, and we were all huddled in the kitchen on couch-pillow beds. The oven was on and open. My mother had tacked blankets up over the entrances to the living and dining rooms. Mary and Jim and my mother were all sick with the flu, coughing and shivering, wrapped in blankets. My father sat in the cold in the dining room, drinking coffee and reading an old newspaper. He called for me.

"Go upstairs and put on a lot of clothes. If you stay in here with me, you might not catch what they have." Steam came out of his mouth when he spoke. "Or you can go in Nan and Pop's—they have their electric heater on."

I nodded and went past him toward the stairs, and I saw, out the bit of the front window not obscured by the darkened Christmas tree, a wall of snow, reaching up beyond the top of the glass. The wind shrieked around the house.

"How high is it?" I asked.

He turned to look at the living-room window. "They said five feet on the radio a couple of hours ago. But it's drifted up around the houses to the gutters. That's some serious snow."

Up in my bedroom, teeth chattering against the cold, I dressed in layers of pajamas and shirts and pants. I put on my socks and sneakers, which I never usually wore in the house.

Outside my ice-crusted window, I saw a tidal wave of white in the front yard, and it sloped down to about four feet in the space between our house and the Farleys'. The street was blocked from view, and I could make out only the roofs on the other side. It felt like we were trapped with the wind in a snow globe.

When I got back downstairs, Mom was sitting at the other end of the dining-room table, a shawl over her bathrobe, smoking and shaking. "We're going to need aspirin and children's aspirin, and some frozen orange juice, a carton of cigs. I doubt the liquor store's open, but get a half gallon of wine if it is," she said.

My father was hunched over the table, writing with a pencil stub on the back of an envelope. "Okay," he said.

"How are you going to get to the street?" she asked.

"I could get out the back door," he said, "but from the looks of it I'd have to dig through the drift in the front to get to the road. But that's like twelve feet of snow. Once I make it to the road, it should be all right. I heard the plow go through last night a couple times."

"You can't go out the front door," she said.

"I'm not gonna. I'm going out the upstairs window. I'll lie flat and breaststroke to the street," he said, smiling. He lit a cigarette. "I'll go in a minute."

"How are you going to get back in?" she said.

"I'll worry about that later." My father turned to me and said, "Go ask Nan and Pop if they need anything from the store."

I went next door, and it was warm. The rings of the little electric heater glowed bright orange. Pop was sitting in the chair in the corner, his head back, lightly snoring, and Nan was on the couch at a tray, doing a paint-by-number.

She looked up and said, "Close the door, quick."

I did and went over to see her picture, which was of a bullfighter. Although she wasn't great at staying in the lines, the blobs of color were starting to become something. "It's good," I said, and then asked if she wanted anything from the store.

"No, but who's going to the store in this mess?" she asked.

"Dad's going," I said. "He's going out the front window upstairs."

A few minutes later, my father, dressed in his jacket, a pair of gloves, and Jim's black skullcap, led Nan, my mother, and me upstairs. We went into Jim's room, and my father started moving the desk and chair away from the windows. I looked out and could see that the snow had drifted up to the edge of the roof. My father removed one of the storm windows from its frame and shoved the window the whole way up. The wind and snow blasted into the room, and we all stepped back. My father said, "If I sink in, throw me a line," and laughed. Then he hoisted himself through the opening, into the storm.

Mom and Nan and I crowded around the window, the snow blowing in our faces. My father crept down the sloping roof and, when he reached the edge, lay down on his stomach. He carefully pushed himself out onto the snow and immediately sank in a foot or two.

"Oh, Christ," said my mother.

"He loves the elements," said Nan.

He started wriggling forward toward the street. He moved very slowly, and I thought the drift might devour him at any second. Halfway there he stopped and just lay still.

My mother called out to him, "Are you all right?"

"Things are shifting a bit," he said.

He started forward again, and when he eventually came close to the street, he got up on his knees and crawled quickly like a crab. Then he went over the edge. I don't know if he heard us, but we clapped. A strong gust pushed us all away from the opening. My mother stepped through the blowing snow and shut the window with a bang. The room went very still.

"It's so dark out already," said Nan.

When we got downstairs, my mother went back into our kitchen and I followed Nan into her house. She put the TV on for me, and I watched a Hercules movie with the sound off while she painted. Last night I hadn't gotten much sleep, with all the coughing and maneuvering in the crowded kitchen. My weariness and the warmth of the heater made me doze. When I woke up a while later, Nan had put away her paints and was frying a pork chop at her little stove. On the TV, Hercules was lifting a giant boulder. Pop was awake now, reading a magazine. He saw I was also awake and said, "You shouldn't watch this junk," nodding toward the television. "You should read a magazine. It's educational. See?" He turned the magazine in his hands so I could see the page he was on. There was no writing, just a picture of a naked woman sitting on the lap of a guy in a gorilla suit. I could feel my face flush red. Nan looked over and laughed. "Put that away," she said. He closed the magazine and threw it down next to his chair.

After lunch Pop brought out his project. I sat next to him at the kitchenette table. He'd been putting together a plastic model kit that had two figures—a Neanderthal man, who stood on one side of the base, and a human skeleton that stood on the other. The caveman was finished and stood, dressed in a leopard skin, with a club in his hand. Pop worked on the human rib cage, gluing each sharp bone in place, and I held the skull, working the movable jaw up and down. Nan passed by every few seconds, doing her daily exercise, walking from the living room to the bedroom one hundred times.

While he worked, Pop sipped at a glass of Old Grand-Dad and told me something that happened once when he was in the merchant marine. His ship was off the coast of Italy, and they were coming into port. It was a beautiful clear day, and the sun was bright. "The town we were heading for came in sight on the horizon," he said. "I thought I was seeing heaven. The buildings of the town glowed pure white in the sun. As we got closer, it looked even more beautiful—even the streets were white. Then we landed and went ashore. And let this be a lesson to you. . . ."

I nodded.

"Our ship had brought the seagulls, and they circled in the sky by the hundreds, thinking we were a fishing boat. That's when I realized that the whiteness of the buildings and streets was from dried gull shit. Over time those birds had covered everything."

When I went back next door to our house, my mother was drinking and smoking at the dining-room table. I could tell by the look on her face that she was in a bad mood, so as cold as it was, I went up to my room and, fully clothed, got into bed and pulled the covers up. Before long I built up some heat in my cocoon and drifted off to sleep. It seemed like only minutes later that Jim was standing next to my bed with a blanket wrapped around him. "Get up," he said.

I opened my eyes, and he said, "It's three-thirty, and Dad's not back yet."

"How long's he been gone?" I asked.

"Like five hours. Even if he crawled, he'd have made it by now."

"What's Mom say?" I asked.

He closed his eyes, tilted his head back, and snored. "She's out cold in the kitchen. Mary's fever's gotten worse. We need the children's aspirin. Nan's got her in her place, wrapped up on the couch. I'm going out to look for Dad."

"Do you feel better?" I asked.

He sat down on the edge of the bed and shook his head. The only other time I'd seen him look as weak was when I went to one of his wrestling matches and he'd lost. I had an image in my mind of my father up to his hips in snow, unable to move, and sinking slowly, like it was quicksand. "I'll go," I said.

"Yeah, right," he said.

I threw the blanket off and sat up. "I can do it," I said, and the part of me that didn't want to was not in my head.

"You'll have to go out the window," he said.

"I'm just afraid of sinking in."

"It stopped snowing, and it looks like there's an ice crust, so you'll slide across it."

I got out of bed and went to the closet for my coat.

"It's getting late, and it'll be dark soon. You gotta go up to the stores and look for him. If you don't see him by then, come right back."

"Okay," I said. My gloves were long lost, so I took a pair of white socks out of the dresser and put them on my hands.

"Put your hood up," he said.

We went into his room.

"Does Nan know about this?" I asked.

"If she did, she wouldn't let you go," he said. Then he stepped forward and pushed up the window. The wind blew in, and I walked forward. He helped me up to the sill, and I scrabbled through onto the roof. The sudden cold, the sight of the houses sunk in snow, stunned me, and I crouched down. The sky was as deep in its gray as the bubble lights were in color.

"Shit or get off the pot!" Jim yelled, and I felt his hand on my shoulder. I looked back once to see him leaning out the window. When I reached the edge of the roof, I got down on my stomach as I'd seen my father do. Jim was right, there was a sheen of ice on the snow. By the time I thought about sinking in, I was halfway across. I pictured myself trapped in snow, unable to breathe. The image scared me, and I went faster until I fell. Thinking I was going under, I screamed. The snow that cushioned my fall was only up to my waist. I stood and caught my breath, amazed that I'd made it. All down the block in front of me, the snow was drifted up on either side, to the edge of the rooftops in giant waves. I remembered when Mrs. Grimm taught our catechism class and told us about the parting of the Red Sea.

I made slow headway, as though in a dream. Beneath the wind it was so silent that at one point my ears made their own sound, and I thought I heard Nan calling my name. I trudged forward toward Hammond Lane at the end of the block, where I hoped the plows had gone through more than once.

The snow started again, giant wet flakes, and night was no more than an hour away by the time I reached Hammond. My sneakers were soaked and freezing. The snow was bunching up under my pant legs, and the socks weren't gloves My nose was running. I had to climb a mountain of plowed snow at the end of the block. It was pretty solid, but coming over the peak scared me because it felt like I was twenty feet up. I scrabbled down the other side to where the road was covered in only a few inches of packed snow. Hammond led straight to the stores. I was tired, but now I could walk easily, and that was a relief. A black car came out of the gloom behind me, its tire chains like a drumbeat. I knew it was Mr. Cleary, the principal of East Lake, because he drove with his left hand on the wheel and his right around his throat, where it always rested. I waved, but he didn't see me.

The parking lot at the stores had been plowed, and all around its edges were giant walls of snow, like a fort. The deli, the candy store, the supermarket, and Howie's Pizza were all dark. At the end of the row, though, it looked like there was a light on in the drugstore. In my mind I saw my father standing at the counter talking to the drug guy with the thick glasses, and I walked faster.

In the window of the store hung an old poster of the Coppertone girl and the little dog yanking her pants down. The lights were definitely on, and I tried to look up the main aisle as I pulled on the door handle. It was locked. I tried it again and again. I moved to the side of the door to look up another aisle but saw no one. I banged on the window. Staring dully into the fluorescent-lit store, I heard a car's tire chains out on Hammond. The sound slowed, and then I realized it was turning in to the parking lot. I looked over my shoulder and saw a long white car. It turned and started toward me, its headlights making my eyes squint. I felt weak and couldn't move. My mouth went dry. The sound of the car's tire chains as it slowly crossed the lot had become my heartbeat. When the car reached Howie's Pizza, the fear exploded inside me, and I bolted around the side of the drugstore. There was a wall of plowed snow in front of me, and I jumped up onto the first ice block. I climbed up and up like a monkey. Behind me I heard the car stop and its door open. When I reached the top, I looked back for just a second. Only after I jumped did I realize that the person standing next to the car was not the man in the white coat but the drugstore guy. It was a sheer twelve-foot drop. When I hit, my knees buckled and I went face-first into two feet of snow.

I got up and turned to go back over the hill but was confronted by a wall of ice. It was unclimbable. I felt like crying, but I didn't. The dark made me think about how great it would be back in the oven warmth of the kitchen. I took a few deep breaths and thought about how to get home. I wasn't familiar with the street I was trapped on, which ran behind the stores. Hinkley lived in this neighborhood, so I didn't go there much. What I did know was that at the end of the winding block it touched the woods somewhere. I thought the drifts might not be as bad under the trees, and I could cut through to the Masons' backyard and then climb over the fences to ours.

I started out and wound my way around drifts of snow as I went. The illuminated windows of the houses, some showing lit Christmas trees, made me feel better each time I saw one. Then the wind picked up, and the snow started to come faster, driving against me. My ears hurt from the cold, and my hands were freezing in my coat pockets. I could barely make out the treetops of the woods, looming darker than the night behind a house I was passing. The snow was fierce, and I had to get in under the trees to get some relief. I walked up the driveway of the darkened house, into the backyard. On my way to the woods, I saw an old wooden garage, the snow drifted against one side. It was open, so I went in to rest for a minute. It smelled of gasoline, but it was a pleasure to stand on the solid concrete floor. Leaning against the wall, I listened to the wind outside and closed my eyes.

I could have stayed there for a long time. I found that my sight had adjusted to the darkness of the place, and I realized that there was a car only a foot away from me. It was a white car. I squinted. A big white car. I thought about how I'd been fooled by the drugstore guy, but then I saw something behind the backseat where the windshield curved down. Resting against one of the fins, I got a better look. It was a kid's baseball hat. When I saw the Cleveland Indian's smile, I turned and looked at the house. A light went on in an upstairs window. I let out a whispered cry and ran. Before I knew it, I was in the woods, running through knee-deep snow.

I don't remember how I got there, but I kind of woke up and found myself banging on the back door of our house. My father opened it and drew me into his arms.

"It's all right," he said, and I realized how heavily I was breathing. I pulled my hood off and shielded my eyes for a moment against the fluorescent light.

"I came to get you," I said, almost crying.

"I know," he said, and pulled me close to his side.

On the floor around us, my mother was sleeping by the entrance to the living room, Mary was sitting up reading an old racing form, and Jim lay with blankets piled over him, staring up at me. He was trembling from fever, but he said, "Nice work."

I pointed at Mary and said, "Is she better?"

"Yeah," said my father. "She sweated the shit out."

Mary looked up from her form. "I sweated it," she said.

Jim laughed.

My father sent me to the bathroom to get out of my wet clothes, and he went upstairs to my room and got me underwear and socks and slippers and two sets of pajamas. My feet itched terribly as they thawed. After I dressed, I came out to the living room, where my father sat on the couch in front of the Christmas tree. On the coffee table were two small glasses and the squat, dark bottle of Drambuie. I sat down next to my father, and he leaned forward and poured out the golden syrup. He struck a match and touched the flame to the liquid in my glass. A blue flame wavered across the surface. We watched it for a little while, and then he said, "Okay, blow it out." I did.

"Give that a minute," he told me, and took a sip of his. He lit a cigarette. "I don't know how you made it. It's rough out there. I was just about to put my jacket on and go back out to look for you."

"Why'd it take you so long?" I asked.

"Well, I went up to Hammond on my way out. And it was plowed, so I started walking to the stores, and about halfway there I look over on the side of the road and see a hand coming out of the snow. At first I thought I was seeing things. So I walked over to it and kicked some snow from around it, and there's a body." He took another sip.

"What'd you do?" I asked.

"I dug the body out. Man, this guy was frozen solid. I mean solid, like a statue. Finally I turn the body over—the eyes were shattered like glass. You know who it was?"

"Who?" I said.

He pointed with the two fingers that held his cigarette. "The guy up the street. You know, the old man with the squirrels."

"Mr. Barzita," I said, and felt the snow in my face. I thought about him sitting among his trees with the gun on his lap, his eyes shattered, and I took up the Drambuie. The first taste was sweet molten lava. Barzita turned to confetti.

"He's plucked his last fig," said my father. "So once I found him, I had to go up to the stores and use the pay phone to call the cops. They told me I had to go back and wait by the body, so I did. I stood there for about two hours, freezing. Finally the cop came, and him and me put the body in the backseat of his car and took it to the hospital. On the way there, we got stuck and had to dig out. We had to help other people who were stuck. It was a big rigmarole. Bullshit on top of bullshit. The cops asked me all kinds of questions. They figured the guy'd gone out to the store early and maybe a plow clipped him in the dark. His neck was broken. After it was over, the cop gave me a ride. I still had to get the aspirin and stuff. On the way, though, more bullshit. Then he got a call and had to drop me up by the library. You know, one thing after another."

My father got up and turned out all the lights except those on the tree. We sat in silence, staring at the colors. I drank only half the Drambuie before I put the glass down on the table.

"Have you squinted yet this year?" he asked. He had this thing about squinting at the Christmas lights in the dark. We both squinted for a while, and then I leaned my head back and closed my eyes.

"Okay," he said, "what's nine times nine?"

I made believe I'd fallen asleep, but I heard Mary from the kitchen call quietly, "Eighty-one."

He's Coming Up the Drainpipe

■ The next day, as soon as he could get through, the heating guy came and fixed the oil burner. It was good to get out of the kitchen. Jim was feeling all better, except he had a cold. He and I went outside in the frigid wind and sunshine to help my father, who had to get to work that night, dig a path to the street and free the cars. I waited for a chance to talk to Jim about what I'd seen, and my father finally went inside for a while.

"I know I was wrong about Barzita," I said, "but now I know where the man with the white car lives."

"Where?"

I told him about the house with the garage that bordered the woods.

"What if he killed Barzita and then dumped the body in the road during the blizzard?" Jim said.

"I didn't think of that," I told him. "I figured I was just wrong."

"If you didn't think of it, it's probably right," he said. "We'll go through the woods, and you can show me the guy's house, but we have to wait till the snow's gone. Otherwise he can track our footprints back home."

"I left footprints," I said.

"Let's hope the storm covered them."

On the days left of our Christmas vacation, we went sleigh riding, had a massive snowball fight with armies of kids, and Jim and I walked to the bay one afternoon because Larry March told us his father said it was frozen solid. Jim said March's old man's head was frozen solid, but we walked out onto the bay, powdered snow swirling around us in the sunlight. There were eruptions of ice that stood a foot or so above the surface. Sometimes the ice was rumpled, sometimes patches were clear and smooth and you could look down into the murk below. If it weren't for me being scared of falling through, Jim would have gone all the way to Captree Island. When I told him I was going back to shore, he turned to me and said, "I know why Mary won't help us."

"Why?" I asked.

"Pop and her aren't working the figures for the races. He told me the other day, he's waiting for the running of the pigs down at Hialeah. There's no races for him to bet on right now. I'll bet she thinks she's on vacation like Pop."

That night, standing before Botch Town, we asked Mary if Jim's theory was right. She didn't say anything but stepped forward to the board and scrutinized it. We stood there for a while until Jim looked at me and shook his head. He reached around Mary, picked up the prowler figure, and tried to hand it to her. She pushed his arm away.

"No," she said, and looked around the board. She found the white car parked up the block by Mr. Barzita's house and picked it up. When she put it down, it landed right in front of our house.

"When?" Jim said.

"Now," said Mary.

"Now?" I asked.

"Right now," said Mary.

Jim had already taken off up the stairs, and I was close behind him. We went to the front window and looked out into the night. The snow was everywhere, and the moon was full. Jim said, "Oh, shit," and a second later I saw the headlights. The white car crept slowly by. After the taillights disappeared from view, Jim stepped back and sat on the couch.

"I told you," I said.

When we went back down into the cellar to tell Mary she was right, she'd already gone over to her own side of the steps. We heard her over there as Mickey. Then Mrs. Harkmar was telling him he had all the right answers. Jim turned his attention to the board. "The prowler is prowling," he said.

"Who?" I asked.

"Hey, look," said Jim. "She changed that." He was pointing to the figure of Charlie Edison, now in our backyard.

"What's that supposed to mean?" I said, and could tell he'd caught the inch of fear in my voice.

"He's coming up the drainpipe for you," he said.

I laughed, but later, after the lights were out and I was in bed and Charlie was behind my open closet door, I wasn't laughing. That night Charlie spoke through the sound of the antenna singing. Three times I heard his voice come out of the noise and call for his mother. Each time I was just about asleep when I heard it.

Why the Sky Is Blue

■ Back in school, at the start of gym class on Monday, this big weird kid, Hodges Stamper, came up behind me, put his arm around my throat, and choked me. Coach Crenshaw stood there scratching his balls, watching the whole thing. Hodges applied so much pressure that I couldn't breathe. Using the heel of my sneaker, I kicked him in the shin with everything I had, and he grunted and let go. There was spittle at the corners of his mouth, and he was smiling. I slunk away and hid next to the bleachers.

Crenshaw eventually blew his whistle and told us he had invented a new sport for the New Year. "Push Off the Mats," he called it. The middle of the gym floor was covered with wrestling mats. He had us line up and asked Bobby Harweed and Larry March to be captains and to pick two teams. I was chosen third to last; my stock had risen.

"Each team lines up on one side of the mat, facing the other," said Crenshaw. "I blow the whistle, and then you all crawl toward each other. If you stand up, you're out. The idea is to drag your opponent to the edge of the mat and make some part of their body touch the wooden floor. As soon as they touch, they're out. Then you can go help your teammates drag the rest of their guys off."

He told us to line up and pointed to the edge each team should take. Then he yelled, "Crawling position!" and we got down on all fours. He put his whistle to his mouth, waited ten seconds, and blew. We charged forward. While I was crawling, I was frantically looking for one of the two kids weaker than me. I saw one, soft and white as marshmallow, kneeling as if he were in a trance, and I veered toward him.

Before I got there, though, somebody grabbed me from the side. I looked around, and it was Hinkley. He took my leg and pulled me. I went down on my stomach and tried to dig my fingers into the mat. It didn't work. I was sliding along. When he was just about to force my foot down onto the wood, I flipped over on my back and with my free leg kicked him out onto the floor. I sat up in time to catch the look of surprise on his face. Crenshaw blew the whistle and made the "you're out" sign at him.

I turned back to the battle in the center of the mat. Our team had cleared off all their guys except Stamper, who knelt like a mound in the middle of everything, kids swarming all over him. I joined in. He pushed and grunted and spat, but we were too many for him. He finally went over, and we dragged him toward the side like we were moving Gulliver. I looked up and saw Crenshaw smiling at the action. We got Stamper so that his head was out over the wood. He wouldn't let us push his head back, though, so five guys, all at once, on the third Mississippi, pushed down, and it finally hit the floor with a crack. I saw Stamper twice later that afternoon—once when I went to the bathroom and once to get a drink from the water fountain. Both times he was leaning against a wall in the hallway, and both times he asked me if it was lunch yet.

In math, Krapp whipped us with long division, and in the middle of one of his explanations, out the window, across the field, on the baseball diamond, Mr. Rogers appeared as if from thin air, talking, with his finger pointing up. Krapp stared like he was seeing a ghost. The ex-librarian walked the bases through half-melted clumps of snow. As he rounded second, he stopped for a moment to clap. At third he signaled "safe" and turned to view the cheering crowd. Home base was covered by a small ice dune. Rogers climbed it halfway, with a strong wind in his face. Then a police car showed up on the field, and like we were watching a movie, we all got up and went to the window. Krapp said nothing. Two officers got out of the black-and-white car with the blinking cherry on top, and each took one of Mr. Rogers's arms. He kept talking as they loaded him into the backseat of the cruiser. The engine started, and they rolled away toward Sewer Pipe Hill.

Krapp told us to sit down. He closed the math book and checked the clock. It was fifteen minutes until the end of the school day. He went behind his desk and grabbed his chair, lifted it and slowly carried it out in front of the class. Placing it down, he took a seat facing us.

"From now until the bell rings, I will answer any question you have. You can ask me anything except one thing," he said. "You can't ask me why the sky is blue."

You could have heard a pin drop. I felt all of us kids tense like one clenched muscle. No one wanted their Krapp too nice. He looked out over our heads at some spot on the back wall. I stared so hard at the clock that I could see the minute hand move. Almost a whole quarter hour of complete silence. At four minutes to, I thought of a question. In my mind's eye, I saw myself raising my hand and saying, "Where's Charlie Edison?"—but I never did. Finally Hodges Stamper raised his hand and asked, "Is it almost lunch yet?"

"You've had lunch," said Krapp, and then the bell rang.

Jim made me tell him about it three times. He called it "The

Soft Side of Krapp," but I told him about how Krapp sat staring at us, his arms crossed against his chest. "Like he had all the answers," I said. "Kind of like a swami."

"He'll be out on the baseball diamond in no time," said Jim.

A Hundred Bottles Apiece

■ The day the horses started at Hialeah, Jim decided the ground was clear enough for us to go in search of the man in the white coat's house. It was a Saturday, and the sun was shining. There was a light breeze. As we forded the stream behind the old Halloway house, Jim said to me, "We can't keep calling this guy 'the man in the white coat.' It takes too long to say."

"What do you want to call him?" I asked.

We stepped onto the path, and he said, "I had an idea. Remember the name of the nun who told us about him walking the earth? Her name was Sister Joe, so . . ."

"Brother Joe?" I asked.

"Josephine," he said.

"No," I said immediately. "You can't call him that."

"How about Deathman?" said Jim. "Like Batman."

"I don't want to say that," I told him.

"Well, what do you want?" he asked.

I'd thought of calling him Dr. Watson and was about to say it when Jim cut in and said, "No, wait! We're gonna call him Roger—'cause his face looks like a skull, and the flag that has the skull is the Jolly Roger. What do you think? We could call him Jolly Roger."

"Too much like Mr. Rogers," I said.

"Son of Krapp?" said Jim.

"How about Dr. Watson?" I said.

"No, that sucks. We could just call him Mr. White for short," he said.

"Okay," I said, although I wasn't crazy about it, and we both said it out loud a few times to practice.

Going back across the stream at one point, we came upon Tony Calfano's fort—a lean-to made of tree limbs and brush, a standing triangle of logs. Calfano hunted in the woods with a pellet gun. He was in my class and lived around the corner from us, next to Mrs. Grimm. When he'd kill squirrels, he'd skin them and hang their dried pelts on the walls of his fort. I'd come upon the spot by accident only two other times, and both times it gave me a shiver to see it. He'd told me in school that he knew where sassafras grew in the woods and that he'd pick it and make sassafras tea. One time this kid Tom Frost asked Tony why he was out of school, knowing that the cops had been to his house when his mother went nuts. Calfano said, "I had Frost bite on my dick."

Farther on in our journey, we had to pass through a place we called "the crater," a round depression in the woods on the way to the railroad tracks. It was about twelve feet deep and huge in circumference. The edge was a sloping dirt hill, and all across its sunken space knee-high pines grew like grass. Crows perched in the trees at its far edge. We didn't know that area of the woods very well. In trying to find the back of Mr. White's house, we would have to travel almost to the end of the trees.

Whenever we saw a backyard off to our right, we'd sneak up cautiously, staying well hidden, and look to see if there was a wooden garage standing by itself. At first we went all the way to the tracks and didn't find the house and had to turn back and look again. There was one with a garage in the backyard, but when I looked at the house, I didn't see that high window where the light had come on. I shook my head, and Jim laughed.

"Did you really see this place?" he said.

"Yes."

"Were Laurel and Hardy there?"

I gave him the finger.

"Okay," he said, and we looked some more, traveling back and forth along the western edge of the woods. Finally he said, "Forget it," and started to head home. When we got to the middle of our path across the crater, he stopped and turned west. "Let's look over here," he said. We walked through the low pines to the western edge and climbed up the embankment. There we found a place of giant pines with boughs that swept down to the ground. I had a sudden memory of running around them through the night in waist-high snow and knew that we were close.

"This is it," I told Jim.

We entered an area where we'd never been before. It was more like a forest, with tall pine trees, their brown needles covering the ground. The branches were so high above us that when the sun occasionally snuck through, it was like a beam out of Flash Gordon. The fear was building in my muscles, and my head was going dull. Then, through the pines, I saw the edge of the garage and immediately crouched down. I whispered to Jim, and when he turned and saw me, he dropped, too. I pointed toward the garage. He couldn't see it from his angle, so he crept back to where I was and looked.

A minute later we were behind the last row of pines and had a clear view of the garage, the backyard, and the house. Its afternoon peacefulness made it scarier to me. We knelt there for a long time, listening to the breeze and staring at the windows. I thought of Charlie Edison trapped inside there, and my mouth went dry. I was losing strength through the bottoms of my sneakers.

Jim turned to me and whispered, "If anything happens, run home and tell somebody to call the cops," and then he was off, across the short space of open ground to the back of the garage. I couldn't believe he'd gone, and I didn't want to be left alone. As I started toward him, though, he looked back and held up a hand to make me stop. He stood upright and walked out of sight around the side of the garage that couldn't be seen from the house. At every second I expected the back door to squeal open, the light to go on in the upstairs window. After a very long time, Jim appeared behind the garage and waved for me to come.

I ran up next to him, and he whispered, "The car is gone. He must be out killing someone."

I stopped walking.

"Come on," he said. "Hurry up. I want to show you something."

I took a deep breath before stepping into the shadow of the garage. There were oil stains on the concrete floor, and shelves lined the walls, stacked with empty Mr. Clean bottles, all turned out the same way to show the bald guy with his arms folded. Jim grabbed my arm and said, "Look back there."

He pulled me slowly, farther into the garage. I saw a huge silver box lying across almost the whole width of the place. It hummed with electricity.

"What is it?" I asked.

"A giant freezer," he said.

An image of Barzita, eyes shattered, frost on his chin stubble, arms twisted and solid as an ice pop blossomed in my head, and I pulled my arm out of Jim's grip. "No," I said, and took off at top speed. As I passed the back end of the shed, I heard car tires on the gravel of the driveway. That's where Jim passed me. We got back into the woods and then stopped and got down to catch our breath. We still had a full view of the backyard, and we watched.

"Did he see you?" I asked Jim.

"No way," he said.

The sound of the car door closing in the garage shut us up. We saw him come out and head toward the back steps. He wore a white rain hat, and over his thin wrist he carried a black umbrella. Mr. White was bony, with a big Adam's apple and a sharp nose. He reached for the railing leading to the back door and then stopped. He turned slightly and looked over his shoulder into the woods. When he took two steps directly toward where we hid, I felt Jim's grip on my ankle, telling me not to run. Mr. White stopped again and sniffed the air. At one point I thought he was staring right into my eyes.

He finally backed away toward the steps and then climbed them. We ran like hell the minute the door closed. Halfway across the crater, we started laughing, and it made me run faster. We didn't stop until we were almost home.

"He killed Barzita, froze him, and when the snow came, he dumped his body in the road," said Jim.

"Do you think?" I said.

"What do you think?"

"I'm wondering about all the Mr. Clean," I said.

"Me, too," said Jim.

"Maybe he cleans up the death with it," I said.

"A hundred bottles apiece," said Jim.

What Time Will D Meet C and A?

■ Mary broke from the gate of her vacation like Pop's favorite horse, Rim Groper, and was all over Botch Town at least once a day. Whenever Jim and I went down into the cellar after our homework, all the figures would have moved. Mr. Felina was in his driveway, Peter Horton was on his way toward Hammond, and Mr. Curdmeyer was spending a lot of time in his grape arbor in the middle of winter. The first things we always checked for were the prowler and the white car. The prowler prowled up and down just outside the school while the white car passed Boris the janitor's house.

"He's in two places at once?" said Jim.

"He's got powers," I said.

"Do you think he splits himself and one of him spies on people and the other kills them?" he asked.

"Probably," I said.

We went back to looking for the right configuration that would tell us where Mr. White would strike next.

"What are we gonna do if we figure it out?" I asked.

"We'll need to do something," said Jim.

We asked Mary about a dozen times how she figured the stuff out, and she just shook her head. Then one night when we were studying Botch Town, we heard Mrs. Harkmar's voice from the other side of the cellar. She was explaining to Mickey and the other students how her system worked.

"This is very complicated, so if you feel stupid, it's okay," said Mrs. Harkmar in a flat voice, like a robot. "First, they're off, and then you start counting—one, two, three, four, five, six, seven. Then one, two, three, four, five, six. Then one, two, three, four. One, two, three, four, five, six. Like that. Then you start to add a lot with multiplication. Fast and faster on the back turn. See them in your head. See it. They're coming into the home stretch. Follow each one. Where are they going? Will they win, place, or show?"

We heard the ruler hit the desk and knew that Mrs. Harkmar had finished the lesson.

Jim looked at me and shook his head. We laughed, but we made sure that Mickey couldn't hear us. A few minutes later, Jim put his hand in his pocket and pulled something out. "Oh, I forgot to show you this."

He handed me what looked like a baseball card. It was a New York Yankee card, an old Topps. The player, a painting instead of a photo, was named Scott Riddley. He had a Krapp flattop haircut and a mustache, a glove on his right hand. It said he was a pitcher.

"I got that in Mr. White's garage," he said. "It was leaning against one of those bottles of Mr. Clean."

"Really?"

He nodded.

"It's old," I said.

"From 1953," he said. "I looked on the back."

I never understood the stuff on the backs of baseball cards. "Where?" I asked.

He turned the card over and pointed at a number, and I nodded without really seeing it.

"Mr. White collects Mr. Clean bottles and old baseball cards," he said.

"Yeah?"

"Well, go write it down," he said, and pointed to the stairs.

I thought of Mrs. Harkmar's lecture the next night when my father got home from work early and decided it was time I learned math his way. We sat at the dining-room table, the red math book open in front of us. My father had one of his yellow legal pads on which he sometimes did problems for fun, and I had my school notebook. He gave me one of the pencils he collected. On his night job as a janitor at the department store, he sometimes found half-used pencils in the trash. He sharpened them till their points were like Dr. Gerber's needles. "These are good pencils," he said.

I nodded.

When he wrote numbers, his hand moved fast and the pencil made a cutting sound. He crossed his sevens in the middle. We started with him asking me the times tables. I knew up to five, and then things went black. He asked me what was six times nine. I counted on my fingers, and at one point the digits in my head that I'd imagined as bundles of sticks turned into eyes. Rows of eyes, staring back at me. I figured in silence for a long time, feeling the right answer slip away. I gave my answer. He shook his head and told me, "Fifty-four." He drew six bundles of nine sticks and told me to count them. I did. Then he asked me another one, and I got that wrong, too. He told me the answer. On the next one, he went back to six times nine. "Fifty-one," I said. He got red in the face, yelled, "Think!" and poked me in the chest with his index finger.

By the time we got through with multiplication, he was sweating. We moved on to my homework—a word problem. Planes and trains all going somewhere at one hundred miles an hour, all leaving at different times, passing each other, laying over for fifteen minutes, with passengers A, B, C, and D, each getting off at Chicago or New York or Miami. I tried to picture it and went numb. My father drew an airplane with an arrow pointing forward. Then he drew lines like triangle legs to two different spots I guessed were on the ground. He wrote out *"100 miles an hour."* He connected the dangling legs of the triangle with a straight, slashing line. He wrote A, B, and C at its points, the top point being the plane. He wrote D outside the triangle and drew a box behind it and wrote *"Train Station"* in script.

He said, "How far is Chicago from New York, and what time will D meet C and A? Figure it out, and I'll be back in a little while." He got up, went into the living room, and turned on the TV. I sat there looking back and forth from his drawing to the book. I couldn't make anything out of it and eventually had to look away. For a while I stared at the screaming faces made by the knots in the wood paneling. I looked out the window at the night and at the light over the table.

In the middle of the table was a brass bowl with fruit in it. There were some bananas, an orange, and two apples, and they were all going brown. Three teeny flies hovered above the bowl. I stared at it for a long time, too tired to think to look elsewhere. It was like I was under a spell. My arm came off the table, my hand holding the pencil straight out toward one of the apples. When I jabbed, I jabbed slowly, letting the pencil slide through the rotten outer skin and into the mush below. I stabbed that apple three times before I even knew I was stabbing it, so I stabbed some other fruit. The pencil made neat dark holes.

"What's your answer?" said my father, returning to the table.

"B," I said.

I saw him glance over at the fruit. "What's this shit?" he asked, pointing at the brass bowl.

I said, "It went bad, and I wanted to warn people not to eat it, so I poked holes in it while I was thinking."

He stared at me, and I had to look away. "Go to bed," he said.

As I shuffled away from the table, I heard him crumple his drawing of the airplane triangle. "B, for 'bone-dry ignorance,'" he said with disgust.

Up in my bedroom, the antenna was silent. Instead I imagined the aroma of Mr. White's pipe smoke. The smell was so strong I could just about see it. George was out of bed more than once, pacing the floor, sniffing the closet. The next morning came like a punch in the face.

Do Something

■ Three nights in a row, we noticed that the white car was somewhere close to Boris the janitor's house. On the fourth night, it was parked in his driveway. Jim lifted the car out of Botch Town and said, "We have to do something now."

"It's Boris?" I asked.

He nodded. "If we tell Mom or Dad, we'll get in trouble for not telling them sooner, and if we tell the police, we'll still get in trouble. We should call them and not say our names but tell them everything we know and who we think will be next. Then we hang up."

"No," I said. "If you call, they can trace it. I saw it on *Perry Mason*. We need to write a letter, no return address."

Jim liked the idea and told me to go get the notebook. I returned to the cellar, and he told me every word to write. Here's what he said:

We know who killed Charlie Edison and Mr. Barzita. There's a very white guy who drives a long white car and looks in peoples windows. We call him Mr. White. He lives in a house on one of the streets behind the

Stores. The woods reach the edge
of his back yard. He has a freezer
in a wooden garage where he keeps
his car and he killed Barzita and
froze him and then dumped him in
the road during the blizzard. Next
he's after Boris the Janitor.
Do something. Charlie Edison
is in the lake behind East Lake.

I wrote as fast as I could, but my hand cramped. Jim finally took over and finished it. As he tore the letter out of my notebook, he said. "Let's send one to Krapp, too."

"Same as the police?" I asked.

"No, I have a special message for him," said Jim. He picked up the pencil and leaned over the notebook. He wrote only two words and then ripped the page out and held it up. In big, sloppy letters it read:

YOUR KRAPP.

We laughed hard.

"His address is in the phone book," Jim said. "Look it up for the envelope. I'll get the stamps."

I took a deep breath when I went out to the mailbox on the corner. The street glistened under the light poles, and steam rose from the lawns. Taking a look up the block, I saw no headlights coming, so I started out at a slow jog. I had the two anonymous letters in my coat pocket, and I left the coat unzipped so as to run better. I made it to the corner halfway to Hammond in no time flat. The only thing that slowed me was the sight of

Mr. Barzita's house across the street It crouched in the dark
perfectly still behind a net of crisscrossing fig branches. When I
reached for the handle of the mailbox, I looked down and saw
what I thought was a clump of snow transform into a dead kit-
ten lying on the frozen ground, its mouth open. It had sharp
teeth, and its fur was pure white. A few inches away, someone
had left a bowl half filled with milk, now frozen. I dropped the
letters into the box and took off back home at top speed.

Not on Your Life

■ Nan reached way back into her bedroom closet and pulled out a long, dark brown billy club with a woven royal blue tassel around the handle. "That's the dress one," she said. She handed it to Jim.

"Oh, man," he said.

Mary reached for the tassel.

Nan went in for another and brought forth the club with the dice. It was shorter and blunter than the dress club, and blond in color. Inlaid into its side were two yellowed dice, showing six and one. She handed that one to me, and I could feel the energy go up my arm.

Next came the blackjack, shining like a scorpion, and Nan demonstrated on her palm, thunking it repeatedly with the rubbery weight. "You can break a skull with it," she said. Jim reached for it, and Nan laughed. "Not on your life," she said, and put it away.

Mary went over to look at the glass Virgin Mary filled with Lourdes water on the dresser, but Nan called her back and handed her a real police badge. Then, from out of her bathrobe pocket, she drew the police revolver. It had a wooden handle, and the rest looked like tarnished silver. She held it above our heads in her right hand, her grip wobbling. Jim's hand went toward it, and I ducked slightly. Mary held out the badge.

"You can't touch this. In case of an emergency, I keep it loaded," Nan said.

"*You're* loaded," Pop called down the hallway.

Nan laughed and put the gun away. She let us handle the clubs for another few seconds, and then when Jim made like he was going to crush my skull, she asked for them back. We couldn't believe it when she let Mary keep the badge.

"We'll split it," said Jim.

Mary said, "No," and left the bedroom. We heard the door to our house open and close, and she was gone. Nan gave Jim and me each a ladyfinger. We sat with Pop at the kitchenette table, where he smoked a Lucky Strike. Nan made tea and sat down with us.

Proof

■ After the drudgery of *Silas Marner*, Krapp dusted the chalk off his hands and stepped away from the blackboard. "It seems," he said, "that someone has written me a letter." His face flushed red, and his jaw tensed. When I heard the word "letter," I almost peed my pants. *Don't look away*, I reminded myself.

"Someone has sent me a letter, I think, telling me who I am," he said. He reached into his shirt pocket and pulled out a neatly folded square of notebook paper. He opened it and turned it to the class. We read it. Tim Sullivan had to cover his face with both hands, but no one made a sound. "I think it was one of you," he said, staring up and down the rows into each person's eyes. "Because . . . the writer missed the contraction." When he got to me, I did my best not to blink.

"In fact," he began, folding the letter and returning it to his pocket. He rubbed his hands in front of us. "I know who it was. You forget that I see your handwriting all the time. I took the letter and matched the handwriting to its author on one of your papers. Now, would the guilty party like to confess?"

I knew that Jim would never confess. He'd just sit there and nod slightly. That's what I intended to do, but inside I was getting weaker by the second. Part of me wanted so badly to blurt out that it was me. But then I realized that it really wasn't me, it was Jim, and he wasn't even here, and that's when Krapp slapped his hands together and said, "Will Hinkley, come forward." To hear it made me hollow inside, but I automatically laughed. No one even noticed me, because everybody had begun whispering. Krapp called, "Silence!"

"I didn't do it," Will said, refusing to get out of his chair.

"Come up here now," said Krapp. He trembled like George with a sneaker in his face.

"I didn't write you any letter," said Hinkley, his Adam's apple bobbing like mad.

"I have the proof," said Krapp. "Go to the office. Your parents are waiting there with Mr. Cleary."

Will Hinkley got out of his seat, red in the face and with tears in his eyes. As he opened the door to leave the room, Krapp said to him, "No one tells me who I am, young man."

"You're Krapp," said Hinkley, and he ran down the hall, his sneakers squealing at the turn. The door swung shut, and Krapp told us to take out our math books.

All through the travels of A, B, C, and D from Chicago to New York at a hundred miles an hour, I thought about the cops opening the other letter. I saw them jump into their black-and-white cars, turn on the sirens, and then arrive at Mr. White's house. They crash in the back door, their guns out. Inside, it's dim and smells like Mr. Clean. They hear Mr. White escaping up the attic steps. By the time the cops reach the attic, all they find, in the middle of the floor, is a pillar of salt.

Jim didn't like it when I told him what happened. "That rots," he said.

"Why?" I asked.

"Because now the cops are gonna think Hinkley wrote the other letter, too, and he'll get all the credit when they catch Mr. White."

"We could have just told and gotten the credit," I said.

"Yeah," said Jim.

"Tim told me Hinkley's punishment is that he has to stay after school every day for the rest of the year and roll the trash barrels down to the furnace room," I said.

"Hinkley can take the credit," he said.

My mother had a bad night that night. She was fierce, her face puffy with anger. The air went thin, and it got hard to breathe. She was yelling insults at my father, cursing, drinking fast. My father sat at his end of the dining-room table, smoking a cigarette, head bowed. Mary and Jim headed for the cellar. I ran to my room, lay on my bed, and cried into my pillow. Her voice came up through the floor, a steady barrage that, like the blizzard, swelled into a howl, receded, and then swelled again. It went on and on, and I never heard my father say a word.

I eventually dozed off for a little while, and when I awoke, it was quiet. I got out of bed and carefully went down the stairs. The lights were out, and there was a lingering haze of cigarette smoke. I heard my father snoring from the bedroom down the hall. Going into the kitchen, I looked around in the dark for the bottle of wine. I found it on the sink counter and grabbed it by the neck.

At the back door, I undid the latch as quietly as possible, opened the storm door, and then pushed open the outer wooden door. Half in and half out of the house, one foot on the back porch, I heaved the bottle into the night. It clunked against the ground, but I didn't hear it break. When I turned back into the house, I jumped, because Nan was standing there in her bathrobe and hairnet.

"Go get it," she said.

I started to cry. She stepped forward and hugged me for a minute. Then she whispered, "Go."

I went out into the night in my bare feet and pajamas. It was freezing cold. I walked all around the area I thought the bottle had landed, but only when I stubbed my toe on it did I see it.

Back inside, Nan wiped the dirt off with a towel. I showed her where I'd gotten it from, and she replaced it on the counter. While she was locking the back door, she told me to go to bed.

Scenes from Perno Shell's adventures twined around my wondering what they had to do with Mr. White. I was almost certain from the smell of smoke that he'd read all the books I had. Either he just liked to read kids' books or it was a clue of some kind. But how could I know? The figures of Shell and Mr. White passed each other in the desert, on the Amazon. They became each other and then went back to being themselves in hot-air balloons. I saw them talk to each other, and then I saw them wrestle each other, Shell all in black and Mr. White in his overcoat and hat, on a rickety little bridge high above a bottomless lake. *"The Last Journey of Perno Shell,"* I said. George woke up, looked at me, and went back to sleep.

Driving Back to Yugoslavia

■ It was the day the temperature finally rose above freezing, and we were allowed back on the playground after lunch. The ground was still hard as a rock, and the dark clouds threatened more snow. I was on the way out toward the fence to talk to Tim Sullivan when I passed Peter Horton, and he was telling two other kids, "Boris's gone."

"Boris?" I said, and went over to where they were standing.

"My dad was there when they went to his house last night," said Peter.

"Who?"

"The cops," he said. "He didn't come to work for, like, four days and didn't call. Cleary sent the cops to see where he was. He was gone."

"What do you mean, 'gone'?" I asked.

"His car was gone," said Peter.

"He's driving back to Yugoslavia," said one of the other kids.

In my mind I saw a barrel of the red stuff with a broom leaning against it in the dim light of the furnace room beneath the school. I looked for Boris—his plaid shirt, his missing teeth, his five strands combed over a bald head—but only his voice came to me. "You are talking dogshit," he said. I pictured a cop throwing our letter in the trash along with the pink hatbox that held the footprint.

When I finally got out to the fence where Tim was, he asked, "Who'll clean the puke now?" and the saliva slid to the corners of my mouth.

By the time Jim and I arrived in Botch Town that night, Mary had already been there. Boris was off the board. The white car was turning onto Hammond, and the prowler was at the edge of the woods behind Halloways'. Jim called Mary over to our side. As soon as she came through the curtain, he asked her, "Where's Boris?"

Mary turned and walked to the back wall. She lifted something off the big pipe that ran to the sewer. When she returned, she showed us it was Boris.

"Where is he?" said Jim.

"Away," said Mary.

"How do you know?" I asked.

"I heard it in school," she said.

"She doesn't know any more than we do," said Jim.

"Did the prowler get him?" I asked.

"I don't know," she said.

Mary stepped backward toward the curtain. Just before she went through, Jim asked her, "What *do* you know?"

"He's cold," she said. "Very cold."

The next morning we were dressed and out early. The sky was overcast, and a light snow fell around us as we made our way through the woods. Neither of us said a word, and the journey went so fast it was as if the woods were shrinking. We were suddenly there, like in a dream, peering through the branches at Mr. White's backyard. There was a numbness throbbing in my head, and I felt weak. Jim scanned the windows for signs of movement and said, "Same as last time." He crouched low and ran for the garage. For a whole minute, his back to the wooden wall, he stood perfectly still, and we listened.

I looked to the house for the thousandth time. When I looked back, Jim was gone around the side. A second later he was back, waving me to follow him. I couldn't move at first, but then he whisper-yelled, "Hurry," and it put me in motion. I joined him, and we walked around to the front.

Again I hesitated in the shadow at the edge of the entrance. The cold concrete-and-oil smell put me off. I turned and looked behind me to where the driveway curved around toward the street. Jim was already at the back of the place, his hand on the freezer latch. It squealed when he opened it. He got his fingers under the lid and was trying to pull it up.

"Help me," he said. "Hurry up."

I ran to help him. Together we lifted the heavy lid like the top of a coffin. A light came on inside, reflecting off the walls of ice. It was big enough for a body, but there was no body there. It was empty.

"Shit," said Jim, and he was about to lower the lid when I saw something crumpled up in the corner.

"Look," I said.

He saw it and said, "Get it. I can hold this by myself for a second."

I let go and dove halfway in to grab the piece of wadded orange paper. I knew what it was before I put it in my pocket. Sliding out, I helped Jim lower the lid. With two inches left to go, we just dropped it and ran. The sound of it latching echoed behind us. We were out and around the garage in a flash. At the edge of the woods, we crouched down and rested, watching the house.

"Where's Boris?" said Jim. "Mary sent us on a wild-goose chase."

"She just said he was very cold. Maybe he's in the lake."

"The lake's still frozen," said Jim.

"Let's get out of here."

"Wait a second," he said. He brushed away the pine needles on the ground and dug around until he found a good-size stone. Seeing the way he gripped it, I got up and started running. I ran a hundred yards before I heard the crash of window glass, and then I heard Jim running behind me. We didn't let up until we were all the way to the stream behind Halloways'.

"Let me see the clue," he said, working to catch his breath.

I dug into my pocket and pulled out the ball of orange tissue paper.

"A snot rag?" said Jim.

"No," I said. I opened the paper, and as the folds came away, inside was revealed a length of black ribbon.

"Fig Man," he said. "His Halloween treats."

I nodded.

"How'd you like that throw?" he said. "Right through the upstairs window." He laughed.

I jumped the stream. "Now he'll know we were there," I said.

"He knows less about us than we know about him," said Jim. He jumped, and off we ran.

At dinner we learned from my mother that the cops wouldn't even consider Boris a missing person until another week or so went by. She went on to tell us about how he left his family and ran away from Communism. "Boris came all that way to be the janitor of East Lake School," she said, and laughed.

As soon as the last word was out of her mouth, we heard the sirens coming down the block. Jim was the first away from the table, but we all—my mother, Mary, and me—were at the window when the three cop cars screamed past. We went for our coats and shoes, even my mother.

She told us to stay close to her, and we followed. It wasn't as cold as it had been. The skies were clear, and the moon was out. Other neighbors were either ahead of us or just coming out their front doors as we passed. We saw Mr. Mangini, Mr. and Mrs. Hackett, the woman my mother called Diamond Lil, and the tired old Bishops with Reggie between them, talking a mile a minute.

Jim walked up behind me, leaned over, and said, "Maybe they found Boris's body."

I nodded, and Mary looked over, bringing her finger to her lips.

The action was definitely at East Lake. As we passed Mrs. Homretz's house, we could see the police cars pulled up on the field between the school and the woods, their red lights flashing. A crowd of people from the neighborhood was being held back by a cop. We joined the group. Mr. Mason, a thin man with big glasses, like a grown-up Henry, told my mother that Tony Calfano had shot out all the windows of the school with a pellet rifle. We heard more little bits and pieces of the story from other people. Mr. Felina said, "Apparently he just went from window to window, like clockwork, and shot each one."

Jim grabbed me, and we wove our way through the crowd until we were near the front. Across the field we saw the broken glass everywhere, reflecting the moon. From there I could see that some of the windows had no glass left and some just had huge jagged holes, like Mr. Barzita's frozen eyes. The cop who was keeping us back told everybody as much as he knew. We listened to him, and he said that the suspect was still there when they arrived. "He's in the back of the patrol car," said the cop. "We have the gun."

Cleary pulled up then and parked in the bus circle. He got out of his car, wearing a rumpled suit. Moving stiff and slow as a sleepwalker, he came over to where we all stood.

"Please, go home," he said, even letting go of his throat to raise both his hands in the air. "Go home and call your neighbors and tell them no school tomorrow."

The kids in the crowd were told to shut up by their parents.

Jim and I looked at each other and smiled. "No school for you," he said. "Tony Calfano is my new hero." He made like he had a rifle and was shooting from the hip. "I should do the same at the junior high."

"No school," Mary said on the way home. No one else was near us, but my mother kept her voice low. "Our taxes are going to have to pay for that," she said angrily. "Who gave that crazy guinea a gun?"

Well after we put ourselves to bed, Jim knocked on my door. He let the light from the hall in and took a seat at the end of my bed. "Did you think it could be Mr. White's revenge for my busting his window?"

"What?" I asked.

"What happened at East Lake. Maybe he possessed Tony to break the windows."

"He has powers," I said.

"Yeah," he said. "It's starting to get scary."

"Is Boris dead?" I asked.

"Here's what I think," he said. "Mr. White killed him and then put him in his own car and drove it way out onto the ice of the bay. The ice melts, it cracks, and Boris and his car are gone."

"Maybe," I said.

Like That

■ It was late afternoon and raining hard outside. Mary and I were in the cellar, staring at Botch Town. Jim hadn't gotten home from school yet. She told me to sit down in Jim's chair.

"You have to stare hard at one person," she said.

"Who?" I asked.

"You pick," she said.

"I'm going to stare at Mr. Conrad," I said, and pointed.

She stepped up next to the chair, leaned over, and started whispering numbers into my ear. Numbers and numbers, like string that held my head in place. They came in torrents, then showers, and then I didn't notice them at all. What I noticed was that a piece of clay had crumbled and fallen off the back of Mr. Conrad's head. I noticed his ears, and his pose, slightly hunched. He was standing in front of his house, looking across the street toward the Hayeses' place. It was all cardboard and clay, but something was shifting at the edges. I saw the lawns and the house across the street with its shrubs and yellow door. The color of the door caught my attention, and then I heard Mary say, "Equals," and for just a split second I was in a bedroom and Mrs. Hayes was naked on the bed. She was smoking a cigarette, and her legs were open. I blinked, and she vanished back into the hole in Mr. Conrad's clay head in front of his cardboard house.

"Like that," said Mary.

After she went into her schoolroom and the lesson had begun, I noticed that Boris the janitor was no longer on the sewer pipe but now rested on top of an old end table halfway between Botch Town and the pipe.

I wasn't sure if my head hurt because of what Mary had done or if everything was just too much to think about anymore. The four-thirty movie on TV was *Mothra.* There were two tiny twins in it who lived in a birdcage and sang like the antenna. I fell asleep when Mothra's caterpillar was swimming across the ocean and woke once when he had wings and was destroying a city. The next I knew, Jim was calling me for dinner.

At dinner Mary told how this kid in her class, Gene, who walked with steel crutches and was called "the Mechanical Crab," puked. "Mr. Cleary came in and cleaned it," she said.

My mother laughed into her wine.

"Did he use the red stuff?" asked Jim.

Mary nodded.

"Did he make a face?" I asked.

"Almost," said Mary.

Jim put his right hand to his throat, tightened his nostrils, and shifted his eyes side to side. My mother laughed so hard she coughed. Even when Mary and I stopped laughing, my mother kept on coughing. It went on and on. She held her cigarette away from her with one hand and used the other to cover her mouth. Her face went red, and tears came to the corners of her eyes. The harder the coughing got, the less sound came out. Jim got up and slapped her hard on the back. She took a swing at him, and he jumped away. A moment later she caught her breath. "You're gonna kill me," she said, still laughing.

Welcome, Lou

■ After the Pledge of Allegiance and the collection of lunch money, when Krapp was telling us about George Washington cutting down the cherry tree, a knock came on the classroom door.

"Come in," Krapp called. In stepped Mr. Cleary. He held the door with his shoulder and said, "I want you to meet the new janitor, who'll be taking over until Boris comes back." I pictured Boris sitting behind the wheel of his car at the bottom of the bay. Charlie was in the passenger seat. Cleary stepped in and to the side, opening the door more. A tall, scrawny man in gray work clothes came forward. "This is Lou," said Cleary. The man's shirt had a white oval that held the name Lou stitched in red.

Krapp said, "Welcome, Lou."

Lou lifted his head, and I saw how pale he was. The light was on his hair, and it was White. The shivering started in my legs and ran up my spine. Mr. White mumbled, "Thank you," and stepped back into the shadow of the hallway.

Before leaving, Mr. Cleary turned to us and said, "I expect you to treat Lou with all the respect you would Boris." Someone laughed for a split second—one of the girls. Cleary scanned the class, shot a look at Krapp, and then left.

I was stunned well past the class punishment of writing a

hundred times *"I must not laugh at Mr. Cleary"* and past the making of George Washington's wooden teeth. On the playground at recess, I stood with my back to the chain-link fence at the boundary of the field, shivering.

Later that afternoon our class passed Mr. White in the hallway on our way to the library. His smell of pipe smoke gagged me and made my eyes tear. With a squeegee on a stick and a bucket of water, he was cleaning the big windows that looked out on the courtyard. He had his back to us as we went by, but after we passed, I glanced over my shoulder and saw him watching.

In the library, now under Krapp's control, perfect silence was the rule. I sat with a book open on the table where the sunlight streamed in through the courtyard window. My eyes were closed, and I repeated to myself what Jim had said: "He knows less about us than we know about him."

When I eventually opened my eyes, I saw Mr. White out in the hallway through the glass panes of the library door. He was slowly rubbing with a dirty rag. His eyes darted quickly as he looked from kid to kid to kid and back again. Before he could look at me, I closed my eyes.

That night Jim gave me his penknife. "Keep it in your coat pocket," he said. "Go for the face." I tried to picture myself stabbing Mr. White in the cheek and heard metal hit bone. Jim's advice was "Don't let him get you by yourself." He told me six different ways to escape from Mr. White. One was to crawl between his legs and run, and another was to kick him in the nuts and run. He repeated all six.

The next day it took me twice as long as usual to walk to school. Mary even told me to hurry up. The whole time I kept shoving my hand into my coat pocket to check for the knife. Once in the building, as we passed the main office on the way to our classrooms, I looked down the hall to my right at the door to the furnace room and pictured Lou standing amid flames.

I stopped walking and thought about running home. Then, between the main office and the door at the end of the hall, I saw the entrance to the nurse's office.

I made it to my desk in Krapp's room on time. After holding out until well into the lecture about the solar system, I put up my hand. He noticed me, and although he hadn't asked a question, he pointed to me and said my name.

"I feel like I'm going to throw up," I said.

"Oh, no," he said, and in less than two minutes he wrote out a pass.

The windowless hallways were empty and dim. I moved quickly, afraid that at each turn I'd come face-to-face with Mr. White. When I reached the hall lined on one side with courtyard windows and saw the main office, it was like coming out of a tunnel. I ran the rest of the way to the nurse's door.

Mrs. Edwards was thin and old. She kept her gray hair long and always wore her white nursing cap and uniform. I never saw her give out any medicine or cure anybody of anything, but she was nice. If she bought your story, she'd send you home. Mary, who visited her frequently, had told me that if the coffee in Mrs. Edwards's cup was dark, she'd make you stay, but if it was light, she'd call home and have someone come and pick you up.

The nurse asked me what was wrong with me, and I told her. When she went into the little room in her office where she kept supplies and a cot for sick kids, I stepped closer to her desk and looked into her cup. There was coffee the blond color of the club with the dice, and inside I felt like Pop winning a double. Mrs. Edwards came back and choked me with a wooden stick, checked my ears with a flashlight, and banged my knees with a rubber hammer. Then she told me to go lie down on the cot in the sickroom.

"Take your sneakers off first," she said.

It was dark in the small room, with the exception of a sliver of light coming in the half-closed door to the larger office. I lay there peering at the opening, listening hard to hear if she was calling Nan. She made a phone call, mumbled for a few minutes, and hung up. A second later the door opened wider, and she was standing over me.

"I'm going out to use the lavatory," she said. "I'll be right back."

I nodded, hoping I looked as miserable as I was trying to. She pulled at the door, leaving it a bit ajar. I heard the outer office door open and close, and then silence. In my thoughts I pictured the cup of light coffee and saw Nan getting into the blue Impala. For a few seconds, I was pleased with myself, until another thought broke through. Jim and I hadn't told Mary that Lou was Mr. White. Jim had said not to, because it would scare her too much. Now she'd be left at the school with him roaming around and not know. She'd have to walk home by herself. I tried to talk myself out of its being a problem, but in the end I knew I couldn't leave her. As soon as the nurse came back, I'd tell her I was okay. A little while later, I heard the door to the office open and close. I got off the cot and went to talk to Mrs. Edwards, but just as I reached for the doorknob, I smelled pipe smoke. Through the opening I saw a bristled broom head pushing red stuff around the floor. I nearly cried out. I heard Jim's voice in my head, telling me to hurry up in Mr. White's garage. I stepped quietly backward, got down on the floor, and slid under the cot. My cheek rested against the cold floor as I stared hard through the opening into the outer office.

Three times I saw the broom go by, followed by Lou's big sneakered feet. He was working his way across the office, getting closer and closer to the sickroom. I thought of the penknife in my coat pocket back in the closet in Krapp's room. Then he was right outside, his shadow blocking the light from the office. Even above the pounding of my heart, I heard him sniffing the air like an animal. He pushed the door open, and as his left foot moved forward, I heard Mrs. Edwards's voice. "Hi, Lou."

He backed away from the door and turned around. "Just about done here," he said, and moved out of sight. I slid out from beneath the cot and got onto it, knowing that Mrs. Edwards would be looking in to check on me.

"Okay, that's it," I heard Lou say.

"Thanks," said the nurse.

Lou had left my door open wider than before, and as he passed by on his way out, he turned his head and stared in at me. When he saw me lying there, his eyes widened. He hesitated for a fraction of a second and then smiled.

I told Mrs. Edwards I was better, and she sent me back to class. On the trip through the hallways I scurried like an insect but slowed when I passed Room X. The teacher was at the blackboard writing numbers, and I saw Mary sitting next to the Mechanical Crab, her eyes closed, mumbling to herself. I didn't see Lou again for the rest of the day. When I found Mary after school, I told her to hurry, and we walked quickly toward home. On the way I told her that Mr. White was Lou. She nodded but said nothing.

Another sleepless night, and the next day my mother made egg-salad sandwiches for our lunch bags. Their fart stench swirled around me as we walked to school. Jim had told me he'd come up with a plan by that night, but we had to go another whole day. He knew I was on the verge of just telling our parents everything. In the meantime he taught Mary some karate moves. Every step we took was dreadfully slow. When we passed Mrs. Grimm's house, Mary said to me, "I'll poke his eyes like Moe."

"Good," I said.

By the time we got to school, almost late, we came through the front door, and there was Boris the janitor in his baggy shirt and work gloves, pushing the broom. It was just us and him in the foyer of the school.

"Boris, where were you?" I said to him.

He stopped sweeping and looked up. He shrugged. "I run away," he said.

In the following days, Boris's story came to us through our mother at dinner as she relayed whatever gossip Nan had picked up from the neighborhood ladies. She told us that someone had put a letter in Boris's mailbox that said they were after him. He got scared and ran away for a while. He visited a cousin in Michigan. The police were investigating it, but Boris had lost the letter. My mother laughed at this last fact. "That figures," she said. "Sounds like he was on a bender."

For Jim, Boris's return called into question Mary's powers. Even with all she had been right about, he let this one thing convince him we'd been fooling ourselves. "It makes sense that Mr. White has Mr. Clean bottles at his house," he said. "He's a janitor. Barzita did get hit by the snowplow, and Charlie must have fallen into the lake by accident. It's all coincidence." I went along with him because I also wanted it to be true.

All Mary said was "Who sent the letter to Boris?" I never asked, "What about the orange paper and ribbon?"

Spring stuck its big toe into winter, and we let the investigation drop as the days grew a little brighter, a little warmer. I was slowly forgetting my fear, and at night, without the howling of the winter wind, the antenna was silent. Charlie no longer had a voice. His sullen, sodden presence behind the open closet door became increasingly easy to ignore, to pretend it was nothing.

Children of All Ages

■ My mother had seen them setting up the tents in the empty lot next to where she worked in Farmingdale. Every night at dinner, on our way to Bermuda, we detoured to the circus. On Saturday we finally went—us three kids and our mother. She put on lipstick and curled her hair, but she was still pale in her turquoise dress and green overcoat. Her perfume was suffocating.

She smoked with the car windows closed, the sharp haze burning my nose hair as we watched the towns roll by. On the radio, Elvis sang "Are You Lonesome Tonight?" We passed the college, which rose up out of a vast field like a city from a science-fiction movie. Jim was always happy to go anywhere, and Mary wanted to see the clowns. I didn't care about the circus, but I made believe I was excited.

We parked at the edge of a wide field. The ground was total mud, and on the walk to the tents my mother lifted her whole foot out of her stuck shoe more than once. We gathered before a stand where a midget with a mustache sat. He wore a top hat and a coat with red and white stripes.

My mother paid for our admission, and the midget looked angrily up at us as he handed her the four tickets. We stood around until there were no more people coming from the parking lot. When he'd sold the last ticket, the midget stood up and lifted a megaphone.

"Ladies and gentlemen and children of all ages," I think he said, but anything that came after was muffled.

"What's he saying?" asked Jim.

My mother shrugged and tossed her cigarette into the mud.

The midget's harangue went on and on. From somewhere he'd gotten a cane, and every once in a while he rapped the tabletop in front of him. Mary put her hands over her ears. When he finally finished, we moved slowly past him with the rest of the crowd. In amid the maze of yellow tents, I did catch a spark of excitement, because there was a whole row of them filled with the sideshow. Paintings, full of color and wild images, which hung outside each tent, told what was behind its flaps. The first one in the row was for Sweet Marie, a fat woman. The picture showed a woman like a Thanksgiving Day parade balloon, perfectly round, sitting on a bench knitting.

"Sweet Marie," said Jim, and he pointed to Mary.

Mary shook her head and said, "You are."

My mother led the way into the dark tent. Other people were already inside. Beneath one bare bulb, like the sun of Botch Town, up on a small stage that bowed under her weight, sat Sweet Marie. She had on only a skirt and a bra, so you could see all the mounds and folds and blobs of fat. There was a light blue bow in her hair, and her face was like a beer belly with eyes and a mouth. My mother whispered, "Disgusting," and sent us up front for a better look. Jim led me right to the edge of the stage in front of her. The air there was thick with the smell of straw, canvas, her body odor, and cigarette smoke. I looked up at her face and only then noticed that she had a goatee beard. I backed away.

"No pictures," she said. "If you want a photo, I have signed photos here for a quarter." She held one up. The shot was of her lying on a rug in a bathing suit big enough to drown in.

Scrawled in Magic Marker, I think it said *"Sweet on you, Marie."* People started leaving.

"You'll look, but you don't want my picture," she said with an edge to her voice. "Buy a picture."

My mother called us to her, saying, "That's enough of this." We followed. Outside, she said, "Good Christ, this is a dump," and laughed. "Let's see what else they have."

The painting for Mr. Electric was of a young, muscular man, drawing lightning bolts down from dark clouds. Inside the tent we found an old guy with glasses and a World War I flying helmet covered in sequins. He put a lightbulb in his mouth, and it lit up. The next tent housed a guy in an old-fashioned uniform with gold fringe on the shoulders and a hundred buttons. Admiral Gullet swallowed swords and fire. Jim and I liked it that when he burped, smoke came out. The rubber lady was in a box with three sides so we could see in, and there was a sling around her right arm. My mother laughed about that for the next two tents.

The last tent in the row of sideshows was one you had to pay extra to enter. "The Blood-Sweating Hippo" was the attraction, but there was no painting for it. It was top secret. My mother hesitated at the entrance and said, "It's almost time for the show in the big tent. If we have time after that, we'll come back to this."

Jim was disappointed, but he said, "Okay." Even I wanted to see the Blood-Sweating Hippo, but we turned and walked away. My mother bought us cotton candy—plumes of blue wrapped in a paper cone. The first bite was like eating hair, until it suddenly melted into straight sugar. We found seats in the wooden bleachers and looked out into the well-lit center ring.

The midget with the top hat who'd sold us our tickets stepped into the spotlight carrying his megaphone in one hand and a whip in the other. Some of the lights around the audience went out. He lifted the megaphone and said, "Ladies and gentlemen and children of all ages." Like earlier, I couldn't make out anything he said after that. When he finally stopped mumbling, he turned and faced the main entrance to the tent. An elephant came in with a woman riding behind its head. The huge beast's trunk dragged in the sawdust, and it moved slowly, lumbering back and forth with each step. The midget cracked the whip and yelled something with the word "pachyderm" in it. The elephant stepped into the center ring and laboriously made its way around the circumference. When the whip cracked again, a flap in the elephant's backside opened and giant, steaming turds just fell out like cannonballs on an assembly line.

"The greatest show on earth," said my mother.

We saw a trapeze act, a lion tamer, and then came the clowns. They drove into the center ring in a little car. Explosions came out of the tailpipe. The door opened, and fifteen clowns jumped out one after the other. Mary counted off every one. She stood up and waved to them as other kids did. They tooted horns and lit firecrackers. Crazy hair and ripped clothes—they were like bums off the street with painted faces and gloves. Each one wore a hat with a feather or a tassel or a flower coming out the top.

The clowns went up into the bleachers all around the ring, shaking hands, squirting water out of flowers they wore on their lapels, getting too close to people. Everybody was yelling and screaming, and the band was playing "Happy Days Are Here Again." One clown made his way up toward where we sat. Mary stepped into the aisle to meet him. He had a flowerpot hat, gloves without fingers, painted teardrops, and glasses. Leaning over her, his face right in Mary's, he put out his hand to shake. Her smile turned in an instant, her whole face collapsing into fear. She ran back to her seat and leaned into my mother. The clown waved and was gone.

At the end they shot the midget out of a cannon. A puff of

smoke, an explosion, and then he flew across the center ring into a net that dropped him onto a pile of old mattresses. As he took the football helmet off his head and bowed, I wondered what he did at night. I saw him in a shack, playing cards with Admiral Gullet and Sweet Marie. They discussed the death of the elephant, but in his head he was thinking of the cannon.

Before Jim could even ask, my mother started heading for the hippo tent. "The Blood-Sweating Hippo," said Jim, putting his hand to his forehead. I trailed after them with Mary, who was walking slowly.

"Come on, let's go," I said.

She held out her hand. I took it and made her run with me to catch up.

The guy at the tent entrance taking the money told us we had only ten minutes, because everything was closing down. "I can't guarantee he'll sweat blood in ten minutes," he said. It cost a quarter a person, and we all went in. This tent was bigger than the other sideshow tents. There was a light at the center, but it was pitch dark around that.

"Low tide," my mother said of the smell.

We made our way to a circular enclosure and peered over the walls. There was a lightbulb above the ring that lit the slick hide of the hippo. The creature lay there, in straw sodden with its own piss, huge and unmoving. All it did was breathe. We stared at it for as long as we could. Then Jim picked Mary up and held her so she could see. She pointed to the edge of the enclosure at something I hadn't noticed before. There was a track that went around the rim of the circle, and on it was a turtle. A few seconds later, she pointed to another spot, and there was a rabbit.

"The tortoise and the hare," said my mother.

"What does that have to do with a hippo?" I asked.

"Ask the midget," she said.

"Let's look some more," said Jim. My mother joined him. I

was going to take another peek, but when I turned to see where Mary was, she was gone. I walked back into the shadows of the tent and called her name. After searching around the entire perimeter and not finding her, I told my mother.

"She probably went outside," she said. "Go see."

I ran toward the front of the tent, a rectangle of late-afternoon light guiding me. At the flap I asked the guy who took the money if he'd seen my little sister. He pointed past the tents. "She went out there," he said. I took off in the direction he indicated and saw her standing out past the circus in the muddy field. I called to her, but she wouldn't come. When I got to her side, she was looking at the ground. A crocus was growing up out of the mud. It hadn't opened yet, but inside you could see yellow.

"Mom says hurry up, we're leaving," I told her.

In the car on the way home, Jim called Mary "Sweet Marie" about twenty times. Finally my mother told him to shut up. She asked us each what our favorite part of the circus was.

"The midget getting shot out of the cannon," said Jim.

I told her I liked the hippo.

"What about you, Mary?" she asked.

There was silence, and then Jim said, "The clowns?"

"I thought you liked clowns," said my mother.

"He wasn't a clown," said Mary. "It was Mel."

"Who's Mel?" said my mother.

"Mister Softee," she said.

My mother and Jim and I laughed, but Mary never even smiled.

"Softee's in jail," said my mother.

Something Holy

■ Sunday morning my parents couldn't get out of bed. My mother called Jim to her and told him to take me and walk to church. Mary got out of it because they didn't trust us to take care of her on such a long journey. We got dressed and put on white shirts and ties. Our Lady of Lourdes was quite a walk from our house, and I dreaded making the trip in my good shoes, soles as hard as rock. Before we left, Nan gave us money to light candles for her.

On the way out the front door, I asked Jim, "Why do you light the candles?"

"I don't know," he said. "It's something holy."

The day was warm, and birds were singing. There was dew on the lawns. When we reached the intersection of Willow Avenue and Feems Road, Jim turned.

"This isn't the way to church," I said.

"I know," he said, and smiled.

I stood my ground.

"Go to church if you want," he said. "I'm going to get a chocolate milk at the deli and sit behind the stores."

"You have money?" I said.

He reached into his pocket and pulled out the candle money. "I'll share it with you."

For about two seconds, I thought of church—Father Toomey,

dead already, yelling at everyone; the bells; the songs. "Okay," I said.

Jim had enough for a chocolate milk and a big chocolate-chip cookie. We sat on milk crates in the alley behind the deli, out of sight in an alcove.

"What if we get caught?" I asked.

"No one ever comes back here but kids," he said, and then held up the cookie the way the priest holds up the host and broke it in half.

After we finished eating, Jim got up and went to the edge of the alcove and stuck his head out to look around. When he looked in the direction of the drugstore, I saw him pull his head back quick. He came over to me.

"Hinkley's coming on his bike," said Jim.

I got off my milk crate. He motioned for me to get flat against the wall while he snuck back to the opening. I saw him hunch down, and just as I heard the sound of the bike tires, he pounced. Before Hinkley's eyes could even go wide, Jim had an arm around his throat and was dragging him off the bike. The bike hit the ground, the front tire spinning. Hinkley struggled to get away, but Jim punched him in the face, and he went down on all fours.

"You hit my brother with a rock on the lake," said Jim, and kicked him in the ribs. Hinkley went over on his side, gasping for air.

"I heard for that letter we wrote Krapp you have to roll the barrels to the furnace room," said Jim, laughing. He walked over to the bike and picked it up.

Hinkley got to his feet. He lunged at Jim and tried to tear his grip off the bike handles. Jim pushed Hinkley aside with one arm and kicked out two front spokes. "How's the furnace room?"

"It stinks," said Will.

"What's that mean?" asked Jim, cocking his foot as if to kick again.

"Were you down there with Lou?" I asked.

"Oh, that washed-out guy? Yeah." He laughed.

When Hinkley laughed at Lou, we laughed with him.

"What about Lou?" asked Jim.

"I only saw Lou one day. When a kid pukes and they get it with the red stuff, after a while it forms into like a red ball. I watched Lou take one of those out of the barrel and put it in the furnace. It sizzled and smelled like hamburgers."

"What was he like?" I asked.

"Really white," said Hinkley.

"Did he say anything to you?" asked Jim.

"Yeah, he told me if I found out for him who threw a rock through his window, he'd give me ten bucks. I didn't know, but I told him I'd heard it was Peter Horton so he would give me the money."

Jim let go of Hinkley's bike, and it dropped onto the ground. He stepped away, and Hinkley went for the handlebars. Jim moved quickly, grabbing Hinkley's arms and locking them behind his back. He called us faggots as Jim turned him toward me. "Punch him in the face," said Jim.

I stepped up, but Hinkley was kicking the air, trying to keep me away. Jim kneed him in the back and told him to take his punishment. "Hit him!" yelled Jim. I just stood there, looking at Hinkley's face. "As hard as you can!" Hinkley squinted and turned his face to the side. Finally Jim called me a pussy and just let him go.

Hinkley sprang for his bike and was on it in a second. He rode thirty feet away from us and then stopped and yelled back, "I know where Lou lives! For another ten bucks, I'm gonna tell him your sister helped Peter Horton." Jim took off after him, but Hinkley was gone.

When Jim and I returned to Botch Town that night, we found that Mary had never left. Boris was back at his house working on his car, Charlie was in the lake, and Mr. Conrad stood in the Hayeses' backyard, leaning against the house. Mr. Barzita had been retired to the shoe box where Jim kept the figures of all those who'd died or moved away from the neighborhood. With a black crayon, in block letters, he'd written on the lid "Hall of Fame." It didn't matter what you did on Willow Avenue while you were there; everyone wound up in the Hall of Fame. We found Barzita in among the others, lying on top of Mrs. Halloway, and Jim laughed.

Sure enough, the white car was parked in front of Peter Horton's house. The prowler was in the Hortons' backyard. Jim asked Mary how long the car had been there, and she said, "Three nights."

"That's about how long it was parked outside of Boris's before he ran away," said Jim. "Mr. White's gonna do something soon."

I pictured Mr. White trying to lift Peter's huge body over his shoulder.

"Yes," said Mary.

"What?" I asked.

"Three," she said.

"Three?" said Jim. "What's that mean?"

"One more than two," said Mary.

"What about Peter?" I asked.

She shook her head and said, "I don't know."

"Okay," said Jim, "you can go play."

Mary went through the curtain to her side. When we heard the class start, Jim leaned in close to me and whispered, "Should we tell her about what Hinkley said?"

"Do you think he'll do it?" I asked.

"No, but . . ."

"What about we tell her if we find the white car in front of our house?"

Jim agreed, and then he told me his new plan. He'd dug around in the couch cushions and under the bed and come up with enough money to buy flashbulbs for his camera. "We'll catch him at the scene of the crime," he said.

Instant Evidence

■ We knew that if my mother was talking while she was drinking, she'd drink faster. At dinner Jim had a thousand questions about Bermuda, and before she could start to clean up the plates, I started talking to her about Sherlock Holmes. I think Mary knew what we were up to, and she went to her room. After a while my mother had drunk so much she just started talking on her own. She smoked like mad and told us about a place called Far Rockaway and when she and my father lived in Kentucky near Fort Knox. She told us about a library there in a mansion run by two old women, blind twins, who knew where every book was and how sometimes the local doctor took a pig instead of money for curing someone.

When she moved to the living-room couch, we went with her. Jim and I nodded every now and then to let her know we were listening. If we saw her smile when she told us something, we laughed. Eventually her eyes closed, her cigarette burned away in the ashtray, the half-filled wineglass tilted toward the floor. Words kept coming out, but more and more slowly making less and less sense. The last thing she said was "You're bad at bad," and then she was out cold. Jim grabbed the glass before it spilled, and I stubbed out the cigarette. Together we took her shoulders and gently moved her back so her head rested on the pillow. Jim sent me to get a blanket and the big red book. We set her up with the book open on her chest and then went next door to tell Nan we were going to bed.

Upstairs in my room, I dressed and, as Jim had instructed, pulled the covers up over my pillow to make it look like I was asleep. Every stair step creaked under our sneakers on the way down. We crept into the kitchen, and Jim turned out the light there and in the dining room. Slowly, so as to not make a sound, Jim opened the back door. It squealed as it swung wide enough for us to pass through. We slipped out into the yard without a hitch. It was nine-thirty, and we had till midnight, when my father got home from work.

We walked around the corner of the house and crossed the lawn to the street. There was a breeze that smelled like the ocean. Peter Horton lived all the way up near Hammond, and we turned in that direction. Most of the houses we passed were darkened, and some had only a light on in an upstairs bedroom window. We stayed out from under the glow of the streetlamps, crossing back and forth, trying not to scrape our feet on the gravel.

Jim wore the camera around his neck on a thin strap, and it bounced off his coat with every step. Across from Mr. Barzita's house, he led me up the side street toward Cuthbert Road. It was a clear night, and away from the streetlamps you could see all the stars. Jim gave me the sign to be extra quiet. We went up on a lawn on the right side of the street and headed around that house to the backyard. We passed right beneath a lit window. My heart started pounding, and my ears pricked up on their own like a dog's. Behind the place it was completely dark. We had to weave around lawn furniture and croquet wickets. Luckily, the back fence was a split-rail. Jim went over the top, and I slid through the middle space into the Hortons' backyard.

Their place was older than the other houses on the block, and bigger—three stories of busted and cracked stucco and a porch out front with columns. Their yard was bigger, too, more than double the size of ours. They had no lawn, but there was a thicket of tall pines surrounding the house, front and back. The fallen needles made for quiet walking.

We crept around the side of the house and crawled in under the branches of a big pine. From there, if we crouched, we could see the road and the house. The lights were out inside, and I thought of all the tons of Hortons, sleeping. They were big, lethargic people, every one with moon eyes and slow wit. They dressed like people in old brown photographs. Four boys and three girls. The father had something that looked like a ball sack coming off his chin. My mother told me it was called a goiter. He wore the same white T-shirt every day, his stomach sticking out, and the mother had dimples on her elbows, dresses like worn nightgowns. They seemed to have come off a farm somewhere, as if a twister had lifted the place and dropped it and them onto Willow Avenue.

The street was empty in front of their house. Two cars went by, and I tensed with each one. That's when it struck me that Jim's plan was crazy. I wondered how he was going to get a photo of Mr. White. Did he expect to catch a shot of those pasty hands around Peter's throat?

"Hey," I said to him. "This is crazy."

"I know," he said. "What if I get a good picture, though?" he whispered.

I shook my head.

"Instant evidence," he said.

"What time is it?" I asked.

"Ten at the latest."

Standing still there in the dark beneath the tree made me cold, and I started to shiver. Jim crouched, watching the street, his camera in both hands at the ready. Another car passed. I think it was Mr. Farley. A long time went by. I yawned and took hold of a branch. Closing my eyes, I thought about how much it felt like we were in Botch Town instead of somewhere in real life. For a moment I was tiny and made of clay. Then Jim tapped my leg.

When I opened my eyes, the first thing I saw, through the opening in three crisscrossing branches, was the white car pulling up to the curb just beyond the halo of a streetlight. It glided in without a sound. Mr. White rolled down his window and lit his pipe. We could see that he had his hat on and wore his overcoat. Before he even tossed his match out, I could smell the smoke. He sat there, smoking and looking at the house through the pines.

Jim and I were frozen in place, and the smoke came stronger and stronger, until my eyes started to water. We shouldn't have smelled it so much, and I started to think it was finding us for him. I wanted to run, and I touched Jim's shoulder to tell him we had to leave. He held his hand up and pointed. Mr. White was tapping out his pipe against the side of the car. He rolled up the window.

When I saw the window go up, I breathed a sigh of relief, but then the car door opened and he stepped out. He put his hands in his overcoat pockets and headed straight for us. There was no way he could see us, and I thought he'd turn and go toward the house, but he didn't. He came on, taking long strides straight toward our tree. I turned to run, and just as I did, I saw the flash go off. The next thing I knew, I was leaping through the middle space in the split-rail fence. Jim just jumped right over it without touching, the camera flying out behind him on its string. I didn't know if Mr. White was right behind me, but I wasn't going to turn around to find out.

We made it to the front lawn of the house whose yard we'd passed through earlier and then stopped when Jim put his hand on my shoulder. We were both winded, but it was clear that Mr. White wasn't coming through the backyard.

"He'll come in the car," said Jim.

Just as he spoke, the metal gate in the fence of the yard across the street opened with a squeal. We looked up. I knew right away it wasn't Mr. White. The figure stepped past the deeper shadow of the house. It was a teenage kid in a black leather jacket and a white T-shirt. He waved for us to come to him. I was unsure, but he waved more frantically, and finally Jim took off toward him. I didn't want to be left behind, so I went, too.

The guy leaned over and whispered, "Stay quiet and follow me."

We went through the gate, and as soon as we did, headlights appeared, turning off Hammond and onto Cuthbert. I had to really move to keep up with Jim and the other guy. He led us through the backyards, and it didn't take long to see he knew where he was going. Every place where two fences didn't quite meet and you could squeeze through, every place where there was a lawn chair or a tree branch to help you over a fence, every path among the trees and bushes, he knew without thinking. We moved like Barzita's squirrels from one end of Cuthbert to the other.

We came out of the backyards where Myrtle intersected Cuthbert and hid behind a lawn swing.

"We'll wait here," said the guy.

I noticed that his hair was combed forward in a wave and that he wore white Converse. A thin silver chain with a crucifix on the end looped down across his chest. A moment later the long car rolled slowly by. We could see Mr. White in the driver's seat, his head swiveling left to right and back again as he looked from lawn to lawn. The car stopped in front of one house for a while and then started up again and disappeared down the street. Once he was gone, we ran at top speed across the asphalt of Myrtle and Cuthbert, into the backyards that bordered the backyards of Willow Avenue. We moved through them like fish in water.

The guy took us to the Curdmeyers' grape arbor. Once we were under the trellises, he stopped. "You're just across the street," he said. "Watch for headlights."

"Do you know the man with the white car?" Jim whispered to him.

He smiled on one side of his mouth. "Sure," he said. "I've seen everything."

We thanked him for saving us and turned to head out across the Curdmeyers' yard toward the front. "Come out again some night," he said, "and I'll show you guys around." Jim and I looked back, but he was gone.

Sneaking into the house was a delicate process of slowly opening doors and cautious stepping. The warmth and total silence made it seem as if the house itself was sleeping. As we passed through the kitchen, I saw that the time was eleven-thirty. My mother was exactly where we'd placed her on the couch. We crept past her, and just before we reached the stairs, she said something with the word "palatial" in it. Jim looked back and smiled at me. More quietly than Mr. White, we made it to the landing outside our bedrooms. I went into my room, and Jim followed me. He stood at the entrance and whispered into the dark, "Do you know who that was?"

"Who?" I asked, dropping my coat on the chair.

"Ray Halloway."

Say Cheese

■ Ever since the day of the circus, my mother was in a strange mood. I'd seen it happen before. Her anger was somehow turning into energy. I could almost hear it percolating in her head. After dinner she no longer sat smoking and staring. Now she was near frantic, her nights filled with projects. She painted, she wrote, she created a TV commercial for a contest put on by Hebrew National salami. She told us all about it and sang the song she wrote, set to the tune of "Hava Nagila." One of the lines was "Even the all-knowing swami eats Hebrew National salami." At the end, she said, there should be balloons and confetti and cannons shooting salamis into the air. We told her it was great. She sent it off in the mail with high hopes, and the next night she started on a painting of Mount Kilimanjaro.

My father didn't change. Every morning at five o'clock, his alarm would ring. He'd sit up in his underwear on the edge of the bed, hunched over, breathing heavily and grunting every few seconds. He'd groan and then lurch to his feet. He'd dress in his work clothes from the day before. He'd comb his hair with water, and by five-twenty he'd be sitting in the kitchen, sleeves rolled up, with a cup of instant coffee, smoking. His gaze wouldn't stray from the clock over the back door. At five-thirty he'd stand and place his cup on the counter.

Next door, Pop had his own contest going. Every day after figuring the horses, he'd take out a bag of candy and lay it on the table. The contest was to make up a new name for the candy. He gave pieces of it to all of us—hard caramels with chunks of nuts in them. I could feel the brown spackle sucking out my teeth. In his boxer shorts and a sleeveless T-shirt, he sat chewing and jotting names along the edge of an old newspaper.

"*Nuttos.*"

"*Crackos.*"

"*Chewos.*"

Nan started every morning by squeezing half a lemon into a glass of boiling water. She drank it steaming hot, all at once, moving her lips and gulping till it was gone. The hot water was followed by a bowl of cold prunes in their own juices. "Why don't you just use dynamite?" Pop said. After breakfast she walked a hundred times from one end of the apartment to the other in her robe and hairnet.

Mary sat in the corner of the fence, back behind the forsythias, smoking a cigarette. The day was overcast and breezy. I saw her from the kitchen window, and she was talking to herself.

Jim and I took a visit to Botch Town. After turning on the sun, Jim lifted the figure of Ray that had long lain on its side from behind the Halloway house. He then picked up the figure of the prowler. Holding them out to me, he said, "I think these are the same guy."

I nodded.

"Maybe when his parents moved, he ran away and came back here," said Jim. He put the figure of Ray on the board and put the prowler carefully into the Hall of Fame so his pin arms wouldn't damage the others already resting there peacefully.

"Where's he living?" I asked.

"I bet in his old house. It's still empty. That's why Mary left him behind it."

"Wouldn't somebody try to find him?"

"Maybe not, because he's eighteen," said Jim.

"But what's he doing here?"

"We'll ask him all that."

"Not for a while," I said. "I don't want to get caught."

"Ray knows what Mr. White is doing," said Jim. "He can help us save Peter Horton. Besides, he's cool, isn't he?"

"He's great at running," I said.

"I wonder if he eats out of the garbage," said Jim.

I pictured Ray in the moonlight, lifting a trash-can lid and finding a pink hatbox filled with dirt.

Later Jim finished off the film in his camera by taking shots of everyone. He got one of Nan in her bathrobe and hairnet shaking her fist at him and smiling. He caught Pop smoking a Lucky Strike, reading the horse paper, his glasses perched at the end of his nose. Mary held her badge out, my mother stirred a big pot of the orange stuff, my father stared, and Jim snapped away. George hunkered down at the end of his leash to take a crap in the backyard, and Jim raised the camera. The dog had his back to us, but I called, "George. Hey, George. Georgie."

Jim aimed, saying, "George, say cheese. Say cheese." George looked back over his shoulder at us and growled, his bottom teeth bared. Jim snapped it, and then he had Mary take one of him and me, standing side by side in front of the shed.

A Lot of Screaming Ensued

■ While Krapp broke a sweat for the Little Big Horn, I tried to spy on Hinkley. He sat two rows across and one seat up, so I only caught his profile—the red hair, the freckled milky skin stretched taut over his cheekbones. I didn't believe he had the nerve to tell Lou that Mary had helped Peter Horton break the window, but I watched him. It was the sight of his Adam's apple bobbing up and down in his skinny neck that eventually made me unsure. As Krapp started to act out Custer's last stand, Hinkley cast a glance over his shoulder like he heard me thinking about him and caught me staring. The instant he looked in my eyes, he turned away.

"He stood like this," said Krapp, legs spread apart, his hands holding invisible six-shooters. "He was the last guy left, standing on this little hill. All around him was a sea of Indians on horseback with bows and arrows." Krapp aimed and fired with the guns that weren't there. "Custer was a crack shot and killed an Indian with every bullet he had left, but then the arrows came. . . ." Krapp took one in the back, and Tim Sullivan lost it. "When the guns were empty, he pulled his sword from its scabbard." The sword came out in slow motion, and he held it pointing toward the ceiling. More arrows hit Krapp, and he twitched with each strike. He made a face that was supposed to be agony but looked more like Custer's last dump. By the time he let the whole thing go, we were all laughing. He looked confused and just about to get pissed off, but instead he smiled. A moment later he took a bow. There was silence, a pause, and somehow all at once we thought to clap for him.

By the end of the performance, I was certain Hinkley had done it.

Out on the playground, I found Peter Horton and told him that Hinkley had taken ten dollars from Lou the janitor and lied about who'd broken the window.

"Why'd he do that?" said Peter.

"To get the ten bucks," I said.

"He didn't know who did it?"

"He just said it was you to get the money. Lou thinks you did it. *Now* do you get it?"

"But I didn't do it," said Horton, pacing back and forth. His face grew red, and there was a saliva bubble between his lips. His eyes were wider than ever. Finally he lumbered off, looking for Hinkley. I followed at a distance. Peter traipsed through a kickball game and right between two kids trading baseball cards. Hinkley was talking to a couple of girls when Horton's fingers closed around the back of his neck, then landed a slow-moving punch that came as if through water but hit like a torpedo. Hinkley's whole body shook. Krapp was on the scene in a shot, threatening trips to the office for all involved. I kept my distance and watched as Krapp helped Hinkley to his feet. His nose was bloody, and he looked dazed. Krapp told him to brush himself off and go to the office. Peter was already on his way across the field, crying. As Krapp yelled at him to get going, Hinkley looked around and found me. He smiled, the blood running down across his lips.

Hinkley and Horton never came back to the classroom that afternoon, and word got around that they were suspended and their parents had to come for them. Krapp was doing geometry circles, triangles, dashed lines—with three different colors of chalk—white, blue, and pink. My mind was numb from it. "That's the point," said Krapp, and there was a knock at the door. He went out into the hallway, and we could hear someone talking to him. Krapp stuck his head back in and called my name. The first time it went right through me. The second, I woke to it and felt instant embarrassment. I got out of my seat and walked to the door. He leaned close and whispered to me, "You're wanted in the office."

Cleary sat behind his desk in his camel-hair jacket and black tie, his drastic crew cut and sideburns that Jim said he put on like a helmet every morning. His hand was around his throat, and his look was, by Mary's scale, dark coffee. It was so quiet that I heard the brass clock on his desk tick. Out the window behind him, I saw the gates to the school, the blue sky, and the way home.

"Have a seat," he said. "Do you know why you're here?"

I sat in the chair, facing him across his desk, and shook my head.

"We had an incident on the playground today," he said, "between Peter Horton and William Hinkley. Did you see it?"

I nodded.

"I hear you told Peter Horton something that got him mad at Hinkley," he said.

"Maybe," I said.

"Maybe?" he asked, and then proceeded to lay out the whole story in perfect detail. He knew about Lou and the ten dollars, the rock through the window, the lies, all of it. "Did you start this fight?" he asked.

As he spoke, I was scared, but once his words evaporated, I started really thinking. "It was unfair what Hinkley did to Peter," I said. "I wanted to warn him in case Lou went to his parents."

"A noble gesture," said Cleary, raising his eyebrows. "William told me that your brother beat him up behind the deli on Sunday."

"I don't know," I said.

"You were there," he said. "You won't be suspended this time, but I'll be calling your parents to inform them of all this. You may go back to class." His hand swept slowly away from his neck and pointed me to the door.

From what Cleary told my mother, she deduced that we hadn't gone to church on Sunday. A lot of screaming ensued. I took a lesson from Jim and just nodded quietly.

"I don't give a damn about Hinkley," my mother said, "but lying about going to church is a venial sin." I tried to remember if Mrs. Grimm had taught us that one.

My mother was angry, but the worst part was she told my father that he had to take us to church next Sunday. The look of betrayal he gave us was like a slap in the face.

"Are you kidding?" said my father.

"You're their father, you'll take them."

"Bullshit," he said. "I don't go to church."

We let the rest of the week go by without trying to sneak out at night. Jim would have gone, but I wasn't ready to take the chance again. Every night the long white car sat outside the Hortons' house in Botch Town. My only relief was that I'd told Peter about Mr. White being after him because of Hinkley's story. I wanted to believe that was enough. "Monday night," said Jim.

Jim got his pictures back from the drugstore Saturday afternoon. We were standing over Botch Town, using its sun to see them better. Scenes of George and the family flipped by, and then Jim stopped and pulled one glossy black-and-white photo closer to his face. The flash had gone off in the dark beneath the tree and reflected off Mr. White's face pushing through the shadowy branches.

"It's just his head and his hat," said Jim.

"But it looks like it's flying in the dark," I said.

"Yeah," said Jim.

"Did you notice how quiet he was?"

"He has powers," said Jim. He continued flipping through the photos, and when he came to the one of me and him in front of the shed, he said, "You can have that." I put it in my back pocket. We returned to the shot of Mr. White and stared at it for a long time.

"When we get more evidence, we'll send this to the cops," he said.

The next morning, dressed in his brown suit that was so worn it shone, a tie, and his good shoes, my father led us out to the car. Mary and I sat in the back and Jim sat with him up front. "This is just bullshit," my father said, turning around to look as he backed out of the driveway.

At church my father took a seat in the first row, on the left, right on the aisle in front of the altar, and we filed in next to him. The smell of incense was eerie, not to mention the plaques on each of the church's great sweeping arches—the story in pictures of Christ's crucifixion. The thick air, the dim silence, made the place seem filled with time. Each second weighed a ton, each minute was a great glass bubble of centuries. The drudgery of church was the most boring thing I ever lived through. Mrs. Grimm had taught us about purgatory, and that was going to church every day until someone's prayers sent you on to heaven.

The Mass started, and no matter what we were supposed to do—stand, kneel, or sit—my father sat through it all. Jim, Mary, and I followed the routine, but my father just sat with his arms folded and one leg crossed over the other. He watched the priest, and when Father Toomey rang the bell and people pounded their chests, my father laughed. On the way home, he told us, "Nice story, but when you die, you're food for the worms," and then he pulled over to a hot-dog cart on the side of the road.

When we got home from church, Nan came in with some news. She said she had just gotten off the phone with Mrs. Curdmeyer, who told her that Mrs. Horton was dead. "She died in her sleep," said Nan.

"That's a shame," said my mother, and I thought about never waking up. The next thing that went through my mind was the sight of the white car parked in front of our house in Botch Town.

A Silent Island

■ Mrs. Horton's wake was held at Clancy's Funeral Home, an old white mansion with giant oaks looming over it. My parents and Jim and I came up the front steps and into the heavy florist scent of the lobby. The furniture in the foyer was gold with thick carved legs. On a coffee table sat a huge vase of white lilies. Paintings of landscapes in gold swirling frames lined the walls. A grandfather clock of polished wood stood in the corner, its pendulum swinging behind glass. On its face was a crescent moon and stars.

Teddy Dunden's father, who was a fireman during the day, worked nights as an usher at Clancy's, holding the door and steering people to the different death rooms. He was a burly, red-faced man with a gray mustache and curly brown hair. He said hello to my parents, and they greeted him in whispers. He looked at the floor, his hands folded like at church, and led us to a room that was crowded with people, all dressed in black. It was quiet but for the sound of crying up near the front, where I saw the lighted coffin surrounded by flowers.

My mother put her hand on my back and gently pushed me forward, Jim alongside. The closeness of the room and the increasing view of Mrs. Horton's profile made me gag. Death was a silent island, and then we were there, standing over her. I knew if I looked at Jim, we would laugh, so I had to stare down into the grimace of her waxy face. In her sleep she was unhappy. It struck me then that none of the neighbors who'd come to the wake had ever been friends with Mrs. Horton. I crossed myself and turned away.

Peter Horton, his jacket button ready to pop, wearing his clodhopper shoes, sat in the front row like a cartoon cat hit by a mallet. His eyes were big blanks, and when I told him I was sorry about his mom, he grunted.

"Peter's zombie-island," Jim said a few minutes later as we stood at the back of the room near the doorway.

I nodded my head in the direction of Mr. Conrad, who sat by himself in the last row, working at his giant left ear with an open paper clip. "He's digging to China," I said.

Mrs. Farley talked Girl Scouts with Mrs. Bishop. Mr. Hackett wore his Korean War uniform, and I almost expected to see the back of the pants blown out where the grenade had hit his ass. Mrs. Restuccio dozed in her chair, and Larry March's old man quietly told knock-knock jokes to Diamond Lil.

My father talked to Mr. Felina and Mr. Farley. My mother sat next to Mrs. Hayes, nodding at a long story. People prayed on the kneeler in front of Mrs. Horton's coffin, walked away, and came back a few seconds later for more. An older woman with a black lace doily on her head was saying the bead prayers, and the Horton children milled slowly through like solid ghosts from Dorothy's Kansas.

Leaning back against the wall, I was about to shut my eyes when Mr. Horton suddenly stood up from his chair, goiter bobbing, and looked toward the ceiling. He introduced himself and started talking to Jesus. At first everybody looked up, and then they all lowered their eyes when they realized nothing was there. "I was thinking the other day about Time, Jesus," he said. Everything he said ended in "Jesus," and at every mention of the name, spit flew from the corners of his mouth. When Mr. Horton asked Jesus to make his wife wake up and live again, my father walked back to us.

"Go outside and get some air," he said, "but don't go far." He looked over his shoulder as if to check whether Mrs. Horton was stirring. Jim and I didn't have to be asked twice. In the lobby we wove our way through a crowd of crying people letting out from one of the other death rooms. Mr. Dunden opened the door for us, and we walked down the long flight of steps. We walked back to the stone benches around a wishing pond beneath giant oaks. Stars were visible through nets of barren branches. The cool night air smelled like the ocean.

"Did Mr. White kill her?" I asked.

"I don't know," he said. "Maybe he couldn't get Peter, so he got her instead. Then again, maybe she just died."

He Kills People

■ The stench of oil paint and turpentine was every-where, as if something chemical come to life. It made every hair on the back of my neck stand up. I sat next to my mother in the dining room and watched her. She was in her usual chair by the window at the end of the room, and before her on the table was a very short easel with Mount Kilimanjaro on it. To one side of her was a palette on which she mixed colors from fat silver tubes, and on the other was an old encyclopedia open to a page that showed a picture of a gazelle. With a brushstroke of burnt sienna and a touch of yellow, in two fluid movements, she formed the outline of an inch-high gazelle in the foreground of her canvas. She made three more, all in different poses, just as quickly. She added gray-and-white horns and black-and-white markings, and they looked real. They stood on an open plain bordered by a jungle of emerald green palm trees. Behind the trees rose the great mountain in varying shades of blue and gray, and the sun glinted off its snowcapped peak.

"It's done," she said. She stood up, wiped her hands on a rag, and took a step back to admire her masterpiece.

I pictured gorillas living in that jungle and wondered if any of them ever climbed the mountain and walked through the snow.

"What do you think?" she asked me, pushing the little easel away from us so it sat in the middle of the table.

"I want to go to Africa," I said.

She smiled and lit a cigarette. Reaching down beside her chair, she hoisted up the half-gallon jug of wine and refilled her glass. She sat then, quietly assessing the painting. In those few seconds, I saw the recent burst of energy leaking out of her. As usual, it had lasted for a little more than a week or so, and she'd used it all up. Like a punctured blow-up pool toy, she seemed to slowly deflate while shadows blossomed in her gaze. She stubbed out her cigarette and said, "It's okay." All the brushes went into the old coffee can of poison-smelling turpentine, and all the caps were put back on the silver paint tubes. She picked up her wineglass, cigarettes, and ashtray and went in to sit in the corner of the couch. I followed her and sat at the other end.

"It won't be for a while," she said, her eyes closed, "but I saw the next painting I'm going to do."

"George's portrait?" I asked. The dog, over by the stairs, lifted his head for a moment.

She smiled. "No. There's a tree at the arboretum. A giant, ancient tree with tendrils that reach to the ground. I want to paint every leaf of it in summer in the late afternoon."

She was still but for her shallow breathing. Between two fingers of her right hand, an unlit cigarette seesawed. The wineglass was as close to spilling without spilling as possible. I grabbed the wineglass and ashtray and set them down on the coffee table. Then, creeping over to the cellar door, I whispered for Jim. He came upstairs with Mary, who we sent to get the Sherlock Holmes while we positioned my mother's head on the pillows and lifted her feet.

I was already dressed, and Jim had stored our coats in the cellar earlier. We put them on and zipped up in the kitchen with the lights off. As we were getting ready to go out the back door, Jim said to Mary, "What do you have to do?"

"Go in, kiss Nan good night, and tell her everybody went to bed, and then go to bed."

"Right," said Jim. "Let's not Mickey this up."

She walked over to where he stood and kicked him in the leg with her bare foot. He laughed without making a sound.

"What if Mr. White comes?" Mary whispered.

"His car's been all the way up on Hammond since Mrs. Horton croaked. He's not coming here," he said.

"What if he does?" she said.

"Call Nan, and she'll get her gun," I said.

Jim and I went out into the night. The door hushed closed, and as I went down the steps, I turned and looked back at Mary's face peering out of the yellow square of light that was the kitchen window. We crept to the edge of the house and then made for the street. For the last day, Ray Halloway's figure had been hanging out over near the school in Botch Town, so we turned in that direction.

We saw a bat flying crazy under the streetlamp across from the Hacketts' house, and Mrs. Grimm's white cat, Legion, was prowling in the ivy on the Calfanos' lawn. Otherwise the block was quiet. It wasn't quite ten o'clock yet, so there were still a fair number of lighted windows. As we wove our way around the glow of the streetlamps, we listened for the sound of tires on the street behind us, checked now and then for the brightness of headlights. Ahead of us rose the silhouette of the school. We passed the gates. The ring on the flag rope clinked against the metal pole. There was some sweet flower smell blowing out of the woods.

We crossed the bus circle and were just stepping up onto the sidewalk in front of the main door when a pebble hit the ground at our feet. We stopped cold and looked around. Fear grew in me, and then a noise came from above.

"Pssst."

We looked up, and there was a person leaning over the edge of the school's flat roof. I knew it was Ray the second I made out the white T-shirt. Slowly my eyes adjusted, and he came into view. He had an unlit cigarette in the corner of his mouth.

"Meet me over at the gym door by the baseball diamond," he whispered. Then he pushed up with his hands and was gone.

We ran as quietly as possible across the parking lot and the basketball court, keeping to the shadows along the wall of the school. The gym was three stories of solid brick. If you jumped off the roof of the main school building, you wouldn't get hurt, but to fall from the roof of the gym was certain death. We followed the asphalt path around the corner of its enormous wall and stopped short at the metal door. I looked out across the baseball diamond in the moonlight and thought of Mr. Rogers, wherever he was, seeing the same thing.

Both of us jumped when the metal door groaned open. I was halfway back to the basketball court before I heard Jim laughing. Turning around, I saw him and Ray waving me back.

"Come on," said Ray as I drew up next to them. He put his hand lightly on my shoulder, and I stepped inside behind Jim. The door closed with a bang.

Inside the sleeping school, it was pitch black, and the smells of red stuff, old books, bad breath, and the slightest trace of that day's baked haddock were so much more powerful in silence.

"How do you get in here?" asked Jim as Ray led us across the polished wooden floor.

"There's a door up on the gym roof. There's no lock on it. When the weather's too cold, I stay down here in the furnace room. I was here all through the snowstorm."

He opened a swinging door, and we stepped out into a hallway of the main building. We walked through the darkened corridors, passing Krapp's room. The door was open, and when I looked in, I half expected to see the glow of his white shirt— him sitting at his desk with his head down.

"How do you get on the roof?" asked Jim.

"There's a pipe that runs up the wall at the back corner of the school by the playground—for the oil or something. I get my foot onto that, pull myself up, and reach my fingers over the edge of the roof. Once I'm on the roof over there, it's easy to get to the ladder that leads up the side of the gym."

"I don't think I could do that," Jim said.

"Well," said Ray, "not many people can."

We entered one of the halls that ran along the courtyard. The enormity of being in the school illegally was just beginning to dawn on me.

"Do you ever get afraid of heights?" asked Jim.

"No," said Ray. He stopped and turned to look out into the courtyard. We halted beside him. A little wash of moonlight fell there, and we could make out the dead weeds and stone bench. "The only thing I worry about," said Ray, pointing through the window, "is falling in there."

"Why?" asked Jim. "The roof's not even that high there."

"Because there's no way out. They built it without a door, and there's no place to get a foothold or a leg up. If I fell in there, I'd be trapped and have to try to break a window to get out. After Calfano busted all the windows, they wired them with alarms, and if they break, the cops come." He turned and continued past the main office and the nurse's office, striding confidently as if the school belonged to him. "Did you ever wonder why they have a bench in there?" he asked over his shoulder. At the end of the hall, he opened the door to the furnace room and held it for Jim and me to enter. As I passed by him into the warm total darkness, I noticed he didn't have his white sneakers on, but instead he wore a pair of pointy black shoes kids called "cockroach killers."

"Hold on a second," he told us. The door swung shut behind him. "I have a flashlight right here. I can't use it in the school, because someone might see the beam." A light flicked on, and there was Ray's head like a flame in demonic shadows, smiling. I almost ran but realized he was holding the light under his chin. Jim and Ray laughed.

He led us down a ramp and onto a concrete floor. Moving the beam around, Ray showed us Boris's office: a corner that contained an old desk with dozens of cubbyholes all stuffed with papers, a swivel chair with a tuft of stuffing coming out of the seat, and a workbench. In another corner stood at least ten barrels on rollers. Ray walked over to one of them and shone the flashlight on its contents. The red stuff.

"What is this shit anyway?" he asked.

"Pieces of eraser?" I said.

"Chemical rubber bits," said Jim.

He showed us the furnace, a potbellied man of metal with numbered-gauge eyes within circles of glass, a spigot nose, and two pipe arms reaching out and into the walls. The latch on the furnace door squealed when Ray opened it to reveal small blue flames dancing in its depths.

"They only use this to get rid of trash," he said. "The oil burner's over there." He turned and illuminated it with the flashlight. "That heats the school.

"Over here," he said. He ducked under one of the furnace's long arms and into a passageway that ran beside it. Once past the back of the machine, the alley got narrower. Eventually I had to turn sideways and scrape myself along the smooth stone walls. Two steps through and the walls opened immediately into a vast underground cavern supported by concrete columns.

Ray held the flashlight out in front of him and pointed it away from the foundation of the school. "I don't know how far it goes on," he said. "I went in there once and came to a place where I could hear running water up ahead, like a little waterfall, but then the flashlight batteries ran out and I had to make my way back through total darkness. I think it's an air-raid shelter. You know, in case the Russians drop the big one."

He continued, "I keep my stuff over here," and led us in among the columns. He shone the light into a corner made by the foundation of the school and the walls of the cavern, where a sleeping bag was spread out near a collection of paper bags. Next to the bedroll was an electric lantern. He leaned over and turned it on, and a greater light came up around us—warmer and yellower than the harsh flashlight beam. He slipped out of his jacket and sat down Indian style.

Jim sat and finally I did, too. It was like we were having a campout in a nightmare. There was too much darkness for me, and I was breathing fast. Ray rummaged in his jacket pocket for his cigarettes and matches. Once he had them, he reached into a brown paper bag and brought out a clear plastic sack. He laid it down in front of us and said, "You want some candy?"

When I got a good look at it, I saw it was the half bag of candy Pop had thrown out. He'd eventually given up on the contest and wrote the words "hard shit" on a three-by-five card and sent it in to the candy company. Then, with the back of his arm, he'd swept the half-full sack off the table and right into the trash can four feet away.

Jim saw me looking at the candy and shifted his eyes. I knew he'd caught it.

"What are you doing here?" he asked Ray.

"There's two reasons. First, I'm looking for something," said Ray. He took a drag of his cigarette and stared into the lantern.

"Mrs. Conrad's ass?" said Jim.

Ray laughed, "Well, there is a lot of ass. But I lost something. I'm here looking for it."

"What?" I asked.

He said nothing for a moment, and I thought I'd pissed him off. Finally he said, "That part's a secret."

"What about Mr. White?" asked Jim.

"The guy in the white car?" said Ray. "Yeah, I know all about him. I watch him. That's the other reason I'm here, to warn everyone about him."

"He kills people," I said.

"I know," said Ray. "I saw that he was watching Boris's house, and I knew he wanted to get rid of him to take his job and get closer to the kids. So I wrote Boris a letter and put it in his mailbox to scare him away for a while."

"We think he killed Charlie Edison," said Jim.

"He did," said Ray. "Behind the stores last fall. He crept up on him like a bad thought, broke his neck, and then threw the kid into his car. He kept him in that big freezer until after the cops dredged the lake. Then he got rid of him in there."

"How do you know?" I asked.

"I saw it. And I saw him break Mr. Barzita's neck like a Popsicle stick on Halloween night. I watched through the old man's basement window. He's killed a lot of people, mostly kids."

"Mrs. Horton?" asked Jim.

"I think she just died from being too fat," said Ray.

"Does he know you know?" I asked.

"He knows I'm watching him," said Ray, flicking his cigarette. "He tries to catch me all the time, but I'm too fast for him. I haunt him constantly."

"How come you didn't tell anyone?" asked Jim.

"How come *you* didn't?" asked Ray. "If someone finds out I'm here, they'll send me back to my parents' house."

"That's bad?" I said.

Ray nodded. "If I find what I'm looking for here, I'll never have to go back there." He sat quietly for a time, staring. When he finally looked up, he smiled and said, "I'm going out to make the rounds. You guys should come for a while. We'll see some stuff." From one of the brown paper bags, he retrieved his sneakers and changed out of the black shoes.

"Nice shoes," said Jim.

Ray shrugged. "I took them from the Blair kid. Right out of his closet."

"You go in houses?" I asked.

"During the day when everyone is out. I can get in any-where. That's how I get the stuff I need," he said, tightening the laces of his right sneaker. "I only take what I need," he added, a little defensively.

We left the school through the door in Mrs. Plog's kinder-garten room, which led out into the playground with monkey bars and a slide. Jim couldn't help himself from spinning the whirly thing as he went past. Ray opened the gate and let us out, and then he took off across the field. We followed at a run as he crossed the bus circle and went up onto the grass, where he knelt down next to a fence that bordered the school.

When we finally caught up and were crouched next to him, he said, "Okay, no matter what happens from here on, you can't say a word. Follow me. If you don't know what to do, watch my hand signals. Walk on the sides of your feet when we're near the windows. Watch out for kids' toys lying around in the back-yards."

Jim and I both nodded, but I wasn't sure if I was going to be able to keep up with them. It didn't matter, though, because a few seconds later we were running through backyards, climb-ing over split-rail and picket fences. When Ray finally stopped, I almost ran past him. He waved over his shoulder for us to fol-low as he moved from the back of the yard toward the house. I saw where he was headed—a lit window at knee level on the first floor.

Ray leaned over and rested his hands on his thighs as he peered into the bright rectangle. Jim and I came up on either side of him and assumed the same pose. Inside was a heavy man sitting in a chair with his back to us, watching TV. His head was bald, with big wrinkles of fat where his neck met his shoulders. On a small table next to him was a tall object that looked like the base of a lamp without the shade or bulb but with a hose attached. The man held the end of the hose and was doing something with it near his face. Finally all became clear when a great bluish stream of smoke formed a cloud like a dark thought above his head. It was the kind of pipe the giant caterpillar on the mushroom had in *Alice in Wonderland*.

We were off. Because I couldn't see too much, the sounds of the night became clearer—the bubble of a pool filter, television laughter, an owl in the woods, and between my deep breaths the whisper of cars passing, twenty blocks north, on Sunrise Highway. We broke out of the backyards and crossed Cuthbert, went through another yard, and climbed over a fence to reach the houses on Willow.

Our next stop was the Steppersons'. There was a side window that you could look in if you stood on the fence whose last post butted up against the house. Ray quietly climbed up. He stood there perched in midair for a long time. The glow from the window lit his face, and I watched his expression slowly change from its usual alertness to something slower and more distant. When he was done, he dropped to the ground silently and helped Jim get up on the fence. Jim looked for only a couple of seconds. Then it was my turn. Ray grabbed my forearm as I stood balanced on the fence rail. I could feel the wiry strength in his arm as I looked into a bedroom. Todd Stepperson, who was in the grade below mine, lay in bed, asleep. His room was a mess—toys and clothes all over the place. I noticed that at the foot of the bed he had a collection of stuffed animals, and in among them was a kind of baby doll called Thumbelina that had a string you pulled in the back to make it squirm. Mary had one, and Jim and I used to pull the string and roll it down the stairs to see it writhe when it hit the bottom.

Ray held on and helped me to land without making a sound. We didn't run but walked quickly away from the Steppersons' house and around the two rusted cars parked in the back corner of their yard. There was no fence to slow us as we crossed into the next yard, then the next. We ran through a string of yards, and even though we were traveling along Willow, the street I lived on, I lost track of where we were.

I couldn't fix our position until I caught up with Ray and Jim standing outside a lighted playroom window watching Marci Hayes pull off her jeans. She stood there in her white underwear and a yellow button-down shirt, her blond hair loose to the middle of her back. Next, a button at a time, the shirt came off. Jim's mouth was wide open, and he had a look on his face like he was about to cry. Ray was smiling. Marci unhooked her bra and turned to the side to remove the strap from her shoulder, and there they were—not too big, with dark nipples. When she slipped out of her underwear and that pink ass was staring him in the face, Jim staggered forward slightly and stepped on a twig.

Marci's head turned sharply. Like a shot, we were gone. From the bushes at the back of the yard, we watched as she came, now dressed in a nightgown, to the window and peered out.

At the Bishops' a phonograph was playing "Take Me Out to the Ball Game," booming loud through the windowpanes. Reggie was in feet pajamas decorated with little cars. The music stopped, and we watched as he lifted the needle to start the record again. "No more," said Mr. Bishop, coming into the room. From where we stood, we could see the bald spot in his gray hair and a profile of his weariness. He kind of sagged like old laundry and waved his hands in front of him.

"But I'm not tired yet," said Reggie. The music started again. He ran over to his father and, putting his feet on his dad's shoes, slung his arms around the old man's neck and clasped his hands. Mr. Bishop staggered forward as Reggie let his body go slack. His father moved around the room slowly, lurching back and forth, doing the box step. At one point he stared directly out into the night at us, but I had no fear those eyes would see me.

We passed silently by Dan Curdmeyer, sitting in his grape arbor in the dark, asleep, a beer on the table in front of him. Ray motioned for us to go on ahead, and he walked carefully over to where Mr. Curdmeyer sat. In one swift movement, he lifted the glass, drained it, replaced the glass, and was suddenly back by our side. There was something impossible in his speed. We crossed the side street by Mr. Barzita's house and wound up behind the Eriksons'. A light shone in their dining room, but it was empty. Ray took longer looking into the empty rooms.

All three of us stood on the wooden deck around the pool in the Felinas' backyard and watched Mr. and Mrs. Felina lying in bed together talking. They looked comfortable on their pillows as they smiled and laughed. We watched for a long time. Finally they stopped talking, and she rolled close to him. I thought they were going to sleep, so I got ready to go. Before I could take the first step down the deck ladder, though, Ray tapped my shoulder and pointed. I looked up and saw that the bedcovers had been thrown aside. The Felinas were completely naked, Mrs. was on her knees, and Mr. had a giant boner. Jim started laughing without making noise, and the suddenness of the whole thing made me laugh, too. I thought Ray would be mad at us, but he joined in. We watched until the show was over, then ran on to see Boris the janitor sleeping in front of the TV, Mrs. Edison in her dining room by candlelight with a bowl of water in front of her on the table, Peter Horton sitting at his too-small desk, sobbing.

"That's just one night," said Ray. We walked leisurely down Willow Avenue, sticking to the edges of the lawns instead of the street. "There's lots more to see."

"Thanks," said Jim and I echoed him.

"The next time you come out, I'll have a plan to catch Mr. White," Ray said.

We left him outside the Farleys'. He ducked into the back-yard, and we ran across the front lawn to our house. A few minutes later, we were each in our respective rooms, dressed in our pajamas. I'd just gotten into bed when I heard my father come in. I lay there wondering what Ray might be seeing and what he was looking for. It struck me that out of all we had seen, it was Peter Horton and his sorrow that kept returning to me.

Something's Coming

■ Pop and I were out in the backyard inspecting his trees. I carried an old coffee can with some stinking black mixture in it. He had a big old stiff-bristled paintbrush. He dipped it into the can and leaned over, painting the bottom few feet of a tree trunk all the way down to the ground. It was a beautiful afternoon. The sun was actually hot. Pop wore only a sleeveless T-shirt and shorts, and I had no coat. Before painting each tree, he'd look it over from a distance, and then he'd get in close, rubbing the bark and lightly touching the buds he could reach. He said there would be a lot of cherries come summer and that the bugs would be bad.

When we finished with the last tree, we sat across from each other at the picnic table. He dumped the can of tree paint into the grass and put the brush on the bench next to him. He lit a Lucky Strike and said, "I want you to do me a favor."

I nodded.

"Come around here behind me. I want you to look at something on my back." He set his cigarette on the edge of the table and lifted his T-shirt as I went to stand behind him. The tattoo dog was waiting for me, blue and swirling.

"Look at the dog," he said. "What color are its eyes?"

"Red," I told him.

He pulled his shirt down and waved at me to sit. He lifted his cigarette and said, "I could feel it."

"What's it feel like?" I asked.

"It itches, sometimes to the point where it burns. I haven't felt it in a long time. That's not red ink. Those eyes usually show just the color of my skin."

"Is it Chimto warning you?" I asked.

He nodded. "Something's coming. Some dark crapola's on the way, and it's getting close."

"What are you gonna do?" I asked.

"Nothing," he said. "What can you do? You just wait to see where it lands and then start shoveling. It's good to know that it's coming, though. Early warning, you know?"

"Is it all bad stuff?"

"The old Javanese who gave me the tattoo told me that when the eyes turn red, it means serious trouble is approaching. I told him, 'Sure, whatever,' and he started in with the whalebone needles. About halfway through the job, he gave me this kind of gum to chew, like tree resin. It tasted like licorice, and it made me tired and kind of dizzy. After chewing it, I could hear, just outside his shack, a giant dog snarling and barking."

"Has the dog ever saved your life?"

He pointed at me and said, "That's what it's all about."

I nodded, unsure what he meant. We sat there for a while without speaking. The leaves were coming back, and I noticed that the grass was getting greener. The sun felt great. Eventually I got up and started toward the house.

"You and your brother sneaking out at night wouldn't be a good idea right now," he said.

I turned around and looked at him. He put his finger to his lips.

Shut Up

■ I told Jim all about my conversation with Pop.

"Shit" was his response.

"I don't think he's gonna tell," I said.

"The dog's eyes really were red?" he asked.

"Bright red."

"The dog sees Mr. White," he said.

"That's what I thought."

"Well, if the dog sees him, how come Mary doesn't see him? The white car's been up on Hammond for a couple weeks now in Botch Town."

We went in search of Mary and found her in her room, lying on the wood floor, putting together a jigsaw puzzle of a forest path. I was surprised she wasn't gabbing with Sally O'Malley and Sandy Graham. Jim must have felt the same way, because he said to her, "How come you're not Mickey as much anymore?"

"Shut up," she said, fitting a piece into the puzzle.

Jim told her about Pop's dog tattoo, and then he asked her how come the white car hadn't moved.

"Make a Mr. White," she said without looking up.

"He's not in the car?" I asked.

"Thank you," she said, and told us to leave.

I tried to fit the dog's warning, Mr. White on foot, Ray,

and all the rest of it into some sort of pattern I could analyze. I went out into the backyard to get some air. Jim followed me.

"He's coming for Mary," said Jim.

"We should tell Dad," I said.

"No. Ray knows everything about it. We should find out what his plan is first," said Jim.

"I'm not going," I said.

"Then I'll go by myself," he said.

"What if Mr. White finds you before you find Ray?" I asked.

He shrugged and said, "That's a chance I'll just have to take."

That night after dinner, Nan came in to tell us that the police had been across the street that afternoon.

"Where?" my mother asked.

"The Hayeses' place," said Nan. "The daughter heard someone outside her window the other night."

"Did she see who it was?" asked Jim.

"It was too dark," said Nan.

Later, down in Botch Town, Jim brought the prowler back from the Hall of Fame and painted him completely white, even the steel-pin arms. The eyes still glowed through from underneath the paint. In the middle of his work, he looked up and said "Marci Hayes" to me, and we both laughed.

Make the Moon

■ "Make the moon," said Krapp. "I don't care how you do it."

He passed around a book with pictures of the moon.

"Craters," he said. "Round and gray with craters. Papiermâché, clay, paper, plaster—it doesn't matter, but it's got to look like the moon. Hand it in next week. Thursday."

The Night Watch

■ The men met in our backyard on Saturday as the sun was going down. My father said Jim and I could sit out with them for a while if we kept quiet. Mr. Mason, my father, Mr. Farley, Dan Curdmeyer, and Mr. Conrad sat in lawn chairs back by the forsythia bushes, which had begun to sprout yellow buds. There was a warm breeze, and it was more night than day. Mr. Conrad had brought a six-pack and a flashlight. Curdmeyer had brought two of each. Mr. Farley was the last to arrive, with a bottle of whiskey and a stack of Dixie cups.

I sat next to my father's chair on the ground and Jim sat in his own chair. Mr. Conrad offered my father a beer. "Thanks," said my father, and he laughed. Mr. Farley started pouring cups of whiskey and passing them around. Almost everyone was smoking; Curdmeyer had a pipe. When all the men had a little paper cup, Mr. Mason held his up and said, "To the night watch."

They took a sip, and then Dan Curdmeyer said, "Where's Hayes? It was his daughter, wasn't it?"

"I don't know," said Mr. Mason, shaking his head. "My wife made me set this up."

They all chuckled, low, almost embarrassed.

"I had my kids rig trip wires in all the backyards except this one. Two sticks with fishing line and a can with stones in it. If we hear them, we're supposed to run and catch the Peeping Tom," said Mason.

I pictured Henry and the horrible dumplings, rattling soda cans.

"Run? After a few more of these," said Farley, "*crawl* will be more like it."

"Drinks outside," said my father. "Not a bad plan."

"If we hear someone, will you guys go after them?" asked Mason.

"Sure," said Mr. Conrad, "I'll kick their ass." A second later he broke into a grin.

"We'll see how it goes," said my father, and after that the talk turned to the weather and money. The drinks flowed. Cigarettes flared and were stamped out. A curse word was thrown in every now and then. The men's laughter was distant, as if they were laughing at something they remembered more than what had just been said. Full night arrived, and it got a little cooler.

Mr. Farley talked about a new machine-gun system that was being made at Grumman, where he worked. "A thousand rounds a second," he said.

"How big are the shells?" my father asked.

Farley held out two trembling fingers about five inches apart. He smiled as if it were the most amazing news. When Farley was finished going on about the miraculous design, Mr. Conrad took a matchbox out of his pocket, set his drink down, and picked up the flashlight he'd brought.

"What have you got there, Jake?" asked Curdmeyer, who was already slumped back in his chair.

Conrad slid open the matchbox and shone the flashlight on it. He held the box out to my father, who put his drink on the ground. The small square dropped onto his palm. I stood up so I could see better. Lying on cotton inside the little box was the tiny brown figure of a naked woman.

My father laughed. "Which ear did that come out of?" he asked.

"One goes straight through to the other," Conrad said.

Farley laughed.

My father passed it on to Curdmeyer, who looked and said, "How did you shape it?"

"Paper clip, my thumbnail, a straight pin . . ."

"This was a pretty big ball of *earwax*," said Farley when it was passed to him.

"I've always had a lot of wax," said Mr. Conrad, and shyly nodded his head.

"You made this from your earwax?" asked Mason when it was his turn to view Conrad's creation. He grimaced like it was a turd. "That's bizarre."

"He's got a whole chess set made from it," said Curdmeyer.

Mr. Mason shook his head and handed the matchbox back to its owner. After that they talked about the army, and I lay down on the ground where I'd been sitting.

"At Aberdeen, in basic, there was this lieutenant," said my father. "I was just thinking about him the other day. He was a little skinny Jewish guy with glasses. The sleeves of his uniform came down almost past his fingers. His pants were too big. Everybody laughed at him behind his back and wondered how he'd made rank. Then one day they had us standing in trenches, tossing live grenades. You pulled the pin, waited, and then you had to throw it up over the top of the trench. So one of the guys lobs it, and it hits the lip of the trench and falls back inside. Everybody froze and just stared at the grenade, except for that lieutenant. I'm talking like in less than a second he leaps into the trench, grabs the grenade, and tosses it over the top. Amazing. It exploded in midair, and some of the shrapnel fell into the trench, but no one was hit. From that day on, no one ever gave a shit about how his uniform looked." He punctuated his story with a drag on his cigarette.

Mr. Farley spoke like a sleepwalker. "Our unit was part of the invasion of Normandy. North coast of France. What they called 'the hedgerow.' The Nazis were dug in up high, and there was swamp to one side of us. They had a whole panzer division up there. We made this push that later came to be known as the Breakout at Saint-Lo.

"I can't even begin to describe the slaughter. Not a day goes by without me remembering it." He went quiet, and I thought for a second he'd fallen asleep.

"What happened?" asked Conrad.

Mr. Farley woke from his reverie and said, "The terrain was crazy, and we'd gotten to a point where we had to get word back to the main force. The road was blocked, and they needed a runner to go overland with a message. The colonel picked this skinny kid, he couldn't have been more than seventeen. I still remember his name—Wellington. He was useless as a soldier, but he was fast as hell. They gave him the message and sent him on his way. He ran back across the battlefield we'd just fought through. The message got to where it was going, but Wellington never returned to the unit. Later we found him in a field hospital. Apparently he'd had to run over the dead. It was the only way. Had to step on them as he went, but he got the message through."

"Was he wounded?" asked Mason.

Farley shook his head. "As soon as he delivered the message, he lost his sight. Struck stone blind from what he'd seen."

In the silence that followed, I must have dozed off, because when I came to, Jim had gone inside and the subject had turned to the Yankees. I never cared about baseball, but I knew some of the names. Mr. Farley was talking about a new player, Thurman Munson. He said, "I think he's going to be good. He's got that real determination."

"Yeah," said my father, half asleep.

"I agree," said Curdmeyer, puffing on his pipe.

Mason was silent, but Jake Conrad said, "He doesn't look like him, but he reminds me of that old screwball pitcher the Yankees had."

"From when?" asked Farley.

"Maybe early fifties," said Conrad.

"Are you talking about the Riddler?" Farley said.

"Yeah," said Conrad and laughed.

"Riddley was his name," said Curdmeyer. "He jumped out a hotel window in Cleveland. He was determined, all right. They said he was hooked on pills."

"Scott Riddley," my father said, leaning over to tap my back. "You better go in to bed," he said.

"In a minute," I said, and he didn't insist. The ground had gotten cold, but I was so sleepy that even the mention of Riddley couldn't excite me. "Tell Jim," I reminded myself.

I woke some time later to silence. In the house, the dining-room and kitchen lights had been turned off. Out in the yard, Mr. Farley's chair was empty, and the rest of the men were asleep. Conrad clutched his Dixie cup. Mr. Mason sat straight and was almost snoring. I lay listening to the night, and I think I had a feeling about it like the one Mrs. Grimm told us that people have about church. It started me shivering. I got to my feet and turned toward the house, picturing my bed. Just past the cherry tree, I heard something—a clinking sound from a few backyards over. Maybe the Masons' place?

Was it Ray or Mr. White? I stood there trying to decide whether or not to call my father. Before I could figure it out, Mr. Conrad's big ears had scooped up the sound and he was standing. He went around the circle nudging each of the men and putting his finger to his lips. I returned to them and joined the tight circle they formed.

"Your backyard," Conrad whispered, pointing to Mason. Mason looked toward his house, worried, and adjusted his glasses.

Curdmeyer said, "Two stay here, and two guys go down the block, get around behind him, and flush him this way."

"I'll go," said my father. He turned to me, and I thought he was going to send me in, but instead he said, "Go sit on the front steps, and if you see anyone but us, scream. If he comes after you, run in the house and lock the door."

It was decided that Jake Conrad would go with my father. I followed them as they left the backyard and then split off to take up my position on the front steps. If it was Ray, I knew I'd somehow have to warn him or help him get away. I wished Jim were with me. There was a little ball of energy lodged between my throat and stomach. I couldn't just sit on the steps but instead stood out by the street, looking nervously up and down the block.

I saw my father and Conrad on our side of the street, at the very edge of the glow from the lamp in front of the Hayeses' house. When they stepped off the asphalt and headed across the Masons' front lawn, I lost them to the shadows. Then I waited, trying to quiet my breathing so I could hear better. My heart started going, and I couldn't stand still. I walked across the driveway between the cars and stood at the edge of the Conrads' yard. I thought I heard the sound of change jingle in my father's pocket, but I wasn't sure.

Five seconds later I heard Conrad yell, "Whoa!"

I felt the running in the ground before I saw him. Ray came out of the dark across the Conrads' lawn. Behind him I heard my father say, "Over here!"

"Put your hand out," Ray whispered from the dark.

Just as I did, he went by, leaping over the back of Pop's car in one bound. A second later I realized that there was a folded piece of paper between my fingers. I slipped it into my pocket and watched as my father and Conrad ran past me up the street. I turned and looked up the block, and somehow Curdmeyer and Mason were there just past the Dundens'. Ray made a quick turn into the Dundens' backyard, and Mason, who'd seen what was happening and started running, was right on his heels. I ran to catch up to the action, my father and Conrad already moving across the Dundens' lawn toward their backyard.

Curdmeyer and I got there at the same time. Mason and Conrad and my father were standing in front of the Dundens' shed. As we got closer, Mason put his finger to his lips and pointed. My father leaned over to Curdmeyer and whispered, "He's in there."

The men quietly formed a semicircle around the shed door. Conrad lifted his flashlight but didn't turn it on. Mason motioned for me to open the door. I looked over to my father, and he nodded. My hand was trembling. I grabbed the latch and pulled on it. Conrad hit the flashlight, and I ducked away, not wanting to face what was about to happen.

When I looked again, Mason was standing in the shed with the flashlight, pointing it into one corner after another.

Conrad lit a cigarette. "Houdini," he said.

"I could swear he came in here," said Mason. "I heard the door open and close."

"Okay," said my father, "we lost him, but let's look around the streets a little."

"Did anyone get a look at him?" said Curdmeyer.

"Yeah," said my father. "He's just a kid."

"Did you see his face?"

"No."

"I saw his face," said Mason. "But I've never seen him before."

"You know who he looked like?" said Curdmeyer. "That kid who used to live up the block." He pointed.

"You mean the people who moved before we came in?" said Mason.

"Halloways," said my father. "They've been gone for a while."

"But it *can't* be him," said Conrad.

My father flashed a worried glance in my direction.

"That's right, I forgot," said Curdmeyer.

When we got back out into the street, they decided to break up and walk the block for a little while. I went with my father, and we headed around the corner toward the school. Who knew how late it was? The ordeal at the Dundens' shed had drained me. My father didn't say anything. We got to the school, went through the gates and off onto the field toward Sewer Pipe Hill.

Suddenly he stopped in the middle of the field and cocked his head back. "Look at the stars," he said.

I looked. There were more than I'd ever seen before.

He pointed toward the north. "Do you see the bright one there?" he asked.

I nodded, although I wasn't sure which one he meant.

"The light from that star could have taken a thousand years to reach us. If we could dissect that light and study it, we could see a thousand years into the past. Time travel," he said.

I thought of someone on a planet going around that star, sending me a message. "Likewise," he said, "someone out there is seeing a thousand years ago from here."

"Ten centuries," I said.

"Right. Times tables. Good." He clapped once and said, "Let's go home."

We met Conrad and Mason on Conrad's lawn. My father told them we hadn't seen anyone. They said Curdmeyer had already gone to bed. "Did you guys see anyone?" asked my father. Conrad shook his head, and Mason said, "Just some old guy walking over on Feems Road."

"What'd he look like?" asked my father.

"He was too old. Besides, he was wearing an overcoat and hat. I'd be surprised if the guy could run."

"It's kind of late for a walk," said my father.

"No shit," said Conrad. "I'm going in."

"I've had enough," said Mason.

We headed home.

Before I turned off the light in my room, I checked the note in my pocket. Unfolding it, I read,

WORKING OUT THE TRAP.
WATCH YOUR WINDOW.

I was going to tell Jim, but I was too tired. I fell asleep, looking out at the stars.

Jonah and the Whale

■ We sat in the alley behind the deli on overturned crates, passing a carton of chocolate milk back and forth. Jim had predicted that my father wouldn't return to church. I was so weary from having participated in the night watch, but Jim pumped me with questions, and eventually I told him everything that had happened. I'd already given him the note from Ray.

"Jumped out a window in Cleveland," said Jim, and shook his head.

"When Curdmeyer said the prowler looked like Ray, I almost puked," I said. "But you know what was weird?"

"What?"

"After they'd already said that the Halloways had moved away, Conrad said, 'It can't be him,' like there was some other reason than that they'd moved. And then Curdmeyer said, 'That's right, I forgot.'"

"What d'ya mean?"

"I don't know," I said.

"Yeah, you do," said Jim. "You just don't realize it yet."

"What's he looking for?" I asked.

"I don't know. . . ." He unwrapped a chocolate-chip cookie and held it up like the host again. It broke, and he handed me the smaller part. "The question is, what's he going to do when he finds it?"

When we got home, my mother quizzed us about the sermon. Before I could even blush, Jim, as cool as could be, said, "Jonah and the whale." It was a story we'd learned from Mrs. Grimm.

"What did the priest say about it?" asked my mother.

"Be good or God will swallow you."

Ask the Kid

■ The sun was shining, and I was sitting in Jim's chair, overlooking Botch Town. Mary was standing next to me.

"Can you do that thing with telling me the numbers again?" I asked.

She shook her head.

"Why not?"

"Mickey's leaving," she said.

I wasn't sure what she meant. I turned and looked at her, searching for Mickey. Finally I asked, "Where's he going?"

"Away," she said.

"So?"

"He's got the *numbers*."

"Can *you* still do Botch Town?" I asked.

"Sometimes," she said.

"But not the numbers in my ear?"

"I could try," she said, shaking her head, as if she weren't sure. "Who do you want to see?"

I stood and reached behind the Halloways' house for Ray. Sitting back down, I set the figure in front of me, at the edge of the table. In life Ray was always in motion, even sitting cross-legged by the lantern in his underground camp. In clay he was thin and stiff, standing straight with his arms at his sides. We hadn't really known him, though, when Jim made the Botch

Town version. The figures were only meant to hold the places of the living, but I wondered if in the world of the board, life on the painted Willow Avenue was something different.

Mary started with the numbers, pouring them into my ear like a batch of spaghetti dumped into a colander. The strings of digits swam around inside my head, and I stared hard at the clay Ray. I wanted to know what he was looking for, and I believed that the answer would suddenly evolve into a Technicolor scene before my eyes. For the briefest time, I felt like I wasn't sitting in the chair but actually on the street in Botch Town—and then Mary moved, and I found myself returned to the chair. The second she stopped speaking the numbers, I realized I'd imagined the whole thing.

"No good," said Mary, shaking her head again.

"Never mind," I said.

She mumbled a few words and went over on her side of the curtain. I kept staring at Ray, hoping I'd get something. Before long, though, my glance drifted, looking for Mr. White. I found him lying on his side at the edge of the board up near Hammond, which meant he wasn't close by. I scanned the street, studying the houses and our clay neighbors. Eventually I came to the end of the block at East Lake. When the school came into view, I remembered I had to make the moon for Krapp. It was due the next day. I knew I'd need Jim to help me. I stood up to go see if he was home yet, and just as I reached for the light string, I noticed someone back in the woods standing by the lake. It was Mrs. Edison, her hair fanning out behind her, her thin arms folded over her chest. She was at the very edge of the water, staring out across the sparkled blue.

"Mary," I called.

She came through the curtain.

"How long ago did Mrs. Edison go into the woods?"

"Today," she said.

"When will she be there, outside of Botch Town?"

"I don't know," she said, and turned, going back through the curtain.

I stood looking for another second and then ran upstairs and put on my coat. I got George on the leash, and we went out the door. Once we hit the street, we ran down around the turn toward East Lake. I was breathing heavily, and in my mind I saw Mrs. Edison sitting at her dining-room table staring into a bowl of water. *Maybe Charlie found a way to tell her,* I thought.

It took extra effort for me to venture into the woods. There was still plenty of afternoon left, and it was a nice day, but always lurking at the edge of my thoughts was the fact that Mr. White had been leaving his car at home and Mary seemed to be losing her powers. Halfway up the path, my neck was sore from turning my head so quickly so many times. The occasional sound of a snapping twig made my heart race. George stopped to piss every ten feet, and I let him so he'd be on my side in case Mr. White showed up.

We turned off the path and walked quietly through the low scrub amid the pines. As we neared the lake, we passed through a thicket of oak and I caught a glimpse of the water. Drawing closer to the shore, I saw her. She was no more than ten feet from me. Tall yellow grass sprouted right up to the water's edge. She stood between two pines, her back to me. I could tell she had her arms folded across her chest. Her hair was as crazy as she was. The sight of her stillness overpowered my amazement that she was actually there. From the moment I'd seen her on the board in Botch Town, I'd thought she was going to drown herself.

I dropped the leash, and George took off back through the trees. I ran in the opposite direction to Mrs. Edison's side and made a face my mother would describe as simpering. "My dog got away. Can you help me get him?" I said to her.

She turned her head and looked into my eyes.

"My dog got away, and I have to get him. Can you help me?" I said.

It took a while, like she was waking up, but she smiled and nodded. With her arms still folded, she followed me. I walked through the scrub, and she followed silently, like a ghost. I waited for her at the path and saw George standing a few feet ahead of me. When I took a step in his direction, he bolted.

She joined me, and we walked along together, shoulder to shoulder.

"You were in Charlie's class," said Mrs. Edison. Her voice was calm. She leaned her head toward me but kept her gaze trained on something far ahead.

"Yeah."

"Do you miss him?" she asked.

I told her how Krapp had left Charlie's desk empty so we would remember him all year.

"I think he's in the lake," she said.

I didn't respond.

"He's fallen into the lake," she said. "I can *feel* it."

My throat was suddenly dry, and when I spoke, it came out cracked. "I think they checked the lake."

Abruptly, she stopped walking and opened her arms. I looked up, and it took me a second to realize that she was motioning to George, who stood a few feet away. I crouched down so he wouldn't run. He looked at me and then at Mrs. Edison, whose arms were now open wide. She made a kissing sound, and the dog ran to her. She leaned over and grabbed his leash with one hand while petting him with the other.

"His name is George," I said.

She handed me the leash. "He's a nice dog," she said.

I started walking again toward the school field and hoped she'd follow. She did. We were almost back to Sewer Pipe Hill when she said, "You're going to the junior high school next year."

"I hope so."

When we reached the field, she stopped almost exactly at the same spot my father did to show me the star, and she suddenly put her arms around me. She pulled me to her. Fear and something else ran through me, but I didn't move a muscle. I could feel her ribs and the beat of her heart. A big chunk of a minute passed before she let me go. Then she touched the top of my head and said, "Go home."

I tightened my grip on the leash and ran. At the gate I called back to her and checked to see that she was moving toward the street instead of back to the woods. She was, very slowly. She waved, and I took off.

Even though Krapp's moon needed making, when I got home from the woods, I sat in the corner of the couch and watched the afternoon movie. James Cagney was tap-dancing and singing "I'm a Yankee Doodle Dandy." I escaped into the television and then into myself, huddled in sleep. It was dark when my mother called me to dinner.

Not until the next morning, Thursday, did I remember the moon. I saw its big, creamy face laughing in a star-filled sky just before my father shut the door on his way out to work, waking me. I opened my eyes to the early-morning darkness and felt instant panic shoot through me, straight up from my feet like electricity. Krapp loomed in my thoughts, and he wasn't standing for it.

I went across the hallway and tapped very lightly on Jim's door. There was no answer. "Jim," I whispered. Nothing. I tapped again. Then I heard the springs of his bed, his feet on the floor. He opened the door dressed in his pajama pants. His eyes squinted, and his hair was in a whirl.

"What d'ya want?" he said.

"I forgot to make the moon for Krapp."

A few seconds passed, like he'd fallen back to sleep on his feet. "Is it due today?"

"Yeah."

He smiled and shook his head. "Now you're at my mercy," he said.

"He's gonna kill me if I don't have it."

"You'll be in detention for a week. He'll make you write, five hundred times, 'When Krapp Says Make the Moon, Make It.'"

"I'm begging," I said.

"What time is it?" he asked.

"Dad just left for work."

"Okay," he said. "But later."

"It's going to take a while, isn't it? We should start now."

"I said I'll do it. Go away."

He shut the door, and I heard him roll back into his bed.

I couldn't sit still. I even tried to think of some way to make the moon on my own, but every idea I had vanished as soon as it appeared. What was frustrating was that I could see it clearly, the image from my dream. No matter what else I thought about, it was also there, hovering in the background. I washed and dressed, brushed my teeth and combed my hair. Then I paced back and forth in my room, practicing excuses that I knew had no chance with Krapp.

We had to leave for school by eight o'clock. Mary and I would walk to East Lake, and Jim would catch the bus at the corner across from Barzita's. That morning he didn't get up until seven, and then he decided he needed a shower. I was so mad at him, but I knew not to say anything. He ate his cereal like an old man, lifting the spoon to his mouth as if it weighed ten pounds. He chewed in slow motion, a smile on his face. It was 7:35 by the time he put his bowl and spoon in the sink. We had a little more than maybe fifteen minutes if we hustled. He stretched and yawned.

"Okay," he said, "let's go."

I followed him down the cellar steps. He turned the light on. Then he stood rubbing his chin and his head, saying

"Hmmmmm," like Betty Boop's Pappy. He walked over to the little table next to his chair that held his supply of junk for Botch Town and pushed the mess around with both hands.

The cellar door opened. "What are you guys doing down there?" my mother called.

"I'm looking for my compass for school," he said.

"It's almost quarter of," she said. "You've got to get going soon."

"Be right up," he said.

"The Glory That Was Grease" went through my mind, and I was just about to curse him out when he knelt down and pulled a box from under the table. He opened it, and inside was a plastic bag. After unrolling the plastic, he reached into it and came out with two handfuls of gray clay, the stuff of the inhabitants of Botch Town. He placed the two clumps on the table, rolled back the plastic, and slid the closed box back into its place.

"One moon for Krapp, coming right up," he said, standing, rubbing his hands. He lifted the two hunks of clay and mashed them together. When they were melded into one big piece, he began rolling it, rolling it, rolling it, faster and faster, like he was making a meatball. When it was a perfect sphere, he really went to work on it, pressing into it with his thumb, pinching pieces up, digging with his pinkie nail. I couldn't believe it, but when he was done, holding his creation between his thumb and forefinger at its poles, it really looked like the moon.

"There you go," he said. "Krapp'll never be the same."

"How will I carry it without wrecking it?" I said.

"Easy," he said, and looked down, surveying his junk collection again. He reached in and pulled out an old wooden Popsicle stick and stuck it into the bottom of my moon. "Moonsicle," he said, holding it out to me. "I should sell the idea to Softee."

"Hurry up," my mother called from the cellar door. Jim ran

up the steps, and I followed more slowly, holding the moon in front of me like one of Mrs. Grimm's candy apples.

My mother had already gone out to her car. Mary had her coat on and was waiting for me by the front door.

"What's that?" she asked, pointing.

"The moon," said Jim. He brushed past us and left. "It looks great, doesn't it?" he called back from the front steps.

I'd gotten my arm into one sleeve of my jacket, but as I switched hands with the moon to get the other in, I banged the soft clay against the banister. There was a small dent where it had hit, which I felt like a wound in my side.

All the way to school, kids laughed at my moonsicle and flaunted their own huge creations of baked and painted plaster or papier-mâché balloons. Still, I held that stick carefully, not letting the weight of the clay ball topple it from my grip. It was the only thing standing between me and Krapp.

I got to Krapp's room and was heading for the coat closet when someone gave my elbow a shove. My arm flew straight out, but I held tight. Unfortunately, the moon didn't. It flew three feet through the air and then landed with a plop on the floor. I wanted to turn and see who'd hit me, but just then Hodges Stamper was backing away from the closet. I heard Hinkley laughing as I lunged for the clay. Too late. Without realizing it, Stamper stamped one half of it into a pancake with his heel. I considered just kicking it into the dark part of the coat closet, but then Krapp called for us to take our seats. With one good jab, I skewered the mess that was my moon.

Everybody had a moon project on his or her desk, and each was more amazing than the next. Pat Trepedino's could actually have *been* the moon. I just sat there holding my stick. Krapp started his inspection, up and down the aisles. He made no comment as he went. You could hear him sniffing like a bloodhound for failure. Finally he got to me, and he looked down at the thing I held in my hand. I stared up at him.

"It got stepped on," I said. I darted a glance up the next row and saw Hinkley smile.

Krapp leaned over and, extending his thumb and forefinger, clasped the wooden stick, relieving me of the weight of my flattened moon. Once it was in his hand, he walked up to his desk and dropped it into the trash. It hit with a clunk, and I could feel the other kids wanting to laugh.

He said nothing. Then the other kids were called one at a time to the front of the room to explain how they had made their moons. Only once, when Mitchell Erikson told how his was molded out of Plasticine and how he and his father shot it with BBs to make the craters authentic, did Krapp look over at me and sigh. After the last bell of the day sounded, as I was slinking toward the coat closet, he called me up to his desk.

He waited until the last of the kids was out of the room and said, "Your moon was pathetic. You have till tomorrow to make me a real moon."

I nodded.

"And it better not come on a stick," he added.

Mary was waiting for me outside the school. I told her to hurry, and I walked as fast as I could, breaking into a run when we got to the Masons' lawn. Inside the house I ditched my book bag on the couch and headed for Nan and Pop's door. I didn't even say hello before I told them that I needed plaster.

"What for?" asked Nan, looking up from her latest paint-by-number.

"I have to make the moon."

"You're going to make the moon out of plaster?" said Pop, and he laughed.

"It's for school, and I have to do it today."

Nan looked over at Pop and said, "Go get him some plaster."

Pop put out his cigarette and said, "Yes, Your Highness."

He got dressed in his baggy pants and a button-down shirt, and off we went in the blue Impala. At the hardware store, the guy behind the counter asked, "What do you need it for?"

Pop said, "Ask the kid," as he pulled some bills from his pocket.

"I don't have to ask the kid," said the guy, and he laughed loud. "Making the moon, right?"

Pop just held out his hand for the change.

"I've sold ten boxes of plaster this week."

We left, and as we were passing through the door, Pop said, "Dimwit," and I wasn't sure if he meant me or the hardware guy.

On the way home, he pulled in to the parking lot shared by the deli and Mr. Pizza and the drugstore. He killed the engine.

"Here," he said. "Go into the deli and get a quart of skim milk." He handed me a dollar. "I'm going up to the drugstore to get my prescription. I'll meet you back here in a couple of minutes."

"Can I get a piece of bubble gum?"

"Sure," he said. "Get one for the other kids, too."

I took the money, nodded, and we got out of the car. Pop headed down toward the pharmacy, and I went into the deli. The deli always smelled like a holiday. Rudy, the little German guy who owned it, always wore a white apron. He cooked and prepared everything he sold right in the back of the store—potato salad, coleslaw, meatballs, roast turkey, pot roast, dumplings. It was all displayed on a field of greenery beneath a length of glass curved like the windshield of a car. I slid open the door of the cold case and grabbed a bottle of milk. Rudy asked how my parents were, and I told him, "Fine," as I dug three pieces of Bazooka out of a plastic bucket next to the cash register.

"And you are being good?" he said, smiling.

I nodded, pocketed two pieces of the gum, and took the change. As I left, he called, "Tell your mother I have fish cakes."

Out on the sidewalk, I held the bottle of milk under my arm as I worked to open my piece of Bazooka. I shoved the pink rectangle into my mouth. It took some strong tooth work to turn the little rock into something pliable. While I went at it, I read the tiny comic it came wrapped in. Bazooka Joe, a kid with an eye patch and a baseball hat, and his friend Mort, who wore the collar of his red sweater up over his mouth, were standing next to a rocket ship. Neither the jokes nor the fortunes printed beneath the comics ever made any sense, but I read them anyway, getting my full penny's worth.

As I shoved the crumpled comic into my pants pocket, I felt a hand close around my elbow and a large body push against me. At first I thought it was Pop, but he'd just have called my name. I looked up and realized I was being pushed to the edge of the sidewalk, toward the alley that ran between a high chain-link fence and the wall of the deli. Turning my head, all I saw was a flap of white material.

We turned into the alley. "Move your ass," Mr. White said, a bead of spit hitting my cheek. The thought that at any second he might snap my neck made me go slack, and I dropped the milk bottle. I heard it crash against the asphalt, and when it did, Mr. White shoved me harder, and the wad of Bazooka shot out of my mouth. That woke me up, and I started struggling. But he held on tight, his grip ice cold, and pressed me up against the wall. I tried to scream, but he leaned in next to me, his sour breath in my nose. My throat closed. I pushed off the wall, and he pushed me, and I hit the back of my head against the concrete. Things got woozy, and all of a sudden my arms and legs started to tingle.

Then Mr. White spun away from me, and I saw Pop behind him in the alley.

"What the hell d'ya think you're doing?" Pop yelled.

Mr. White brought his arm up, striking like a cobra, and his fingers squeezed into Pop's left shoulder. Pop grunted once and his knees buckled slightly, but at the same time he swung with his free right hand, a perfect punch straight out of Jamaica

Arena. It hit Mr. White square on the left temple, so hard his hat was knocked sideways, pushing White back two steps, his overcoat flapping. With that momentum he turned and ran down the alley like a spider on his long legs, his shoes clicking on the pavement, his hand clamped to the hat to hold it on. In a blink he was gone around behind the stores.

By that time I was crying, and Pop pulled me into a hug. The broken milk bottle crunched beneath our feet as we left the alley. He led me back to the car and opened the door for me. He got in behind the wheel and put the key in the ignition. "We're gonna get that son of a bitch," he said, rubbing his shoulder. He backed the car out. Next thing I knew, we were parked at the police station.

We sat at a table in a wood-paneled room. There was an American flag on a stand in the corner, and a framed portrait of President Johnson on the wall. A cop sat across from us, pen in hand, taking down what Pop told him. Every once in a while, when he stopped writing to ask a question, the cop wiggled in his seat, full of what I guessed was excitement.

"Have you ever seen this man before?" he asked, and I realized he was talking to me.

"Ever see him?" Pop asked.

I nodded.

"Where'd you see him?" said the cop.

"He was a janitor in our school for a couple of days."

"Boris? At East Lake?" the cop asked.

"When Boris was gone," I said. "His name is Lou."

"I'll have to get some information from the school, and then we can put out an APB," he said to Pop, as if I weren't there.

"I know where he lives," I said.

The cop looked over at me. "Really? Where?"

"Around behind the stores."

"Can you take me there now?"

I nodded.

Pop and I sat in the back of the police car, and the cop drove. We parked outside Mr. White's house. "There's another car on the way. When they get here, tell them I went inside." He drew his gun and held it pointing straight up, checking it. "Stay in the car," he said, looking at us through the rearview mirror, and then he opened his door and went around the side of the house toward the back.

"Dick Tracy," said Pop. He lit a cigarette. "How did you know where this guy lives?" he asked.

I was thinking of being locked inside the freezer in the garage. "A kid in school who lives over here told me."

He took a drag on his butt and considered what I'd told him. "How are you doing?" he asked.

I nodded yet again but didn't say anything.

"Well, my shoulder hurts like hell where he grabbed me. Must have been some kind of pressure point or something."

Another black-and-white car with two cops in it passed by and pulled over to park in front of us. Pop got out and told them that the first cop had gone inside. They drew their guns and went around back. I kept listening for gunshots and death screams, but the day was perfectly blue and calm. The new leaves of the trees around the house rustled quietly.

"I don't know why I went to look for you down that alley," Pop said. "Another couple of minutes and you could have been gone."

"Chimto," I said.

"That dog doesn't miss a trick."

The cops returned a few minutes later. Our officer, his gun back in his holster, got into the car and said, "He's cleared out. Looks like whoever was there threw stuff together quickly. We might've just missed him. We'll tell the school to warn the kids, and we'll run it in the newspaper. Even if he crosses state lines, we'll get him."

Back at the police station I told them what Mr. White's car

looked like, but I was afraid to say any more. Pop called home to let Nan know what had happened. By the time we passed through the front door of the house, my mother was home. She was waiting for me. As soon as I saw her, I started crying again, and she put her arms around me. "It's okay," she said. "You're okay."

Time of the Season

■ And then the Shadow Year rolled on. The thought of Mr. White fleeing town with the police on his tail assured us it was over. We left Botch Town to its own devices and all slept better. Jim took the money he'd saved from birthdays and holidays and bought an old guitar. Mary suddenly stopped figuring the horses and spent more time outside with her new real friend, Emily, from Cuthbert Road. The girl was tall and skinny, with a big nose and long hair that covered her face. She and Mary smoked roll-ups back behind the forsythia. Their favorite song was "Time of the Season."

The only reminder I had of my near abduction was when I saw Pop rub his shoulder where Mr. White had grabbed him. He told me one afternoon, "That guy put the touch on me." Still, that was enough of a reminder so that I never went anywhere alone. I spent my free time writing my own version of Perno Shell's last adventure, and I avoided having to make the moon. My mother called Cleary and told him I had to take it easy for the rest of the school year and that I was going to pass to the next grade no matter what. Cleary didn't argue.

On the final day of school, fifteen minutes before the last bell rang, Krapp got out of his chair and stepped to the front of the room. We were eating cupcakes with sprinkles and drinking soda brought in by Pat Trepedino's mother. The kids were all talking and milling around the warm classroom.

"Well, we had a good year," said Krapp. I think I was the only one paying attention to him. "I hope you remember your lessons and that you all enjoy the junior high," he said, speaking to the back wall. He looked around and then returned to his desk. When the bell rang, there was a loud cheer from all over the school. I was slow gathering my things. I didn't want to leave East Lake in the wild rush to summer but rather to walk one last time down the quiet hallways.

Leaving the classroom, I turned and said good-bye to Krapp. He looked up at me, waved with a flick of his pencil, and went back to his work. As I passed through the door into the hall, his chair tipped back, and just like that, he fell slowly into my past. The halls were as quiet as the night I had roamed them with Jim and Ray. I caught a whiff of the library, the hot dogs and beans from lunch, and, always, the red stuff. My report card, though far from good, showed that I had graduated from the Retard Factory. I went through the open front doors, and summer was there to meet me—a warm breeze, a blue sky, someone mowing a lawn somewhere. Mary was waiting, and we'd never walked home so slowly.

That night I was in the cellar looking for the basketball when I heard Mrs. Harkmar, like Krapp, addressing her last class.

"You all did very good," she said. "Mickey, you were the best. Sally, you did good. Sandy, you'll have to go to summer school, but don't cry." She whapped the desktop with her ruler. "Mickey's moving away, so let's give him a round of applause." There was the sound of clapping. "I'm retiring," she said. "I won't see you again." These last words were spoken in Mary's, not Mrs. Harkmar's, voice. I went back to looking for the basketball and found it under the supply table. As I was heading for the stairs, I heard one more thing. There came a quick

"Yay!" in Mickey's voice, and I figured school had just let out.

On the first weekend night he had free, my father cooked his meal of many meats out on the backyard grill. Hamburgers and hot dogs, chicken and sausage. There was potato salad from Rudy's. We all sat, Nan and Pop included, at the picnic table, and feasted off grease-stained paper plates. Afterward, in the dark, we kids cooked marshmallows over gray coals that glowed orange from within when you tapped them. The adults sat at the table and drank and smoked and talked. A few houses down, a transistor radio was playing "There's a Kind of Hush" by Herman's Hermits.

This Is Cool

■ One night my mother didn't drink. She didn't drink the following night either, or the next. For the first few days of this new routine, she'd go to bed directly after dinner. Losing the wine made her look older and very tired. On the fourth night, she seemed to have awoken, smiling and talking at dinner. There was no mention of Bermuda. Maybe that's where her anger had gone. She took out her guitar and showed Jim a few things she knew about frets and charts. From that point on, the summer got so light it was like a dream. Days were both long and brief, if that makes any sense. I forgot if it was Monday or Thursday. We played basketball over at East Lake, swam in the neighbors' pools, read about Nick Fury and His Howling Commandos, stayed out late, and captured fireflies in mayonnaise jars. I kept away from the woods and in that way managed to forget about Charlie for the most part.

That light time lasted a month or so, and today I'm not sure it ever happened. Then one evening my mother came home from work, toting a half gallon of Taylor Cream Sherry. "Oh, no," Jim whispered when he saw it sitting on the kitchen counter. The late sun was shining through the window, and its rays illuminated the wine. It glowed a beautiful red-amber, and the sight of it made me instantly weak. Dinner was late, it had already grown dark, but none of us kids said a word. Before we'd gotten to the table, my mother had already had quite a few glasses. She sat smoking, her eyes nearly closed.

"Why so quiet?" she finally said, and her voice had an edge to it.

I stared into my soup.

"Look at me," she said. I looked up and saw Jim and Mary do the same. "What's your problem?"

I shook my head, and Jim said, "No problem." I was going to return my gaze to the soup, but I saw something move outside the darkened window behind her. Mary actually jumped in her seat, but my mother was too drunk to catch it. I can't believe I didn't cry out, but there was Ray's face at the glass. He was smiling and holding two fingers up behind my mother's head to make it look like she had devil's horns. Jim couldn't help himself; he smiled. My mother looked at him and said, "Are you laughing at me?"

"No," he said. "I was thinking about this kid in school who could put his whole hand in his mouth up to his wrist. You know that kid?" he said to me.

"Yeah," I said, nodding, but I wasn't sure which one he meant.

Ray motioned to us and then pointed his finger down. He ducked out of sight, and a few seconds later I heard the slightest noise coming from the basement window well next to the back steps. When my mother closed her eyes, Jim looked over at me and smiled. Mary pointed to the floor with the pinkie of the hand holding her spoon.

After dinner we helped clean up, and then my mother headed for the couch to pass out. We each went to our rooms and waited. We'd not seen or heard anything from Ray since the night-watch night when he'd given me the note. There hadn't even been any reports of the prowler. For some reason I'd never really wondered what had happened to him. It was like he'd vanished once the weight of Mr. White had been lifted. Ten minutes after I'd closed the door of my room, Jim was whispering up the stairs for me. I tiptoed down and found him and Mary waiting by the cellar door. My mother was out on the couch, and the sight of her reminded me momentarily of the guitar lesson she'd given Jim. Down we went, laying each foot carefully on the creaky wooden steps. One of the back windows was open and latched up on its hook in the ceiling. The sun was on over Botch Town. Ray sat in Jim's chair, staring out over the cardboard roofs. He turned when we came toward him, and he smiled.

"This is cool," he said, nodding toward the board.

We introduced Mary to Ray and he shook her hand, which made her smile. Jim told Ray about building the town, and Ray kept looking at it, moving his gaze up and down the block.

"He made it out of junk," I said.

"Yeah," said Jim, laughing.

Ray lifted up the figure of Mrs. Harrington to get a better look. He turned her around and smiled at what he saw. Placing her carefully back in front of her house, he turned to us and said, "The white guy was outside your house all last night."

"But the cops told us he was gone," I said.

"You talked to the cops about him?" he asked.

I told him what had happened in the alley next to the store, how Pop had saved me, and all I'd said to the police. "They're after him," I said.

He moved the chair around to face the three of us. "I'm telling you, he was parked outside on the street right here last night. I watched him to make sure he wasn't going to try something."

"Did you make a plan?" asked Jim.

Ray nodded. "I've got something good. Tomorrow night, you two"—he pointed to me and Jim—"sneak out and lead him over to the school. I'm betting he'll be around. It seems now he's after someone in your house. I'll be waiting at the school. You've got to get there a little before him and run around back. I'll leave a ladder for you. Climb it, and I'll be on the roof. When White shows up, we yell at him from the roof. He'll find his way to the ladder, which once he climbs will put him right near the opening to the courtyard. The minute he steps toward that side of the roof, I'll run into him and knock him into it."

"He'll be stuck," I said.

"Right, and either they'll find him there the next day and call the cops or he'll try to break a window and the cops'll come. Then we'll be rid of him for good." He stood up. "Can you do that?" he asked, moving toward the back window.

I shook my head no, but Jim said, "I'll do it."

"Good," said Ray. "I'll be waiting for you." He reached for the edge of the window frame with both hands, got a good hold, and then pulled his body up in one graceful motion. Like a snake, he slithered through the opening and was gone. We stood quietly for a minute, and then Jim pulled his chair over to the window. He stood on it, unhooked the window from the ceiling, and held it while it swung closed.

"Do you think Mr. White was really out there?" I asked.

Jim brought his chair back to Botch Town and sat down. He picked up the white car, which had lain idle by Hammond for months. He blew dust off it and rubbed it clean with his thumb. "What about it?" he said, turning to Mary.

"I can't tell," she said, and suddenly she looked older to me, like she'd grown up overnight. There was nothing Mickey about her.

We'd never even looked later on to see if the white car was at the curb, and the next day Jim didn't say a word to me about Ray. I made sure not to mention him either. As afternoon turned into evening, I started to wonder if he'd really go by himself, but the night crept by, and eventually he fell asleep on the couch watching television. When my mother told me to wake him to go to bed, he made like he was in a daze, but I knew he was faking it. I avoided looking out the front window into the dark and made sure the front door was locked when I went up.

During the following days, we devoted ourselves to summer vacation with the same crazy energy my mother had given to Mount Kilimanjaro. A week went by, and my concern that no one had gone to see Ray began to fade. Still, I listened at night to hear if Jim was sneaking out, but there was only silence. I never mentioned it to him, because I myself was too scared to go, so I had no right to mention it. Always some small part of me expected a face at every window, but I shoved that to the back of my mind and ran harder, swam faster, and thought more deeply when I wrote, in order to fall straight to sleep at night.

Last Chance

■ A week after Ray's visit, I was sitting up late watching *Chiller Theatre* on TV with the sound turned way down. That day Pop and Nan had taken us kids to the shore, and we got to swim in the ocean until Pop's shoulder started bothering him too much. I was sunburned and had that shivering tiredness that came only from the beach. My mother had already gone in to bed, and my eyes were slowly closing. I could hear Jim upstairs, strumming his guitar. The front door was open, and a breeze wafted through the screen. On the tube there were brain eaters from outer space.

The phone rang in the kitchen, startling me. It rang again, and I leaped out of the recliner and went to answer it. I picked it up, expecting to hear my father saying that he had to work another shift, but when I said "Hello," all I heard was breathing.

"Hello," I said again.

There was more breathing, and then a voice said, "Last chance."

"Who is it?" I asked.

"You know," said the voice. I stood frozen, listening, but then the breathing was gone, and all I heard was a dial tone.

Jim came into the kitchen as I was hanging up. "Who was that?" he said.

"I'm not sure," I told him. "It might have been Mr. White."

"What did he say?"

"Last chance."

"Last chance for what?" said Jim.

I shrugged. "It might have been Mr. White, but now that I think of it, it might have been Ray. I don't know. It could have been anybody."

Jim went into the living room and closed and locked the front door. He walked over to the front window and pushed the curtains aside to look.

"Is he there?" I asked.

"I don't see him."

We stayed up late, watching show after show until we heard my father's car pull in and his steps on the path. We took off like a shot and were up the stairs and in our beds before he opened the door. With him home I felt safe enough to go to sleep, but instead I listened to that voice in my memory repeat its message. Half the time it was Ray, and the other half it was Mr. White—his face in front of mine, my back against the wall. I took the second image into sleep with me, and my muscles tensed, my legs jerked.

I came awake to George growling. I'd kicked him.

Treachery

■ The phone call spooked me, and I didn't want to leave the house, but a couple of days later Jim heard about a new development going up over by the Sullivans'. Part of the woods was being knocked down so construction could start.

"There's a hundred hills of dirt swarmed by flying grasshoppers."

"Who told you?" I asked.

"Tony Calfano. I saw him outside the candy store."

"He's back?"

"I asked him what happened to him for shooting up the school, and he told me he had to go to court, and then all these people asked him a million times why he did it. He said he has to go every week to a head doctor."

"Is he crazy?"

Jim shrugged. "What about the grasshoppers? I want to go see them."

"I don't know," I said.

"It's daylight."

"When Mr. White grabbed me, it was daylight."

He finally convinced me by saying we would take our bikes and not stay long. We crossed the school yard on our way there. The sun was blazing hot. We waved to Chris Hackett and his brother playing catch in a heat mirage way across the field. The rows of houses we passed into were old and tall, with wooden front porches and columns. Jim led me on, pedaling at top speed, and we made so many turns I wondered if he even knew where he was going. Finally he stopped at a corner and waited for me to catch up. He was panting worse than I was.

"We should've been there by now," said Jim.

"What did he tell you?"

"I went the way he told me. Maybe he lied."

"He told you he was crazy," I said.

Jim was quiet for a second and then shook his head and said, "That kid never lies. I'm gonna keep looking for a while. Are you going home?"

He knew I was too afraid to go by myself. "Just a little more," I said.

He started out, pedaling more slowly than before. I followed. We traveled three long streets that wound around and into each other. We made two left-hand turns and a right before we caught sight of the woods back behind a house.

"There it is," said Jim, and I looked up toward the end of the street past the last houses. It looked as if God had taken a bite out of the woods. There was a wide expanse of hard-packed dirt formed into hills from four feet to seven feet tall and covered by a boiling shadow. Chirping and flapping mixed together into a buzz that rose and fell in a single note.

Jim made it to the edge of the hills before me. He was putting his kickstand down as I rolled up. "Look at this place," he said. A gray grasshopper three inches long landed on the sleeve of his T-shirt. He laughed and flicked it away. "Come on." He headed up the closest hill and disappeared over the top. I got off my bike and set the stand. Before I followed him, I looked back up the street. It was empty.

Over the hill and into the bugs I charged. I could feel them hitting against me, landing on my skin, battering my head, but they didn't hurt. It was like being in a living blizzard. When I got to the top of the next hill, I saw Jim through the cloud, standing in the distance on a tall hilltop. He was holding a long, flat board and was swinging to beat the band. I headed toward him. On the way there, in a valley between the hills, I found stacked-up sections of an old picket fence crawling with grasshoppers. I grabbed one of the slats, instantly getting a splinter at the base of my thumb. I ignored it in my rush to reach Jim. I had to go over three more hills and then trudge up the steep one he was on. When he saw me coming, he started laughing. "Treachery," he said, and swung twice as hard. I scrabbled the rest of the way up and joined him.

We fought back-to-back, like in the movie where Jason and his men duel with living skeletons. Every pass of the slat brought the sound of a dozen tiny pops. The dead and injured fell to the dirt with broken wings and severed sections that continued to flap and crawl. In the middle of my third swing, I finally felt how exhausted I was after running and riding so far in the heat. I tried to lift the plank again, but I couldn't. I dropped it and bent over to catch my breath.

"Let's get out of here," said Jim. He dropped his bat, too, and jumped halfway down the hill. He waited for me at the bottom. "It's so hot I can hardly breathe," he said. I was too weary to do anything but nod. By the time we got back to our bikes, the insects had become a horror, and I worried I might pass out and they'd eat me where I fell.

We got on our bikes and didn't look back. So slowly, pedaling four times and then gliding till the glide was nearly gone, we made it to East Lake. Just inside the northern gate, we followed the fence out along the boundary. There was a huge maple tree in a backyard whose branches hung over the chain link, making a pool of shade on the field.

We didn't even bother with the kickstands but just let the bikes drop on the ground. Jim stepped into the shade, let himself fall, and then rolled onto his back. It was such a relief to step out of the sun. I knew what it was like now for the neighbors of Botch Town when we'd leave the sun burning all night. I lay down a few feet from Jim and looked up through the tree branches. The five-pointed leaves were red, and in the distance, through their maze, I saw a triangle of blue sky.

"What about those grasshoppers?" he said. "That was the stupidest thing."

"What was happening there?" I asked.

He laughed.

"You were right about Calfano," I said.

"I told you," he said. "Remember you said Calfano was crazy?"

"Yeah."

"I was thinking that the dirt mounds and the grasshoppers is what it's like inside a crazy person's head."

"Mr. Rogers?" I said.

"He had so many grasshoppers they ate his brain."

"Krapp?"

"Krapp craps grasshoppers."

"We know a lot of crazy people," I said.

Jim rolled onto his side, and I turned my head to look at him. He had a piece of grass in his mouth. "Mom's crazy when she gets loaded," he said.

I nodded.

"They're all a little crazy," said Jim.

"What about us?" I asked.

He didn't answer. Instead he said, "You know what I think?"

"What?"

"I don't think Mr. White is after Mary. I think he's after Mom."

"Why?"

"Because she's weak," he said.

I turned back to the triangle of blue and the shifting leaves.

Jim didn't say anything else about his theory. Some time passed, and then he announced, "I'm gonna teach George to dance."

"How?" I asked.

"By holding food over his head and making him spin on his back legs. I saw it on TV. At first you use a lot of food, and then you make it less and less until you don't even need any food, and all you have to do is whistle and they get up and start dancing."

"I saw a thing on TV," I said, "about a kid who was ten years old but he had a disease that aged him to ninety. He looked like a weird little leprechaun."

"Was he magically delicious?" asked Jim.

We got back onto our bikes and went home. I dozed off on the couch in the stillness of the afternoon and slept so hard I drooled.

The Splinter

■ That night after dinner, my mother, already slurring her words, decided to operate on my splinter. She had Mary run and get her a sewing needle. She called me into the living room and told me to sit next to her at the table. I already regretted having told her about my thumb. My mother put on her reading glasses so they perched at the end of her nose. Taking my hand in both of hers, she turned it palm up. There was an inch-and-a-half-long red line at the bottom of my thumb, and at the tip the darkness of the splinter's wood showed through a thin layer of skin.

"That's a bad one," she said.

Mary brought the needle.

"Will you need a sheet for the blood?" asked Jim.

My mother told him to shut up. She took the needle, lit a match, and then ran the silver tip back and forth through the flame till it turned orange. To cool it she shook it like a thermometer.

She grabbed me by the wrist and drew my palm closer to her. The hand that held the blackened needle wobbled as it descended. I took a deep breath and closed my eyes. I didn't feel pain, only pricking. She picked at my skin with the tip of the needle so many times it went numb. A few moments later a sharp ache blossomed through the numbness. I took another deep breath.

She stopped and told Mary, "Tweezer."

Mary ran to the bathroom and quickly returned. I opened one eye and hazarded a peek. My mother spent a few seconds aiming the silver pincers, and then she lunged. Squeezing my eyes shut again, I couldn't see what she was doing, but right at the center of the splinter's dull ache I felt something sliding. She drew the entire thing out, a long gray shard of wood, and held it up to the light.

"Open your eyes." She smacked me playfully. "Look at the size of that," she said.

"Treachery," said Jim.

Two seconds later the door opened, and Nan was standing there. "Gert," she said to my mother. "We have to take your father to the hospital."

"Is his arm bad again?" asked my mother.

"Pains all up and down it, and he's pale and sweaty."

"Let me just get my coat," said my mother. Nan went home to get ready. When my mother stood, she weaved slightly, steadying herself by touching her fingertips to the table.

"Can you drive?" asked Jim.

"Of course," she said, and straightened up.

Nan came back through the door, leading Pop. His right hand gripped his left bicep. He looked sad and so tired. None of us kids said anything. My mother went to his other side, and they led him slowly out the front and down the steps. We followed.

At one point, on the way to the car, his knees buckled slightly, and they had to hold him up. They got him into the car, and my mother got behind the wheel. Looking at us through the car window, she said, "I don't know how long this is going to take. Jim's in charge. Your father will be home around midnight. I'll call you as soon as I can and let you know how long we'll be. Be good."

The car backed out of the driveway, and I tracked the taillights all the way up the dark street. It was a warm and blustery night. I turned toward the house. Jim and Mary had already gone inside.

They were sitting on either end of the couch with George between them. Jim looked over at me as I came through the door and said, "I'm in charge. I could make you both go to bed right now."

Mary, whose legs were curled beneath her, never looked away from the television but said, "Shove it."

Jim laughed.

"What's this?" I said, nodding at the TV as I sat in my mother's rocker.

"I can't believe it after today," said Jim, "but it's about a grasshopper that gets too close to an atomic explosion and turns giant."

We watched it, but Jim was wrong—it wasn't a grasshopper, it was a praying mantis. When the show was over, Jim went into the kitchen and brought us out two cookies each. Mary found a war movie on the tube. A tank rolled over a guy's arm.

About halfway through it, right after a scene where a soldier throws a grenade into a foxhole full of Germans and gets killed, I started wondering how Pop was doing and if they'd made it to the hospital with my mother driving.

"What do you think's happening?" I said to Jim.

"Colonel Candyass just blew up a bunch of krauts," he said.

"No, with Pop."

"I don't know," he said.

"Mom didn't look good."

"They'll probably wind up in the bay with her driving," said Jim.

"No they won't," said Mary.

Ten minutes later the commercial for Ajax Liquid, which supposedly cleaned your kitchen floor like a white tornado, came on, and the combination of cleaning fluid and the whiteness of the animated twister made me think of Mr. White. Jim and I looked at each other at the exact same moment. He jumped up from the couch and turned off the television. I sat forward on the rocker. Mary looked from one of us to the other.

"Get the front door," said Jim as he ran through the kitchen to lock the back one.

"Mr. White?" asked Mary.

I nodded. Jim came back into the living room and stood still, cocking his head to the side as if trying to hear something. I went and checked the front window for the white car.

"It's not there," I said.

"Mr. White moved in Botch Town today," said Mary.

"I thought you couldn't do that anymore," said Jim.

"I was down there this afternoon, and I saw his white car, and the numbers came all of a sudden," she said.

We ran down into the cellar. Jim lit the sun. There was the white car parked in front of our house. "Why didn't you tell us?" Jim said to Mary.

"I thought we were all forgetting about it," said Mary.

"Are you kidding?" he said. He told me to go over on the other side of the cellar to Pop's workbench and get the flashlight and the hatchet. "I'm going up to get George," he said.

George was confused at being on the leash in the cellar, so Jim let him off. The dog went around sniffing at everything. "He's gonna pee," said Mary, and the moment she said that, the lights went out.

"Give me the flashlight," Jim whispered. "I knew he'd turn off the lights. I bet the phone's out, too."

"He's coming?" I said.

"Look," said Jim, switching the flashlight on, "when he gets to the cellar steps, we go out the back window like Ray did." He picked up his Botch Town chair and carried it over to the back wall. Stepping up onto the seat, he handed the flashlight to me and said, "Aim it up here."

I did. He latched the window to the hook on the ceiling. The night came through the opening. He stepped down and told Mary to get up on the chair. "You stay there, and when I tell you to go, pull yourself up through the window into the back-yard." He shone the flashlight on me. "You help her," he said to me. "Then you go through."

I said, "Okay," but I doubted whether I could manage to pull myself up.

Mary got on the chair and reached her hands up to grab the bottom of the windowsill. "I can do it," she said.

"When I tell you, you gotta go fast," he said. "And the min-ute you get outside, start running for the school. Don't wait for us. We'll catch up."

We stood in the dark and waited. Upstairs, the phone started ringing. Jim told us to ignore it, that it was a trick to get us upstairs. He held the flashlight pointed at the cellar steps and, in his opposite hand, the hatchet.

I was shaking, remembering that Mr. White had the power of total silence. Out of nowhere a plan came to me, and I whis-pered it to Jim: "We should get the extreme-unction box and open it in front of him, like Dracula and the cross."

"Forget it," said Jim.

Right after that I heard George give a low growl. His nails tapped across the concrete floor as he circled. It was quiet for a half a minute, and then he growled again.

"He's here," said Mary, and Jim turned off the flashlight. In the silence we could hear someone messing around with the lock on the front doorknob.

I don't know how many minutes passed before we heard the front door upstairs groan open, but in that time I wished I'd told my father everything back when I'd found Charlie. I was too scared to cry. The flashlight suddenly cut through the dark-ness and lit a pale hand sliding down the banister of the cellar steps. It was perfectly quiet, and we watched Mr. White descend as if he were floating. George started barking.

"Go, Mary," Jim said.

I reached up and grabbed for her legs. She was already halfway through when my arms closed around them and I pushed up. I looked back into the light and saw the face and hat, lit like in the photo. He was coming toward us.

"Get him, George!" Jim yelled. The dog lunged forward, and although I couldn't see anything, I could tell from the sounds that he was biting Mr. White's shoes and ankles.

"Go," said Jim, his voice trembling.

I got up on the chair and grabbed the sill. As I jumped, I hit my head on the ceiling but held on, ducked, and went through the opening. Mary was there. She reached down into the well and pulled my arm. Before I got my feet through, I heard George give a sharp cry, followed by the sound of metal hitting concrete. Jim had thrown the hatchet.

"Come back here," said Mr. White in a cold, quiet voice.

I was out. I had Mary by the hand, and we were running. Out of the backyard, under the mimosa on Nan's side, to the street, where we headed for East Lake. I could taste the adrenaline, and my heart was pounding. Mary kept up with me, and we flew past the front lawns. As we ran, I kept listening for Jim, turning my head to glimpse behind us. When we reached the Manginis', I stopped and turned around.

"Don't stop!" Jim yelled from two lawns behind us, and I was so relieved to hear his voice. We turned and ran, and before we made it to Mrs. Grimm's, he passed us and led the way. Headlights flooded the road from behind.

We ran harder. I could hear the engine of the white car and the sound of its tires on the gravel. We flew past the school gate and onto the field, heading for the side of the building.

"Hurry!" called a distant voice that wasn't Jim's.

I looked up and saw Ray's silhouette on the roof. He was waving both his arms over his head. In that moment, although my heart was pounding and I could hardly catch a breath, it struck me as odd how perfectly the plan was working. How could Ray have known we were coming? As we passed the kindergarten playground and headed for the back of the building, I turned and saw that Mr. White had parked in the bus circle and was getting out of his car.

We saw the shadow of the ladder leaning up to the roof of the school. Ray stood above us, whispering, "Hurry."

Jim made Mary go up first and me after her. I'd always been afraid of heights, but at that moment I didn't even think of it. What I did think of was the fact that we were climbing Pop's extension ladder. Ray grabbed us as we got close to the top and helped us up the last few rungs.

"I've been waiting all summer for you," he said to Jim as my brother reached the roof.

"We couldn't get out," said Jim.

All of us leaned over the side of the school and watched Mr. White come slowly around the back corner. When he got close enough, Ray picked up a pebble and threw it at him.

"Okay, he sees us," said Ray. "Let's get in place."

We backed away from the edge. "You guys go over there toward the gym," he said. "If I get him into the courtyard, we'll just go back down the ladder, but if anything goes wrong, we'll have to climb the wall ladder up to the top of the gym. It's bolted to the wall over there, in the shadows."

"What do we do now?" asked Jim.

"When he comes up on the roof, you guys jump up and down and make noise to distract him. I'll crouch next to the opening for the courtyard over there." He pointed. "When he starts heading for you guys, he'll pass the opening, and I'll shove him over the edge."

It had sounded like a perfect plan when he'd first explained it in the cellar, but now the whole thing seemed ridiculous. "Mr. White has powers," I said.

"Shut up," Jim told me, and led us to our spot. We stared at the top of the ladder, waiting.

"Look," said Mary, pointing, as Mr. White's hat and then his face came into view, glowing against the dark like thousand-year-old starlight. He moved cautiously, turning his head quickly this way and that, like a bird, peering into the night.

I remembered then that we were supposed to make noise and draw his attention. I tried to whistle no good. "Hey," I yelled, but it came out as a whisper.

"Over here, White, you turd sniffer!" called Jim. Even Mary was able to get out a "Yeah!"

He pinpointed where we stood, put his hands in his pockets, and took a step forward. In order to reach us over by the gym wall, he had to move a few steps closer to the opening above the courtyard. We waved our hands to keep him from noticing Ray, who was crouched down low like a ball of shadow. White took two long strides, and just when he got as close to the edge as possible, we saw Ray spring up and rush forward. White never turned to look at him, never seemed to even hear him, but took another step. As God is my judge, Ray passed right through him, not around him but *through* him. I froze on the spot. The dark presence of Ray, though he didn't budge Mr. White an inch, seemed to weaken him for a moment, and White hesitated. All of this happened so fast, but it seemed so slow that I caught every detail. Almost. What I missed was the fact that Jim had taken off running. The rest of the action unfolded like a movie.

White shook his head, like he was clearing mental cobwebs, straightened up, and was about to take another step when Jim hit him low and hard. His arms pinwheeling, Mr. White stumbled to the edge of the roof. His jacket flapped, and his hat fell back out of sight into the courtyard. He struggled to right himself at the edge, and one of his hands came down, grabbing Jim by the sleeve of his shirt. Jim grunted and pushed him. White went backward, but as he fell, he grabbed Jim's ankle, pulling him down to the surface of the roof. I saw one arm of the white overcoat and that pale hand clutching the bottom of Jim's leg.

Mary started running before I did. Jim's screams for help sparked me to action. I got to where he was slowly being pulled over the edge in the same instant Mary did. He was struggling to pull himself back. We started stamping the pale wrist and hand, the arm. Finally I jumped up as high as I could and came down on it with both feet. There was a snapping sound that echoed across the rooftop, followed by a high-pitched cry of pain. The icicle grip loosened, and Jim pulled his ankle free.

We didn't notice that White had grabbed the edge with just the fingertips of his opposite hand, but Mary did. She stepped up and finished the job with a single stamp of her foot. We heard the thud below and a wheeze of stale air pushed from his lungs. Stepping closer to the edge, we looked over and saw him lying flat on his back, his coat spread out like wings behind him, his hat next to his head. I could see that his eyes were open and that he was watching us. Jim leaned over the side and spit on him. Mary did the same, and he never moved or called out.

Jim shoved me. "Get going," he said.

We went down the ladder, Jim first, me last, and Mary in between us. Once we got to the ground, I said, "What happened to Ray?"

Mary shook her head.

"I don't know," said Jim. "He's gone."

Before I could ask, "Was he a ghost?" Jim said, "We have to hurry. We gotta get home and call the cops." He started walking fast around toward the front of the building. "The courtyard will hold him for a while, but he's tricky," Jim called back over his shoulder.

We were passing through the front gate of the school, Jim

up ahead, and I turned to Mary and asked her if she, too, had seen Ray pass through Mr. White. The thought of it still made me giddy.

It was a few moments before she nodded and quietly said, "Right through him."

When we got home, the front door was locked. White must have locked it behind him after he'd entered. Jim went in through the cellar window in the back, and we waited for him on the front stoop. While we were standing there, the lights went back on, and I knew that Jim had been at the cellar fuse box. Even before he could open the door for us all the way, I saw George scurrying around his legs, looking no worse for wear. Neither my mother nor my father was home yet. We went into the kitchen, and Jim picked up the phone and dialed. He waited for an answer, and Mary and I stood still and held our breath.

"Somebody's breaking into East Lake School. Check the courtyard," he said in a voice deeper than his own. Then he hung up quick. As soon as the phone was on the hook, we all started laughing. I laughed so hard my eyes watered, and so did Jim's and Mary's.

Mary went to the refrigerator, took out the Velveeta cheese, and cut a big hunk off the end. She threw the orange wedge to George, who caught it in midair with a snap of his jaws.

It was over. I knew because most of my fear left me the same way the crazy energy went out of my mother—all at once, like a balloon deflating. A few minutes later, we heard the sirens coming down Willow. Two cars sped by, flashing red, as we watched from the front window. I knew that the neighbors would leave their houses and walk over to the school as they had the night Tony Calfano shot out the windows, but we let the curtain fall back into place and turned on the television. No one said a word.

Nan and my mother arrived home. They told us Pop had

had a stroke and that he'd be in the hospital for a while. It was late, but my mother poured two glasses of wine for her and Nan. She thanked us for being so good, and we were sent to bed. We told them nothing.

I lay awake till my father got home, and I heard the mumble of talk coming up from the dining room. George climbed aboard. I fell asleep thinking of Charlie, Ray, Barzita, along with other ghosts, slipping through the backyards of Botch Town.

Bang

■ The cops called early the next day and asked my mother to have my father bring me down to the station on Saturday to look at some mug shots. They told her that they'd caught a man they thought might be the guy who had tried to grab me at the stores. When she told me about the phone call, she asked if I was up to going over there, and I nodded.

On Saturday morning the police station was as quiet as Krapp's library time. The same police officer who'd spoken to Pop and me was there to meet us. He showed us to the same wood-paneled back room with the portrait of President Johnson and the flag. Lying on the table was a row of black-and-white photos of men, from the chest up, staring straight out.

"Sit in front of the pictures there," the cop said to me.

I did, and my father pulled up another chair so he could sit next to me and rest his hand on my shoulder. From the time we had gotten out of the car to when we got back in it and drove away, I felt my father's hand on my shoulder.

"Show me," said the cop.

I scanned down the row of faces, and before I even got to it, I saw it out of the corner of my eye, shining brighter than the other photos. I put my finger right down in the center of Mr. White's forehead and looked at my father. He smiled.

"Bingo," said the cop. "Godfrey Darnell, wanted for murder in Ohio, New Jersey, Pennsylvania, Delaware, and who knows where else."

"Will he have to go to court?" my dad asked, pointing to me.

"Not for a while," said the cop. "Darnell will probably be extradited to another state to face charges there first. He's a nut—kills people for, I guess, fun. Mostly kids, but adults, too, when he senses they can't defend themselves. I'd be surprised if he doesn't get the chair. Nobody knows how many people he's killed."

And nobody found out that day either. I kept my mouth shut about Charlie and Mr. Barzita. After we were done at the police station, my father took me to a new hamburger place over in Babylon, Burger King. We sat near the waterfalls in Argyle Park and ate our burgers. "You did very good today," he said.

I nodded.

"What do you think of this hamburger?" he asked. "It's just a cold onion sandwich with mayonnaise."

I agreed with him, even though I really liked it.

A few nights later, after my father had gotten home and gone to bed, a loud bang woke me from a deep sleep. I heard a commotion from below, and I ran down the steps to find out what had happened. The voices led me through Nan's open door and along the hallway to her bedroom. My father was there in his work pants and shoes but no shirt. My mother had on her robe, and Nan was sitting straight up in bed. Jim was there, too, sticking his pinkie finger into a hole in the wall just above the dresser. Everyone was looking in the other direction, though, at the sliding wooden door of the closet. There was a hole there, too.

"I knew that was a gunshot," said my father. He and Nan laughed.

"The gun must have just gotten too old," said Nan.

"*You* won't," said my mother, "if you keep that thing loaded."

It wasn't until after they started talking about how Pop was doing in the hospital that I noticed the crystal Virgin that had held the holy water lying in shards on top of the dresser. The bullet had shattered it. There was a light blue puddle on the wood and water stains on the wall. I left when Nan started crying. Mary passed me in the hall and waved. I went through our dining room to the kitchen and let myself out the back door. As soon as I stepped away from the house and looked up, I smelled a trace of autumn in the cool air. That gunshot was like a screen door slamming shut, a kind of Times Square celebration.

The Shadow Year was over. I could feel it slide out of my head like the splinter from my thumb, leaving an empty space where it had been.

Those Normal Years

■ We fell into one of those normal years, where light and dark mix gently and nothing is clear. There were so many things I didn't understand, so many questions I had. Mr. White was creepy, but at least he was real. What was Ray? No matter how many times I tried to get Jim to talk about it, he wouldn't. "Leave me alone," he'd say, and shut his door. He stayed in his room all the time after school, playing guitar and napping. We didn't hang out together anymore. He grew slower, quieter, and gained weight. One afternoon I found the photo he'd had Mary take of us in front of the shed. I shoved it under his closed door, thinking he'd come out, but he didn't. That night, when I went up for bed, I saw the photo lying on the floor outside his room. I picked it up and saw he'd written *"Shhhhh"* on the back in red pen.

Mary lost all her weird number powers and somehow became normal all of a sudden. I could never figure out if it had just happened or if it had been her decision. She broke out of Room X in the first two weeks of the new school year and wound up with Krapp, who'd been demoted to teaching fifth grade. Sometimes she and I would sit behind the forsythia and whisper about what had happened. One time I asked her why she thought Mr. White read the Perno Shell books. She said, "He was probably studying how kids thought." The next time I spoke to her about the connection with the books, though, she changed the subject to Krapp.

I understood that Jim and Mary were both trying to tell me it was better to forget. I fought it for a while, but on the night before school started again, I took my notebook that held all the information of our investigation and wrapped it three times in waxed paper. After tying the bundle tight with kite string, crisscrossing it length- and widthwise, I left my bedroom, crept down through the sleeping house, passed my mother, unconscious on the couch, passed the bottle standing open on the kitchen counter, and went out into the night. The crickets were singing, the trees were rustling, there was a moon and so many stars. I walked past the picnic table and beneath the cherry tree and went all the way back by the shed. At the trunk of the giant oak, I knelt and shoved the book into a hole amid the tree's exposed roots, burying it deep underground. Then I brushed off my hands and tried my best to forget. The next day I started junior high.

My mother drank, my father worked, and Pop finally returned from the hospital able to talk out of only one side of his mouth. Nan put him through his paces every day, lifting his legs, making him squeeze a rubber ball. "She's trying to finish me off," he'd say. He died on a cold, rainy day just before Thanksgiving, and at the private, family-only ceremony at Clancy's the morning he was buried, I saw him in his coffin, facedown without a shirt, as he'd requested. A week later we learned that Godfrey Darnell had hanged himself in prison.

Years passed. Jim and I went our separate ways. Mary got married and had kids. Too much to tell, and then one evening at the end of summer while I sat visiting with my mother and father out at the picnic table, having a smoke and a beer, they started talking about the neighbors—who was left from the original crew who were there when they'd first moved into the house on Willow. There weren't many, so they reminisced about the ones they'd seen come and go. It was like they were digging into their own Hall of Fame. After a while the Halloways came up.

"Mister was a real bastard," said my mother.

"Big on the belt," said my father.

"Not just the wife but the kids, too," said my mother, flicking her ash.

"A coward," said my father.

"Mrs. Restuccio told me that after they moved to Philly and the older boy was killed, he changed. Found God."

"Found God," said my father, and he barely laughed.

"What do you mean, 'the older boy was *killed*'?" I said.

"Murdered," said my mother. "They found him in a Dumpster in an alley in South Philadelphia with a broken neck. It happened a couple weeks after they moved there. I don't think they ever figured out who did it. Everyone thought it was the old man for a while, but he'd been at work for sure when it happened."

I felt the exact sense of emptiness I had when Jim and I stood in Mr. White's garage for the first time and saw the bottles of Mr. Clean. I made a mental note to call Mary and tell her, but I never did.

At the end of summer that year, I read in the newspaper that some kid fishing at the lake back in the woods had brought up Charlie Edison's remains. The police made a positive identification using dental records, and the speculation was that he'd been murdered by Darnell. Still, they weren't sure, and there was some mystery involved in the fact that the police had thoroughly dredged the lake when Charlie'd gone missing. I, of course, knew the truth of how things had happened. Ray had told us that White threw the body in the lake *after* the dredging. I'd have come forward to clear it all up, but how do you explain to the cops that you got your information from a ghost?

Only days after I read that news, I found a letter in my mailbox. It was made out in red ink with no return address. I almost tossed it into the can, thinking it was some organization begging money for kids. Instead I let it sit for a few days. Then one night when I was drinking alone in my apartment's small kitchenette, I picked the letter out of the stack of mail on the table. Putting down my cigarette, I opened it. Inside, there was nothing but a thin rectangle of cardboard. I pulled it out and, recognizing it immediately, dropped it on the table. Softee's eyes stared up at me, and when I eventually closed mine, I was back in Botch Town, peering in every window, searching for something I'd lost.

Acknowledgments

Unlike my previous two novels, which relied on secondary sources for their semblance of historical accuracy, this book's foundation is built upon the shifting mirage of my memory. The people, places, and events of this story are no more real than the phantom limbs in which amputees sometimes experience severe pain or subtle sensation. The sole reliance on my own rickety brain at least makes these acknowledgments fewer and easier.

I owe a great debt to Jennifer Brehl, the editor of *The Shadow Year* as well as five of my other novels. As always, her intensity of focus, keen critical eye, and innate sensibilities as a perfect reader helped to make this book all it could possibly be. As well, I am indebted to Howard Morhaim, my agent, for his vital guidance and constant good sense. Thanks, as ever, to Michael Gallagher and Bill Watkins for reading this manuscript in various stages and offering feedback. And, really, where would all this be without the love and inspiration of Lynn, Jack, and Derek, who make the act of writing novels seem the right thing to do?